BEST OFFER WINS

# BEST OFFER WINS

*A Novel*

## MARISA KASHINO

CELADON
BOOKS
NEW YORK

This is a work of fiction. All the characters, organizations, and events portrayed in this novel are either products of the author's imagination or used fictitiously.

BEST OFFER WINS. Copyright © 2025 by Marisa Kashino. All rights reserved. Printed in the United States of America. For information, address Celadon Books, a division of Macmillan Publishers, 120 Broadway, New York, NY 10271.
EU Representative: Macmillan Publishers Ireland Ltd, 1st Floor, The Liffey Trust Centre, 117–126 Sheriff Street Upper, Dublin 1, DO1 YC43.

www.celadonbooks.com

Designed by Michelle McMillian

Library of Congress Cataloging-in-Publication Data

Names: Kashino, Marisa, author.
Title: Best offer wins : a novel / Marisa Kashino.
Description: First U.S. edition. | New York : Celadon Books, 2025.
Identifiers: LCCN 2025006654 | ISBN 9781250400543 (hardcover) | ISBN 9781250436580 (international, sold outside the U.S., subject to rights availability) | ISBN 9781250400550 (ebook)
Subjects: LCSH: House buying—Washington (D.C.)—Fiction | LCGFT: Novels
Classification: LCC PS3611.A785325 B37 2026 | DDC 813/.6—dc23/eng/20250425
LC record available at https://lccn.loc.gov/2025006654

The publisher of this book does not authorize the use or reproduction of any part of this book in any manner for the purpose of training artificial intelligence technologies or systems. The publisher of this book expressly reserves this book from the Text and Data Mining exception in accordance with Article 4(3) of the European Union Digital Single Market Directive 2019/790.

Our books may be purchased in bulk for specialty retail/wholesale, literacy, corporate/premium, educational, and subscription box use. Please contact MacmillanSpecialMarkets@macmillan.com.

First U.S. Edition: 2025
First International Edition: 2025

10 9 8 7 6 5 4 3 2 1

*To Nate and our pack, for making our house my dream home*

BEST OFFER WINS

# 1

Ginny calls around ten, just as I'm hanging up with a client. She sounds urgent.

"Margo, it might be perfect."

I have heard this before.

"Four bedrooms, renovated kitchen, great yard. Right over the DC line—before you ask, yes, it's in the top-choice neighborhood. And guess what? No one else knows about it! It's not listed yet."

That part—the "It's not listed" part—stops me mid-sip of coffee. It pulls me up from my little desk by the apartment's floor-to-ceiling window, a hunk of bait just juicy enough to make me forget that it could be wrapped around a sharp, painful hook. Ian comes to a standstill in the kitchen, his hazel eyes zeroing in on me.

"My sister-in-law does yoga with one of the sellers," Ginny continues, at her usual breathless speed. "He told her they're putting it on the market at the end of the month. Apparently, his husband got a big new job out of town, so it's all very rushed. But maybe—and I don't wanna promise anything here—but maybe that means they're motivated enough to take an offer now, *before* they list publicly."

A surge of hope, that familiar poison, makes my heart stutter. This is the fantasy. The urban legend that everyone house-hunting in this godforsaken market latches onto at some point. You hear about a friend of a friend (in my case, it was the cousin of a coworker) who got an inside tip about a house before it hit the market, who swooped in and bought it before the masses could even think about descending. You hope and wish and pray the same thing will happen to you. You take detours through your target neighborhoods, scouting for a moving truck or an estate-sale sign, any hint at all that might give you the jump on a place before it officially comes up for sale. You know the odds aren't in your favor—and yet it has to happen for someone, right?

Right?

"You're sure it's in Grovemont?" I ask Ginny, my voice a stage whisper like I'm afraid the secret will get out. Someone lays on their horn three stories below, a well-timed reminder of why I hate this place so much.

"Sure is, kiddo," she says. "My sister-in-law's been inside. She says it's stunning. I'm in the car, but I'm gonna have Travis send you the address so you and Ian can go have a look from the street. Let me know what you think as soon as you can."

Even before the email from Ginny's assistant lands in my inbox, I feel the thing that I promised myself I would stop feeling: a hunch that this house could be The One. Why else would my real estate agent—of all the rabid, razor-elbowed agents in Washington—have been the one to score such an extraordinary piece of intel? Or maybe it's that I *have* to believe it's the one. Like a self-preservation thing. Because otherwise, I am terrified that we have really, truly, finally run out of options.

Ian and I have been stuck here—in an apartment so small you can vacuum almost all of it from a single outlet—for eighteen increasingly hellish months. The first six or seven of those drifted by in a kind of placid denial. We still fucked like it would be ideal if I got pregnant immediately, like obviously we'd be out of here and settled into the new house whenever the baby arrived. This was always part of the plan, after all, when we decided to sell our starter home. We had to get the money out of it if we were ever going to afford the dream house in the burbs, so it was unavoidable that we'd have to spend a little while renting.

And it's not like we went in totally blind. We sold the last place—a falling-apart row house almost far west enough to count as Logan Circle—in the fall of 2020, the point in the pandemic when everyone realized that if Covid didn't suffocate them, spending another minute within the same four walls probably would. DC, like everywhere else, was already in the middle of a housing shortage and now hordes of buyers desperate for more space were making it infinitely worse. But when you're a gentrifier, this is the moment you pounce. Ian and I had lived in that row house for nearly a decade. We'd debated "Gunshots or fireworks?" almost as frequently as "Thai or Mexican food?" When you invest in a "transitioning" neighborhood, that's just what you sign up for. The payout on the other side—once the city's hottest restaurants have opened a few blocks away, once you're within walking distance of not one, but two Whole Foods—is the reason you slog through.

So, yeah, I knew it might take a minute to find the forever home, but clearly, this was the time to cash in. And who could argue with that logic after the row house, even with its flooding basement and bad DIY kitchen reno, sold in a single weekend for more than double what we'd paid?

At first, my plan seemed to be working. Less than a month after we moved into the apartment, a house that checked all the boxes hit the market. It was a fully remodeled 1940s Colonial (my favorite style), in Grovemont (my favorite neighborhood), well under our budget. I thought maybe we wouldn't even have to pay for a second month on the storage unit.

Then it got twenty-two offers.

Twenty-fucking-two.

"Now you've got the first bidding war outta the way," Ginny had said with a shrug, after informing us that it sold for $25,000 higher than our offer. "It's like a rite of passage, and now we know we'll just have to be a tad more aggressive next time."

But that was ten "next times" ago.

The next few bidding wars played out pretty much the same, except the numbers kept getting worse. We'd go to $1.1 million and fall just short. So, for the next house, we'd stretch to $1,150,000, only for the winner to offer the same amount—all cash.

After loss number five, I froze my eggs just in case.

At that point, we'd been in the apartment about eight months, and trying for a baby for nearly a year. Dr. Warner convinced us it didn't make sense to start in vitro yet—she still thinks I might get pregnant the old-fashioned way once the stress of the house hunt is over. And it's true that if we wound up taking out a loan for multiple rounds of IVF, it could complicate our mortgage approval. But when you're staring down the barrel of turning thirty-eight, you can't afford to take any chances. While we waste away here in real estate purgatory, at least I know I have a viable batch preserved on ice.

Although to be honest, that fact hasn't been as comforting as I'd hoped. Sometimes, when I can't sleep all I can think is *No house, no baby; no house, no baby* on an endless, agonizing loop.

In hindsight, number six (a split-level with a kitchen that needed a full gut) and number seven (a cute-enough Craftsman, but on a very busy street) were duds that only seemed worth trying for because we were starting to panic. Eight, nine, and ten trickled onto the market at such a glacial pace, weeks and weeks passing between them, that I was convinced the housing supply was about to dry up entirely. Which is why, when number eleven finally came on, I decided we had to push harder. It was another Colonial, a couple miles farther from the city than we preferred but still zoned for the right schools. They'd blown out the primary suite so the bathroom could fit a soaking tub. The nursery was right next door. I talked Ian into tapping into our 401Ks so we could raise our budget to $1.3 million—a full $250,000 above the asking price. How could that possibly not be good enough?

By the time Ginny called, my whole nervous system felt like it had been hooked up to jumper cables. We were out to dinner with friends, so I excused myself and answered from the sidewalk: seventeen bids had rolled in. Seven, including the winning one, were all cash.

We were losers for an eleventh time.

I texted Ian from outside the restaurant, then left him there to explain my disappearance and pay our half of the bill. After I spent the weekend holed up in the bedroom, crying and bingeing *Below Deck*, he started hinting that I should go back to a therapist. I convinced him I was fine (because I was), but that was two months ago now. Nothing halfway decent has even come available since.

"What was that about?" Ian asks, coming around the kitchen counter, oblivious to the ring that his coffee mug has left behind on the white quartz.

I brush past him, already en route to get my Nikes by the front door. "Ginny says there's a house that could be perfect, and we have to see it now 'cause—get this—no one else knows about it yet."

He arches an eyebrow. "How's that possible?"

Just then, my laptop dings from my desk. I race back across the room.

"I'll explain in the car. That's gotta be from Travis."

Ian stands behind me, back at the window overlooking the traffic snarling U Street, as I punch the address into Google Maps. He's close enough that I can smell the cloying sweetness of his Old Spice aftershave. I'm sure there was a time when I found his scent appealing—before we were trapped in this glass box, before sex was just another reminder that we didn't have a baby.

I pull up the street view and feel myself deflate.

Ian laughs. "Just our luck."

A tree-pruning truck is parked in front, with a guy up in the lift cutting back a towering maple. The house is mostly blocked.

"This is a good thing," I say, shoving aside my disappointment. "Mature trees are part of why we love the neighborhood, right? And we've been down this street before, remember? We know it's nice."

I have to be the one who keeps the energy up. Because no matter how many houses we lose, Ian will never feel the urgency of this search as deeply as I do. Even after all those bidding wars, he still flinches when Ginny and I remind him that offering six figures over asking is normal, that we simply don't have any other choice.

For a government lawyer, being risk averse is basically a job requirement. Plus, he's about as wired for struggle as his six-foot, golden-boy looks would lead you to believe. He grew up with a dad who coached his little league teams and a mom who sent him to school with homemade cupcakes on his birthdays. Two loving parents who still call us at least once a week to check in. But my childhood, erratic as it was, gave me something even more valuable, something that I have come to accept Ian will never have: hunger.

It's why I ditched journalism to make triple the money in PR. And it's the whole reason I pushed to buy that rundown little row house to begin with—so we could eventually sell it for enough profit to give us the life that my parents could never provide.

"Ian, let's go." My sneakers are on. I'm pulling my hair into a low pony, trying in vain to tuck away the grays sprouting at my temples like tinsel against jet black.

"Babe, sorry to do this, but do you mind going without me and reporting back? I need to be in the office soon," he says. "For a lunch meeting." I clock that he's wearing real clothes. His mop of sandy hair is slicked with pomade.

"Are you being serious?" He acts like he's saving the world at that job. "Ginny needs an answer *now*, Ian. I mean, aren't you pumped? All these months of searching and we've never had an in like this.

Let's just zip up there real quick and I'll drop you at the office when we're done."

He shifts his weight, deciding how much conflict he can endure so early in the day. "Okay, that should work," he says finally. "As long as I'm in before noon."

I wipe up his coffee ring and we're out the door.

...

We're only thirty minutes from the apartment, but we might as well have teleported to another planet.

The sidewalks in Grovemont are pristine. No discarded pizza crusts or other detritus from wasted twentysomethings stumbling around after closing time. No homeless people hassling you when all you want to do is get inside your own building. (Or is it *unhoused* now? Or *people experiencing homelessness*? Whatever, my point is everyone here in Grovemont is experiencing fucking paradise.)

It must be ten degrees cooler here in the summer, with all these giant trees. This is the kind of place where people get into birdwatching and growing their own tomatoes. Where the only time you hear sirens is when the fire department wants to spice things up at the Christmas parade.

Last month, someone was shot and killed outside the high school down the block from our apartment in Shaw. But just seven miles away—here in the most desirable neighborhood in the most desirable DC suburb of Bethesda—our kid will attend the very best public schools in the whole state of Maryland, possibly the entire country.

Of course, I knew the neighborhood would be perfect. I've been obsessed with it for a year and a half. But when we pull up to the actual house, I almost can't believe it's real. Like if I looked from the side, I would see that it was a flattened set from a movie titled *Margo's Dream Home* or *Margo Dies and Goes to Heaven*. It's a white-painted brick Colonial, with a glossy black front door flanked by brass lanterns. It has a lush front lawn and window boxes I'd fill with whatever type of flowers you're supposed to put in those things.

Ian's mom can show me. She loves her window boxes. In fact, this house looks an awful lot like Ian's parents' house. Which feels like it might be a sign.

Ian notices, too. "Well, I at least love it from the outside," he says. "Kind of like my folks' house, don't you think?"

"I have to see the backyard," I say.

"Wait a minute, what? You can't just let yourself into the backyard."

"I think I can. See that gate?" I point it out for him, through the Prius's rolled-down window.

"No, I mean you *shouldn't* let yourself into the backyard, Margo." He only says my name when he really wants to make a point. But I'm already out of the car.

"Come on, we're the only ones parked out here. No one's home. I'll be very fast."

"Margo, do not do this."

"Just a quick peek. I'll be right back."

I know, I know. This is privilege. No one's calling the cops on an Asian girl in head-to-toe Lululemon, at least not in a neighborhood with this much performative wokeness. Practically every other house has a "Black Lives Matter" sign in the yard, though I am willing to bet no actual Black people live on this street. If a neighbor sees me, I'll just say my dog got loose and ran back here or something. It grosses me out, too, but I don't make the rules.

I unlatch the gate and follow the flagstone pathway around back to a patio. When I spot it—hanging from the sturdy limb of an oak tree, in the far right corner of the yard—my breath halts. A tire swing. How many houses have we looked at? Forty-five? Fifty? And it's the first one I've encountered. This doesn't just feel like a sign. This is one.

I consider crossing the lawn to touch the rough, dark rubber. But then I'd be out in the open, even more exposed to any nosy neighbor peering down from their upstairs window. A soft breeze cools my neck; the tire sways just slightly. I long to get closer, but this'll have to do for now.

It's gorgeous today, but it rained last night, so the outdoor sectional and coffee table on the patio are covered. A few steps lead up to the deck, complete with an eight-person teak dining table and a custom, built-in bar with a gas grill and a mini fridge. It looks like they bumped out the back of the house, probably to enlarge the kitchen. After touring about a zillion of them, I've seen this is the typical reno for a 1940s Colonial.

A speck of an airplane cuts a trail through wide-open sky—and it's so pin-drop quiet that I can hear the faint rumble of its engine. The grass is wet and flawlessly green, because it's only April. There's enough of it to feel like a real backyard, but not so much that it'll be all-consuming. We will own a lawn mower here for the first time in our lives—an essential bauble on the charm bracelet of Successful Adulthood.

During the anxious little blip when my parents were homeowners, my dad turned into a total psychopath over the lawn. Now that lawn was *too* big, too much maintenance. He splurged on a fancy built-in irrigation system, yet somehow, somewhere, there was always still a brown spot that enraged him. The lawn wasn't the real issue, I realize now.

My phone vibrates in my hand. A text from Ian: *Done yet?*

I know I'm pushing it, but I need to see the kitchen. It has to be in that bumped-out addition.

I jog up the steps to the deck, then cup my hands around my face so I can see through the French doors. Carrara marble blankets all the countertops, including a massive island—the kind that becomes a natural hub for the happy chaos of a family. The floors are wide-plank oak. The cabinets are Shaker, painted a warm gray, with brass knobs. I'd given up on ever topping that first Grovemont Colonial, the one we lost in that very first bidding war, but this one is so much better. It's like they peered inside my mind and extracted the perfect backdrop for the perfect future.

There goes my phone again. But Ian will have to hang on a sec because I'm imagining myself drinking coffee on one of those cane-back barstools. Wonder if it would help to offer to buy some of their furniture, too. Might be easier for them than moving it out of town. The gas range is against the wall to the left. Looks like a Thermador, probably worth more than the Prius.

There's a breakfast nook just on the other side of the glass. We'll eat most of our meals there. But I spot a more formal dining room off to the right, through an arched opening. That was one of my main complaints about the row house—in under a thousand square feet, there was no space for a real table where we could celebrate, for instance, our baby's first birthday. But here, we'll host all kinds of holidays and legit grown-up dinner parties. We'll get one of those wine-bottle chillers that sits in a stand.

Ugh. More buzzing. It almost hurts to pull my eyes away, but I finally let them flit down to the screen.

*CAR PULLING UP*

Followed only by: *!!!!!!!!!!!!!!!*

Fuck.

I look back up. A man, slender and well dressed, is coming down the hallway from the front entrance, face tilted toward his phone. I plummet to all fours and crawl toward the steps, the dampness from the deck soaking through my leggings.

The last time something like this happened, it was January and freezing out. Ian thought I was running errands, but really, I was here in Grovemont—on the prowl for any hint of an impending sale—when a Cape Cod with a wide-open garage made me slam on the brakes. Inside were boxes, stacks of them. Possibly packed for an upcoming move.

From the Prius, it was impossible to tell for sure, so I parked around the corner then strolled right in, unnoticed. Just as I was figuring out that the boxes were merely storage, mostly full of junk, I heard the knob turning on the door from the inside of the house. I ducked behind one of the stacks, peeking out just far enough to spy a hand tap the button to close the garage. The concrete floor shuddered beneath me until everything was pitch black. I stayed hidden there till I couldn't feel my toes. At last, I ran over and hit the button again, raising the obnoxious door just enough to squirm out from underneath it. No one must have heard because I made it back to the Prius without incident.

Compared to that, the predicament I'm in now isn't so bad. Once I crawl down the deck stairs, I stand up and slink along the white brick till I reach the gate. Quickly scanning my surroundings, I book it toward the sidewalk.

An olive-green Audi SUV is parked out front.

But there's no trace of our beat-up, silver Prius. Where the hell is Ian?

"Hey!"

I whirl around. The man, now on the front porch, narrows his beautiful eyes and strides toward me.

# 2

It's too late to run. My pulse thunders in my ears as he closes in, veering off the flagstone path to head directly for me through the grass.

"Is everything all right?"

The man, a laptop under his arm—the reason he returned home, I'm guessing—looks concerned.

But not mad.

The edge of my right foot still grazes his front lawn. I barely made it to the pavement. But he must not have seen where I came from. Jesus, he's almost as flawless as his house. Tall. Dark waves. Expensive jeans. An Italian model who lives inside the pages of a design magazine.

I steady myself and force a laugh. "Yes! Oh my gosh, I'm so embarrassed. I think I'm just a little lost. And my phone is dead, of course."

"Lost here?"

What he means is: How does someone wind up lost in the middle of a residential neighborhood that isn't near the Metro or any other landmark that would feasibly draw an idiot like me to this spot on the sidewalk, in front of this perfect home.

I remember my Nikes.

"Yeah, um, I was out for a run and I guess I just got a little overzealous. This isn't my usual route."

"Gotcha. Did you take a fall then? Are you hurt?"

I look down at my charcoal-gray leggings, soaked through up to the knees.

"Ugh, yes, I sure did." I roll my eyes at my clumsiness. "But no, thank you, I'm fine. I wasn't watching where I was going." I push out another laugh. "Honestly, I probably should've called it quits a mile ago. But you gotta take advantage of this weather before it's sweaty and disgusting out, right?"

He smiles—he believes me. "For sure," he says. "I won't miss that."

He's handing me an opening. Should I say something about the house?

"Oh, are you moving?" I feign surprise. "This is such a cute neighborhood."

"I know. We love it here. But yeah, to London."

This is my chance. But will it sound unhinged to ask when they're planning to list—if maybe, possibly I could have a sneak peek inside? Or, worse, I might give myself away. Although he *is* being really nice to me. Dammit, here comes the Prius. I lock eyes with Ian in the driver's seat and give my head a slight shake, willing him not to stop. He picks up some speed and keeps going.

But now my "dead" phone is vibrating. The man's gaze darts to my palm.

"Oops, guess it still has enough juice to let me know the battery needs charging!" I hold it flush against my side, out of view, while I reject Ian's call. That decides it, I just need to get out of here.

"Well, good luck," I say. "I love London." I have never been. "Would you mind pointing me to Mass Ave.?"

"Oh, sure, you want to go three blocks that way, then take a right on Redwood. That'll take you straight to Massachusetts."

"Thank you so much. Have a good one!"

I take off in a jog. The man is almost certainly also heading to Massachusetts Avenue, so I know I can't stop until I see the Audi pass. Once it does, I text Ian my location.

"Margo, what the actual fuck?" He gets out so I can reclaim my place in the driver's seat.

"I know. I'm sorry." I buckle my seatbelt. "But everything's fine. And you're the one who left!"

"Because I didn't want to look like some creeper in front of the guy's house."

"So if he'd caught me in the backyard, I would've had to fend for myself, then?"

"You're being ridiculous. I'm the one who told you not to go back there."

We don't say anything for a couple blocks. Fighting about houses is just a thing we do now.

I break the silence. "I'm calling Ginny. The kitchen is incredible. So is the yard."

Since we spoke earlier, Ginny has done some recon with her sister-in-law and learned the sellers are working with an agent from Long & Foster. "It has to be Theresa Reynolds," she says. "Everyone in Grovemont uses her. I'll call her now. Stay by your phone."

I weave down Massachusetts, through Dupont Circle, and hang a right toward the Environmental Protection Agency's headquarters on Pennsylvania Avenue. Ian must still be annoyed, but he pecks me on the cheek and tells me he loves me before getting out. Muscle memory after all these years.

He had a girlfriend when we first met, playing in a kickball league together in 2008. I was twenty-three, making poverty wages as an editorial aide at *The Washington Post*. I'd only moved here from Seattle a year before—still felt like an alien who would never speak the language of a planet where everyone else had graduated from the same Ivies as their parents. I'm not particularly athletic, but the interns and other aides all did kickball, so I figured it was a box someone my age should check.

Ian had been a baseball player through high school, so the team sports thing came naturally to him. I loved how the group always seemed to turn toward him, no matter what else was going on. If he spoke, people wanted to listen. It wasn't that he was obnoxious about it; there was just something about his presence—calm, confident—that pulled you in.

I wasn't sure if he even knew my name, but one Thursday, when postgame beers devolved into an all-nighter in Adams Morgan, still in uniform, we found ourselves alone together in a corner of the bar. That's when we discovered we had something in common: we were both miserable in our jobs. I was sick of being poor and having to fight for every byline. At only twenty-seven, Ian was making more money than I'd ever dreamed of as an associate at Covington & Burling, but spending most of his days doing document review in a windowless room. Talking to me made him feel better, he said, like he was finally being seen. As he leaned across the table to kiss me, I noticed that his eyes weren't brown, that there was some green in them, too. For the first time, I understood what "hazel" meant.

It went on like that for a few weeks, us getting drunk with the team, then making out in bars, until I told him we had to knock it off because he had a girlfriend. He broke up with her a couple days later, and he hasn't left my side since.

My phone buzzes in the cupholder as I come to a stop at a light. A text from Ginny: *Left a voicemail. Will be in touch as soon as I hear anything.*

You'd think by now I'd be numb to the agony of waiting. But this is more barbaric than an upper-lip wax after a sunburn. I've been circling the block for fifteen minutes looking for a parking spot when she finally calls back. (The garage fee in our building is insane and every dollar counts when you're saving for a down payment.) I pull over in front of a fire hydrant to take the call.

"Ginny? Tell me everything."

She lets out a long sigh.

Fuck me.

"I'm sorry, kiddo. We knew this was a long shot. They wanna take it to the open market. But the good news is they're gonna list it soon and it sounds like it'll be in your budget ... though maybe just barely."

I mute the phone and scream. A guy walking a French bulldog jumps back from the car.

I take a deep breath and unmute. "Then you know that means we won't get it. It'll get bid up. Especially with that kitchen."

"You've seen the kitchen?"

Shit.

"Well, no, but you said your sister-in-law thinks it's stunning."

"She could be wrong! You know what I always say, kiddo. If it's meant to be, it'll work out."

Yeah, and look where that strategy has gotten us. It's time to get creative.

"Maybe I'll feel more hopeful if I focus on getting to know the neighborhood a little better, you know, sort of like manifesting that I'll live there one day?" I say, as if I couldn't draw a map of it from memory. "Where did you say your sister-in-law did yoga? Maybe I'll check out a class."

"That's the spirit, kiddo. Gosh, I can't remember. Grace something or other?"

"That's okay, I'll figure it out. Talk to you later, Ginny."

I Google "grace yoga grovemont bethesda." There it is: Power + Grace Yoga, less than five minutes from my dream home.

# 3

Obviously, I can't go in cold.

I may have been a flack for the last decade but I still know how to do my research. As soon as I ditch the Prius, I dash back to my tiny desk in our tiny living room and pull up the database of Maryland property records. In the drop-down menu, I select "search by street address."

Curtis Bradshaw and Jack Lombardi have owned the dream house since 2015—when they paid $730,000 for it. They're about to make a killing.

Their names are unusual enough that the rest should be easy. I find Curtis's faculty profile first—he's an economics professor at Georgetown University, who looks a little like Stanley Tucci. Balding, with severe, black-framed glasses. Good-looking in a nerdy way. Jack, I can tell from his LinkedIn page, is the one I met earlier. He's in commercial furniture sales.

What happens when I search their names together? Excellent. A *New York Times* wedding announcement from June 2012. They're about a decade older than me and Ian. Curtis was forty-two when they got married, he's from Greenwich, and his dad runs a hedge fund (probably explains how they got into the *NYT*). Jack was thirty-nine. On the sidewalk this morning, I never would've guessed he was almost fifty. He must spend a fortune on skin care. He's from a small town in Ohio, and his parents were public-school teachers. Good for him. Self-made, just like me.

Okay, on to social media.

This is interesting. Curtis has more than ten thousand Twitter followers. But why? He's not terribly active or original on the platform—he mostly seems to retweet places like the *Wall Street Journal* and *Bloomberg*. Maybe it's because of the book he touts in his bio, *Falling Apart: How Globalization Kills Quality*. He links to the Amazon page: 239 ratings, 3.5 stars.

It came out more than three years ago, in January 2019. I scroll down a ways, and, yep, this must be the reason he amassed a following. He appears to have done a fair amount of press around it, and he clearly has no qualms about self-promotion. In February that year, he tweeted: *Smart, incisive convo about Falling Apart with my dear friend Andrew Ross Sorkin on Squawk Box. Give it a watch!* with a link to the video.

"Dear friend," yeah right. Also, "smart" and "incisive" basically mean the same thing.

I click play. "Frankly, somebody should have beaten me to the punch on writing this," he tells his bestie, Andrew. "All I did was explore a question that every single one of us has probably considered—why does nothing last these days? Everything from our clothes to our furniture feels disposable, and the reason, of course, is global economics."

I don't really want to give him a sale, but I add the book to my cart anyway.

Jack doesn't appear to be on Twitter, but he is on Instagram, where his handle is @Daddy2Penny. His bio is a single quote: *"What makes you a man is not the ability to make a child. It's the courage to raise one." —Barack Obama.*

A kid lives in that flawless house? The gays really are doing

God's work. The account is set to private but I can at least enlarge the profile photo . . .

Little Penny is Asian. They have an adopted Asian daughter. She's adorable.

It's hard to tell for sure, because she and Jack are wearing matching sunglasses, faces smushed together cheek to cheek, but I'd guess she's about six years old. I'm assuming she's Chinese, not Japanese like me, but I doubt that will matter much to two white guys. Even I have to admit I see something of myself in her—and I hate it when people lump all of us together in one big, generic Asian pile.

I want to keep digging, but the time in the corner of the screen prods me into shutting my laptop. Already five o'clock. Ian will be home from work any minute and I haven't even showered. We're meeting Erika and Heath for cocktails in an hour. Erika's idea—*The four of us are way overdue to catch up!* she texted—but I suspect she and Heath just want a guaranteed table at Jane Jane, since they're a client of my PR firm, Buzz Inc.

I'm in my robe in the bathroom, patting concealer under my eyes, trying to decide whether it truly disguises the dark circles or only amplifies the fine lines, when Ian walks in. I texted him the house update earlier, so he approaches like I'm a plugged-in hairdryer, teetering over the tub.

"Hey, babe. You feeling okay?"

"Hanging in there," I say, with a good-natured smile.

"I'm so glad. Come here." He pulls me in for a hug. "We have to stop putting all this pressure on ourselves. It'll work out eventually."

I am so goddamn sick of everyone telling me that. But we don't have time for a fight right now, so I just nod.

. . .

Jane Jane is packed, as expected on a Friday on Fourteenth Street, the clatter of cocktail shakers instantly conjuring all the hours I logged ferrying drinks in college to bankroll rent and tuition. The manager steers us through the crop tops and high-waisted jeans, through the shirts with one too many buttons undone, to a booth with a brass "Reserved" placard on the table. As soon as we sit, a server appears with a round of some spicy mezcal concoction that they're testing out before adding to the menu.

Erika claps her hands together. "VIP treatment! How fun! Margo, you have the coolest job."

I know she doesn't mean that. We started at the *Post* together ages ago, and she's since climbed the ranks to senior business reporter. *Erika Ortiz* is now a highly respected byline, while *Margo Miyake* is a name on a pitch email that most journalists delete. She looks smoking hot, as usual, in a fitted leather jacket and fuchsia lipstick, choppy chocolate bob laced with golden highlights. I think I may have worn this same striped Madewell blouse the last time I saw her. If she hadn't been such an ally at the *Post*—if she wasn't the closest thing I had to a best friend—I'd probably hate her.

Ian and I introduced her to Heath, back when he was still cute with a full head of white-blond hair. He worked at the EPA, too, until Hillary lost and he joined Sidley Austin (or "sold out," as Ian would tell you). He made partner there three years ago.

"So what's new, guys?" Heath asks, his ample frame stuffed into the other side of the booth. "How's the ol' house hunt coming along?"

Ian laughs, but I catch his jawline tense. "Easy, bro, I think we may need a couple more of these before we get into that." He rattles the ice in his glass.

"Oh no, that bad?" Erika asks, turning down the corners of her neon pout.

"It's fine," I say, eager to move on. "Just the same bullshit. No inventory, lots of competition. You know how it is."

"Yeah, we sure do," Heath says. "I still can't believe how lucky we got."

Ian scoffs. Before he can say something stupid, I pivot to Erika.

"Your place is so beautiful. How's the decorating coming?"

"Well, we're finally making some progress. We just hired Zoe Estelle. Do you follow her on Insta? She's in such high demand, so she can't do the entire house, but she's at least designing the main level. The upstairs is mostly the kid zone anyway."

I grind my nails into my palms. Erika and Heath started trying around the same time as us, but she got pregnant right away. I faked a migraine at the last minute to get out of going to the baby shower, an event made even more intolerable by its venue: the backyard of the $2.5 million Tudor that she and Heath had just moved into in Wesley Heights.

It was the first place they bid on.

Ian and I could never afford that neighborhood—the rare pocket of DC with detached houses and nice lots, and all the other perks of the burbs without leaving the city. Of course, if Ian wasn't so self-righteous about his work, he would've been a partner at Covington long before Heath's résumé ever made it in the door at Sidley.

He got the offer from the EPA on a Friday, only two weeks after we got engaged. When I came home from work, he had a bottle of good champagne waiting on ice. I was confused because the setup had been almost exactly the same when he'd proposed. "Pretty sure we just did this," I joked.

While he explained what was happening, I stared at the dazzling one and a quarter carats on my ring finger and marveled at how heavy they suddenly felt. The offer was for barely half what he made at the law firm. "It'll still be plenty," he said. A reaction that could only come from someone who'd never been broke.

I knew, obviously, that he'd been through the interviews, that he'd been talking an annoying amount about the global warming action group he belonged to in college. I just didn't think he'd follow through with it. He finally seemed happier at the firm—one of the partners had recently brought him on to a fracking case for an important client. And it was Obama's first term, for chrissake, *everybody* thought they wanted to work for the administration. It had all just seemed like a phase.

Heath turns to Ian now, my cocktail sloshing over the edge of its glass as his gut bumps against our table. "How's the agency treating you, dude?" he asks. "Life a little better these days?"

Ian rakes his fingers back through his hair, the tell that he's on edge. I flag down the server for extra napkins to mop up my drink.

"Yeah, yeah, much better," Ian says. "We've got a lot more latitude. We're going after a pretty big fish right now—one you've definitely heard of—for dumping chemicals into a major river."

"Oh yeah? Who is it? Sounds like pharma."

"No way, man. The general counsel's probably in your foursome at Burning Tree tomorrow."

"Yikes, shots fired!" Heath grabs at his chest. Was he always such a douchebag? "Seriously, though, I still can't believe you've stuck it out there."

Erika and I look at each other. This booth is starting to feel like a holding cell. Everyone is quiet while our server sets down the next round. I ask about their son, Luca, and make a half-hearted effort to seem interested in the animal sounds he knows how to make now. But we all know the night has gone terminal.

"This has been so much fun," I say. "We can't wait this long without getting together again."

"I know, it's been way too long," Erika agrees. "Too bad the sitter can't stay. Otherwise, we could do dinner."

"Next time," I say.

On the walk home, Ian reminds me of one of the crunched-up White Claw cans littering the sidewalk. Hands jammed in his pockets. Hunched into himself. Brow hardened into a scowl. Normally, I'd roll my eyes at him being such a baby, but tonight, I get it. "We don't have to do that again," I tell him.

Once we're through the door of the apartment, he grabs me by the waist and pulls me against him. I search his face, genuinely surprised. I can't remember the last time we had a spontaneous fuck.

"Come on," he whispers. "I just want to feel something else."

I let him take us to the bedroom. He finishes fast on top, then makes me come with his fingers. More an act of efficiency than one of passion.

# 4

The first class on the Saturday schedule at Power + Grace Yoga starts at nine a.m., which means I'm in the parking lot by eight thirty. Ian thinks I'm meeting with a potential client, so I left the apartment in a sheath dress over a sports bra. Once I was out of the city, I pulled behind a gas station and wriggled into yoga pants.

Now I watch and wait for the olive-green Audi.

Eight fifty-five and still no sign of it. I am at least thankful that Jack Lombardi doesn't drive a black Range Rover. There appears to be an infestation of those here. I, on the other hand, occupy the only dinged-up, decade-old Prius. A collector's item, really.

At a little after nine, one more Range Rover tears into the parking lot, followed by a BMW. Two blond ponytails bounce into the studio. Still no Audis.

The classes here are fifty minutes long and start every hour, on the hour, until two o'clock. I packed a sandwich and plenty of water, and scouted a convenient public restroom at the Starbucks in this same complex. But judging by how put together Jack was yesterday, I'm guessing he's a morning-class guy. For now, I'm way down the rabbit hole of Zoe Estelle's Instagram, scrolling through before-and-afters.

This woman is a genius, presumably an obscenely expensive one. Fuck Erika.

As the first round of students begins to trickle back out, I see a flash of olive green pull into a spot by the entrance. Jack emerges, mat under his arm, in red short-shorts and a tight gray tank top, white sweatshirt draped effortlessly over his shoulders. All these housewives must worship him.

I wait a couple minutes so he can get settled; then I scramble inside. The girl up front makes me fill out a form and takes my credit card. The classroom is through a glass door to the left. I lean back from the desk to look for Jack. He's in the second row, an open spot still beside him.

As soon as I have my card back, I kick off my Birkenstocks and hustle through the door. Hundred-degree heat blasts me like bad breath. How did I miss that this was *hot* yoga? And, shit, my water bottle is still in the car. But if I go back for it, someone else will swipe my place.

I hike up my leggings, tucking the soft part around my midsection into the high-rise before I make my approach.

"Mind if I grab this spot?" I ask Jack breezily, as if my skin doesn't feel like it's fusing to Lycra.

"All yours," he says. I catch it then—the flicker of recognition. "Have I seen you here before?"

"No, it's my first time," I say, unrolling my mat. "But you look familiar, too."

He snaps his fingers. "You're the woman from yesterday! From in front of my house."

I laugh and bring my hands to my face, just as I practiced in the mirror. "Oh geez, how embarrassing is this? I was such a mess."

"No, no, not at all. Did you find your way home okay?"

"I did, thank you. I can't believe I'm running into you again! So mortifying."

"Don't worry about it. We all have those days."

"I'm Margo, by the way."

"Jack. Nice to meet you. Or, I guess, see you again."

I have a script in my head—about how I'm getting into yoga to relieve the stress of the adoption process. How my doctor thought it would be good for me, which is barely a lie, since she did suggest yoga once. But Jack's phone is between us, face up, and an incoming text brings it to life. Penny is the wallpaper.

"Oh my gosh, is that your daughter? She's gorgeous!"

"Yeah, that's our Penny." He grins. "You know, it's funny, when we were chatting yesterday, I thought, *I wish Penny were with me.*"

"Really? Why's that?"

He hesitates. Just say it, Jack. Come on.

"Well, you know, she just doesn't have a chance to interact with many . . . well, with many Asian women." He cringes. "Oh my God, does that sound completely awful? Am I being totally offensive?"

I laugh. "No, I get it!" Then I drop the hammer. "My husband and I are considering adopting. So, trust me, I know what a big deal all the literature makes about cultural representation."

Jack's mouth falls open; his eyebrows lift to a height our Botoxed classmates could only dream of. He's about to say something, when a firm handclap snaps our attention to the front of the room. A size-zero in a white sports bra beams an even whiter smile at us.

"Good morning, everyone! We've got a full house of regulars today," she says, "but I see a couple new yogis among us. Very exciting! Welcome! I'm Shannon, and this is Fire Flow Level 2. Let's get started in a tabletop position."

Jack mouths: "We'll talk after."

I am squealing inside. Although I might be about to die. I haven't taken a yoga class since before the pandemic, and I don't make it down to our building's gym as often as I mean to. Hence my size-four ass turning steadily into a six.

This warm-up seems doable enough, though. We're on all fours, doing a series of cat-cows, alternating between arching our backs and rounding them.

"Let's do four more," says Shannon. "Remember to stay connected to your breath. That's all yoga is—just moving and breathing." She has good delivery. I can see why Jack likes this place. "Now let's step it out to a plank. And we're holding for ten . . . nine . . . eight . . ."

These are the longest seconds I have ever heard. But I've got this. We're just moving and breathing. Moving and breathing. That's all Shannon says we're here to do.

"Are we feeling spicy this morning?" Shannon asks. "I think we've got a spicy bunch here!"

I do not know what gave her that impression.

"Let's turn it up with some slow-motion mountain-climbers. You're gonna bring right knee to right triceps—hold, two, three, four—now left knee to left triceps—hold, two, three, four. Three more each side, double time, let's go!"

Fuck you, Shannon. Am I about to be sick? Breathe. Just breathe. Moving and breathing. I am moving and breathing.

"Nice work, guys, take a child's pose."

I collapse onto my mat, then peek at Jack. Are you kidding me? He's holding in a head stand, a layer of sweat glinting off every ripple of his shoulder muscles.

"Honey, are you okay?" Shannon is leaning down to whisper in my ear. "If you need to step out, feel free."

"Uh, thanks, I'm fine." I whisper back. "Just haven't done hot yoga in a while."

This is humiliating.

"Okay, team, let's come to the top of our mats for our sun salutation As."

I make it through the sun As and sun Bs, two sets of side planks, and the first flowing series, only because Shannon keeps looking directly at me and saying things like, "Remember, crew, listen to your body" and "Don't be afraid to take it down to the mat for a child's pose" and "If you disconnect from your breath, take a beat to find it again." All euphemisms for: "Hey, chub in the second row, do what you need to do, just don't pass out on me."

Now we're holding in a high lunge, and I'm determined to power through because I have already spent half the class in a child's pose. But I'm losing the feeling in my front leg and the room is starting to narrow. My vision is . . . staticky.

Two hard claps. "Vinyasa!" Shannon stares at me like a doe in high beams. "Everyone, go ahead and take it down to the mat."

I steady myself and attempt to begin my descent, but Shannon is at my side, grabbing onto my elbow. She leans in. "Ma'am, I really think you need to take a water break outside."

Jack casts a side-eye in my direction. He must think I'm a mess.

"Okay," I say. "Good idea."

Being called ma'am by a twentysomething Blake Lively look-alike might be the only thing as devastating as losing eleven bidding wars. The class is almost over anyway. I gulp water from a paper cup in the lobby while I wait for Jack. When he emerges, I see he has my mat.

"Hey, are you okay?" he asks, handing it to me.

"Just really regretting that third round of cocktails last night," I say, looking sheepish.

"Ah. I've been there." He laughs. I notice several women noticing him, noticing me. "Well, if you're feeling up to it, I'd still love to talk adoption. My husband says I'm basically an evangelist for it—always trying to convert everyone."

I smile. "I would love to be your convert."

"We could grab coffee at the Starbucks right there. Or, if you don't mind driving, we could go to Clover. You know it, right, since you live in the neighborhood?"

I have prepared for this.

"One of my best friends lives in the neighborhood. We were

running together yesterday and I'd just dropped her off at her house when you found me. My husband was coming to pick me up on the corner of Mass Ave."

"Oh, got it. Did your friend tell you about Power + Grace, too?"

"Yeah, she was supposed to meet me this morning, but her son is sick. I was already most of the way here, all the way from Shaw, when she bailed, so I figured why not?"

"Shaw! How hip. We've been dying to try Causa."

"Oh! I could get you a table if you want. My firm does their PR."

He gasps. "That is so cool."

Maybe I do love my job.

The eleven a.m. cohort is crowding into the small lobby, so we clear out. Clover is less than five minutes away. It's shabby-chic like the set of an Anthropologie shoot. We grab a table in the courtyard, under an arbor.

"This place is adorable," I say, taking a sip of oat-milk cappuccino. "Does it always feel like you're on vacation in this neighborhood?"

"It really kind of does. We've loved every second here. But Curt, my husband, has an opportunity at King's College in London that he can't pass on. They just asked him a week ago to join their economics department, and we've always said we'd try living abroad one day."

"Wow! That's so exciting. He must be brilliant."

Jack laughs. "Penny and I try to keep him humble."

"And what about you?" I ask. "What will you do in London?"

"That's still TBD." He removes the lid from his pour-over, freeing a wisp of steam. "I do commercial furniture sales here, for big office tenants, so you can imagine that business has been pretty unpredictable lately. I'm looking forward to taking some time off and just being a full-time dad for a while."

"That's great. Especially since I'm sure the move will be an adjustment for Penny."

"Exactly. I want to be one hundred percent available for her. We're doing what we can to minimize the disruption. We're waiting till the end of the school year to go, and then she'll have an entire summer to get acclimated before she starts first grade, or, I guess they call it year two there, don't they?"

I shrug. "I've only visited a couple times." This type of lie starts to come easily, once you've spent enough years in a town where it feels like everyone else was raised by diplomats who summered on Mallorca.

"Penny is extremely social—so I know she'll be fine," Jack continues. "But yes, of course, it's bound to be at least something of an adjustment. My next to-do is figuring out what kind of gymnastics programs they have over there. She just loves her team here, and her coach says she shows a lot of promise."

I'm realizing he isn't an adoption evangelist so much as a Penny evangelist. I need to find a way in.

"So, did you adopt her as an infant?"

"Oh God, listen to me blathering on, when we're here to help *you*. Yes, she was teeny-tiny when she came home. And as you can probably tell, she is the best thing that has ever happened to us."

I bring a hand to my chest. "That's so sweet," I say. "That's the feeling that I'm after. It's really all I want in the entire world—to love a child like that." (Well, that, and a house where we can actually fit a kid.)

"Then you'll be a wonderful parent. But do you mind if I ask whether you've tried . . . other ways?"

I laugh. "Of course not. We started trying a few months before the pandemic. Buzz—that's my PR firm—had finally made me a vice president, so I felt like I was at a place in my career where I could step away for a few months without falling off a cliff, you know? I was thirty-five by then, but my doctor assured me it would be fine."

All of that is true. I was ovulating on time. Taking all the right vitamins and supplements. Choking down whole milk and sardines. Doing everything you're supposed to do.

I let out a sigh. "It just hasn't been that easy."

Jack takes a drink of his coffee now that it's cool enough. "Did you ever think about in vitro?"

A familiar sting sprouts in my gut.

. . .

Walnuts were the tipping point.

After we'd been trying for forever, I convinced Ian to start eating a cup of them every day. I would put them out for him in the morning with his coffee. A cute little sperm-count-boosting ritual, I'd thought. And really, it seemed like the least he could do, given all the sacrifices *I'd* made—caffeine, alcohol, red meat—an especially tall order when you hang out at restaurants and hotels for a living. Plus, he was getting laid every other day!

But one morning, he refused to eat them. He said he just didn't feel like it, that his stomach was unsettled. I felt the incinerator click on inside me—I get hot when I'm angry—and before I could think, I picked up the bowl and threw it as hard as I could at the fridge, walnuts and glass flying in all directions. (If you know where to look, you can still find a dent in the stainless steel.) I get that I probably overreacted, but it was like the rage had swallowed me from the inside out.

So that's when we made the appointment to talk about IVF. We already knew we'd be good candidates for it. Dr. Warner had said as much when we passed our fertility tests with flying colors a couple months before. But she thought it was too soon to give up on conceiving naturally, especially since there didn't seem to be anything wrong with us. Now, we explained, the status quo was becoming untenable.

"Okay..." she said skeptically, appraising us through wire-rim frames, "but this walnut incident concerns me. Is this only about getting pregnant, Margo, or is something else making you anxious? Have you maybe been under more pressure at work?"

It had only been a few days since we'd lost out on house number five. Ian broke in to tell her all about the toll he thought the search was starting to take.

"Listen, honey," Dr. Warner said, "you've come this far. Waiting a few more months won't hurt. Why don't you and Ian focus on getting the house squared away, and then we can revisit IVF?"

When I started to protest, she cut me off: "The research may not be conclusive, but I can tell you from years and years of doing this that stress *can* impact the results. And in vitro is a marathon. It's an enormous commitment, and it can be quite psychologically taxing—it's a lot to take on if you already have a full plate. I just want to make sure you're set up for the best chance of success if we do indeed go this route. And honestly"—she winked then—"I'm still not convinced we'll need to. Who knows? Maybe once you find your house, you'll be able to relax enough that it'll finally happen on its own."

"I appreciate your concern, I really do," I said, "but I think I'd feel better if we just got the ball rolling now."

"Well, the other factor to weigh, of course, is the expense. I'm obviously not your accountant, but I would advise that you take the time to seriously evaluate that piece of this."

I knew Ian was already worried about the cost, so I wasn't surprised when he piped up. "It could turn into a huge stretch," he said, looking from Dr. Warner to me, "and you know Ginny said we shouldn't take out any other loans right now."

My throat thickened then. As the first tears surfaced, Dr. Warner reached across her desk to comfort me. "Do you think it would help to talk to someone? I can refer you to a wonderful therapist. She's right here in the same buil—"

"No." I knew immediately that I'd said it too harshly. Dr. Warner pulled her hand back from the top of mine. "It's just that my eggs obviously aren't getting any younger," I continued, trying to soften my tone. "What if we never get pregnant, and by the time we try IVF, my goods are all, you know, *dried up?*"

Dr. Warner smiled sympathetically. "I think you just need to take a deep breath, Margo."

"Couldn't I at least *freeze* them now?" I asked. "For peace of mind? Just to know I have a decent supply ready to go if we need them for in vitro later on?"

She leaned back in her chair, considering me. "It's an interesting idea," she said. "That *would* be less of a commitment at this point. And I mean, if that's really what would make you feel better, then sure, we can pursue that."

On our way out, Dr. Warner encouraged me to loosen up—"Try to stop putting so much pressure on yourself"—advice that didn't yet make me want to put my head through a wall.

Ian and I have been in a holding pattern ever since. We don't try nearly as rigorously as we used to, especially since we've accepted that we have no idea when we'll have an actual nursery. But we're not *not* trying, either. It's like our life is on ice, right along with my eggs.

. . .

"We looked into IVF for a minute," I lie to Jack, "but I never felt like it was the right option for us. I really feel like it's my calling to give a home to a child who needs one."

"I was the same way," he says. "Curt wanted to use a surrogate so the baby would at least be biologically related to one of us. But that just didn't make any sense to me at all. Like, we have this beautiful life, why not share it with a child who's already out there somewhere?"

I nod, knowingly. "My husband felt that way at first, too. He was so hung up on having his *own* child. It was incredibly frustrating."

Ian and I have never discussed adoption. But if we were out of options, I bet he'd go for it. He has always wanted children, even, he claims, when he was just a kid, which I still find hard to believe. You don't see a lot of little boys playing house, you know? I, on the other hand, wasn't sure about having a baby until I met him—really, until I met his family and glimpsed the life that was possible.

I slurp the dregs of my lukewarm cappuccino. Jack thumbs through his phone, pulling up the contact info for their adoption agency. "You should talk to them," he says. "Hope Springs. They were fantastic. They do all domestic adoptions."

"Oh, really?" I try—badly, judging by Jack's face—to hide my surprise. "And how did you decide on that route?"

"Well, we were somewhat limited," he says. "It's incredibly challenging, and often illegal, for gay couples to adopt internationally."

"Oh! Duh. I'm so sorry."

"Penny is Chinese-American, if you're wondering. Her parents were in Philly."

"Of course. I shouldn't have assumed. I'm Japanese-American."

"No big deal. Happens a lot." He waves me off. "And I'm not saying domestic adoption was easy. There are birth parents here who don't want to place their babies with same-sex couples, either. You guys won't have to worry about that, obviously." He pauses for another swig of coffee. "But make sure you're prepared for the home study process—it'll be months of background checks and interviewing references and coming to your house, and the whole nine. It's going to feel overwhelming at times, but trust me, it'll all be worth it."

*Home study.*

He smiles reassuringly: "Once you're in the thick of it, you can text me, and I'll remind you how empty my life was before Penny."

"That is so generous," I say, before letting out a long sigh. "It's those visits to our house that I'm worried about."

"Why? Because you live in the city? I thought Shaw was full of young families."

"No, it's not the neighborhood, although I do have my heart set on Bethesda. My girlfriend, the one I told you about, loves it here. And the public schools can't be beat."

He nods. "They're the best."

"It's that we've been stuck in a one-bedroom apartment for a year and a half, and we've held off signing a new lease on a bigger place because we're hoping to buy."

"Oh." He frowns. "Yeah, the market is really tough right now."

"You're telling me." I shake my head. "We've really been through it."

As I unspool the whole saga, I think I can see the wheels turning. Maybe I'm projecting. But when I'm done, he just sits there quietly, like he's weighing something. I give him a nudge: "But this is all great for you, right, assuming you two are selling?"

"Yeah, we're aiming to list by the end of the month." He pauses again. I can tell he's holding something back. "You're right, the timing has worked out pretty well for us."

"Maybe we can buy your house!" I say it like it's a joke. We both laugh.

"It *is* funny that we met like this," he says. My heart rate picks up. "And God, we've put so much work into that place—you should've seen the sad kitchen when we bought it. I would love to know that it's in good hands."

Yes, yes, yes. Say it, Jack. An off-market deal has to seem like his idea.

"What's your budget, if you don't mind my ask—"

"One three."

Jack goes silent again. But my pulse is deafening, booming louder than the bass of all those idling Ubers full of drunk morons, clogging U Street on Saturday nights.

"That might be in the ballpark," he says finally. "Well, I'll be sure to give you a heads-up when we know what day it's hitting the market. That way you and your agent can be first in the door."

Fuck.

Now Jack's phone lights up. "Just a sec, this is Curt." He holds up a finger. "Hey, I'm just at Clover with a yoga friend.... Uh-huh ... Sure, that's fine. Okay, see you in a minute."

He turns back to me. "Yay! You get to meet Penny!"

My stomach does a little flip. I guess winning over Jack was only my opening act.

# 5

I spot Penny as soon as Curt's gray Volvo loops around the lot. Her window is down and she's waving at us from the backseat, sporting a jean jacket, her black bangs skimming the top of the mini Wayfarers she was wearing in Jack's Instagram photo. She reminds me of me at her age, only with cuter clothes and better parents.

"Hi, Daddy!" she yells.

A reporter from the *Washington Business Journal* wants to interview Curt for some story about the supply chain, so now Jack is on duty to take Penny to a play date at the park that starts in ten minutes. Curt is dropping her here to save time.

"Hi, sweetie! How's your morning going?" Jack asks while he unbuckles Penny's car seat. "Daddy gets to take you to the park to play with Violet now. Isn't that fun?"

I wave to Curt through the rolled-down passenger window. His head is shaved clean—he must've given up on his thinning hair. The thick glasses are the same.

"Hey, I'm Margo."

"Glad to know you, Margo." He smiles, but there's a softness missing from his eyes. "I'm Curt."

"Sorry, so rude of me!" says Jack, now with Penny next to him on the sidewalk. "Curt, this is Margo, and guess what? She and her husband are thinking about adoption!"

"Oh my, that's wonderful," says Curt. "Jack's the right man to know, then."

"Yes, he's been so helpful," I say, as I crouch down. "And *you* must be the famous Penny."

The little girl grins and shakes my hand—precocious. "You're Daddy's friend?"

"Yes, honey, Margo is my friend from yoga class," Jack interjects.

"I have a friend at school called Margo," Penny tells me. I feel her studying my face. "But you're prettier than her."

Jack exchanges a look with Curt.

"Wow, Penny, thank you. I think you're really pretty, too. But even more important, I can tell you're super smart, aren't you? And I hear you're amazing at gymnastics."

Penny glows. I catch another glance between her dads. Pretty sure I'm nailing this.

"Can you come to the park with us?" she asks me.

Bull's-eye.

"Oh, honey, I'm sure Margo has other things she needs to do today," Jack says.

"That's okay, I could come for a bit," I say quickly. "It's not far from here, right?"

"Really?" Jack looks at me. "You're sure you wouldn't mind?"

"Not at all. Sounds like fun."

Penny takes my hand, the press of her miniature palm doubling my resolve—*No house, no baby*. I know I'm not supposed to care about gender, or even acknowledge it as anything more than a social construct, but I really would prefer a girl.

"Excellent!" Curt says from the car. "Have a great time, you three. Terrific to meet you, Margo." He blows Penny a kiss and drives away.

I follow behind the Audi in my ancient Prius, to Grovemont

Park, where it appears to be rush hour. The lot is a jumble of parents pushing strollers and trying to keep a grip on little wrists. Jack and Penny wait for me by the sign at the entrance. She takes my hand again and leads me to the playground.

This place is like Disneyland compared to the parks I've seen in the city. A sprawling, bright-blue climbing thing that looks like a dragon curls through one side. At the other end, a slide spirals down from an elaborate, Craftsman-style treehouse that, in the right neighborhood, could probably fetch an offer or two. Penny spies her friend on the swings and jets over, pulling me with her.

"Violet! This is Margo!" she yells.

The girl jumps off her swing and runs up to us. She's a few inches taller than Penny.

"Nice to meet you," I tell Violet, as a woman with the same mousy hair as the little girl scurries over.

"Hi there, I'm Violet's mom!" she says loudly, each syllable practically dripping. She doesn't offer her actual name, or a handshake. "How exciting! Did Jack and Curt finally find a new nanny?"

She carefully enunciates each word, her smile stretched to a disturbing tautness. I know what this is—she's not sure if I speak English.

Jack catches up to us before I have to explain. "Hey, Claire, this is our friend Margo. She tagged along after yoga."

The woman's already pink complexion flushes redder. "Oh! I'm so sorry." Now she extends a hand. "I'm Claire. So great to meet you."

Yeah, *so great* that you can now tell the bitches in your book club you have an ethnic friend.

Penny joins Violet on the swings, and the three of us commandeer a bench nearby. Claire is still yammering away, trying to convince me—or maybe herself—that she's not racist. "I'm *so* embarrassed. It's just that Jack has been saying for months they need to find someone. Haven't you, Jack? But I should *not* have assumed." She taps my knee. I want to hit her. "The girls' gymnastics schedule has really ramped up this year, so a lot of us who ditched our help when they started kindergarten are scrambling again."

Jack laughs uncomfortably. When Claire's attention shifts to the girls, he rolls his eyes so only I can see. I shrug in response.

"So, Violet and Penny do gymnastics together?" I ask, packing away my rage.

"Yes, Violet's a fantastic tumbler," Jack says, clearly relieved to find the off-ramp. "She and Penny met in Little Gym when they were only three."

"God, they were just too cute for words back then, right?" Claire chimes in. "Margo, do you have children?"

Not an altogether unreasonable question to ask a full-grown woman hanging out at a playground. But it still hurts (especially coming from a pinched-face twat who probably masturbates to the Lands' End catalog).

"Not yet," I say, pleasantly. "My husband and I certainly want them, though. We've just started exploring adoption."

Claire again turns the color of a diaper rash.

"Good for you," she says. "I'm sure Jack has been a huge help."

"We haven't known each other long, but yes, he's already been awesome," I say, flashing Jack a smile.

Claire starts to say something else but stops when she sees Violet running toward us in tears. Penny trails her.

"Oh my goodness, sweetheart, what's the matter?" Claire wraps her daughter into a hug.

Violet struggles to form comprehensible words between sobs but manages to relay the general idea that Penny has shared the news about London.

Claire whips toward Jack, her thin lips parted in surprise. "Is that true?" she gasps.

"I was just about to tell you myself," he says. "Curt got a senior faculty job—at King's College. It's a great opportunity. But trust me, I'm still in shock, too."

Claire fishes two cookies from the depths of her nautical-striped tote and hands them to the girls, which seems to alleviate some of the drama. Then she rounds back on Jack.

"But London is so far away! And doesn't Curt already have tenure at Georgetown?" Before Jack can answer, she leans in closer to him. "You know Penny is the *star* at gymnastics," she whispers so Violet doesn't hear. "She's really been thriving this year."

This, I've gathered, is one of the shitty parts of having children: if your kid makes a best friend, you have to figure out a way to tolerate their parents, no matter how much they suck.

"Well, yes, Curt does have a nice setup at Georgetown, and this will be a very big change for all of us," Jack starts. "But we'll be able to travel all over Europe. It'll be a whole new education for Penny."

As if he should have to justify any of this. At least the girls seem over it. They're running back to the swings, cookie crumbs crusted onto the corners of their mouths.

"Oh, of course. I'm sure you've been very thoughtful about everything," says Claire. "Penny just seems very happy *here*, that's all. You must've really agonized over the decision to uproot her."

For fuck's sake, this woman is like a yeast infection in human form. But maybe I can use this....

"I'm sorry to interrupt, but I just have to say that I've never met another six-year-old like Penny. She's so confident and mature." I turn to Jack. "Whenever I'm lucky enough to become a mom, you'll have to tell me how you and Curt did it."

His face relaxes. "Thank you," he says. "That's lovely."

"It's true," I say. "I just can't imagine she'll have any problem at all in London."

Claire clears her throat, then picks at an imaginary piece of lint on her sleeve. Surely, neutralizing that idiot must've won me some points with Jack.

"Margo!" Penny yells from the swings. "Come push us!"

I wave at her and get up from the bench.

"I'll come, too," says Jack.

"Thank you for saving me," he whispers once we're far enough from Claire. "She's just upset because Penny is one of Violet's only friends."

With each push of her swing, Penny asks me a different question: "What's your job?" "Where do you live?" "What's your favorite animal?"

And finally: "Do you want to come over to my house?"

I suck in a breath, waiting for Jack's reaction.

"That's a nice idea, sweetie," he says, while he pushes Violet next to us. He turns to me: "Would you and your husband want to come over for dinner this week?"

A fizzy warmth spreads through my chest.

"Oh my gosh," I say, "we would love that!"

Jack and I settle on Wednesday at six. I should really start calling her Lucky Penny.

# 6

"Margo, are you out of your mind?"

Ian tosses the remote down on the coffee table hard enough that the battery cover pops off the back. He's still in his gym clothes, but the endorphins I was counting on have clearly already waned.

I knew he wouldn't take this well. Which is why I waited till now to tell him. When I got home from the playground yesterday, the timing just didn't feel right. He was going to the Nats game with coworkers, so it wouldn't have been fair to put him through a fight first. Then they lost to the Mets five-nothing and he was in a terrible mood. So, really, this is the first reasonable opening I had.

"It's not like I asked to come to dinner," I say, keeping my tone calm so I don't escalate things. "Jack invited us. All I did was go to a yoga class and make conversation."

"Are you listening to yourself? Do you actually believe that? You didn't just 'go to a yoga class.'" Ian holds his fingers up in air quotes. "You stalked this guy."

I roll my eyes. "You're being so dramatic. I did not *stalk* him. Ginny said her sister-in-law loves that yoga studio and I've been meaning to get back into practicing anyway. It seemed harmless."

"Then why did you lie to me about where you were going?" Ian rises from our gray couch and comes toward me in the kitchen.

"Because I didn't want to worry you! I had no idea if I'd even run into him at all, and you can be so irrational."

"That is some good shit right there." He laughs dryly. "Yeah, I am the irrational one."

"Ian, come on, you know this isn't a normal market. We have to be strategic if we ever want to get out of this place."

"We've offered six figures over asking on almost every single house!"

"Exactly! And we're still here! We need an edge, and I got us one, as fucking usual. You're welcome."

"Give me a goddamn break! *You're* the whole reason we're here in the first place!"

"Yeah, because I'm the one with the balls to strive for something."

So much for staying calm. He stares at me, unblinking, gripping the back of that counter stool so hard it looks like his knuckles might burst through his skin.

Then: "Fuck you, Margo." His voice is barely more than a whisper.

I narrow my eyes. "What did you just say to me?"

"I said, 'Fuck you.'" He's back to full volume, doubling down. "You're acting like a fucking bitch."

Is he playing misogyny bingo or something?

"Yeah, let's hear it, Indiana!" I'm clapping now, like a lunatic. "You can take the boy outta middle America!"

"I am not listening to this."

Ian grabs his keys and wallet off the shelf by the entry and picks up his gym shoes without stopping to put them on. He slams the door so hard the walls shake. Some Sunday morning entertainment for our neighbors.

He's never called me a bitch before. And we have had some other epic blowouts.

The last time he stormed out like this, we were living in the row house. That time, he slammed the door with so much force the latch jammed and we had to call a locksmith to fix it. It was August 2020, and pouring so hard it sounded like the rain was inside.

I'd just given Ginny the go-ahead to list.

"Do you remember that I live here, too?" Ian asked, as he paced back and forth, fingers entwined in his hair. "I don't understand why you think you can decide this without me."

"I don't think that at all." I was looking up at him from the same gray couch—from Room & Board, one of our first grown-up purchases—my legs folded into a crisscross. "You're the one who said when interest rates fell below three percent, you'd be ready to sell, and now they have. So, I was simply relaying to Ginny what you already told me."

If I'd learned anything from my parents' fucked-up marriage, it was that making the other person think they're in control when they're really not is often the easiest way to win a fight. But Ian would not back down.

"We're in the middle of a pandemic, Margo, and you're almost guaranteeing that we'll wind up in some apartment building, with two hundred other people touching the door handles and the elevator buttons and blasting their droplets or whatever all over the goddamn place. I'm just asking for more time to think about it."

"Well, I'm willing to wear a mask and wash my hands for a couple months if it means we can make a mountain of cash, then turn around and buy a nicer house than we ever imagined because the banks are practically giving away mortgages."

"Don't you remember when you thought this house was nice?"

That had made me laugh—which of course made Ian madder—because at that very moment, I had no doubt our basement was flooding. We'd made a lot of improvements by then, mostly thanks to Ian's dad flying in from Indianapolis to help. But the basement required a real waterproofing contractor, and we'd resisted spending the money.

"Be real, Ian," I said, "we probably have two inches of standing water below us."

"This place *could* be enough, though," he said. "We could keep fixing it up. We would at least be safe here until there's a vaccine."

"And when's that going to be?" I asked. "We don't have forever. We're trying to start a family now, right? Unless you don't care about that anymore."

"Jesus, Margo, do not hold that over my head. I'm not saying no. I just need to think about it some more."

By that point, I was out of patience.

"Okay, well maybe *I* need to think some more about the baby."

I didn't mean it, of course, I just needed a conversation-ender. Ian's mouth dropped open. After a beat, he started to say something, then thought better of it and turned to leave. I saw him grab a mask but not an umbrella, heard the explosive bang of the front door. A couple hours later, he showed up soaking wet, knocking on the back door because he'd broken the front handle.

"Fine," he said, when I let him in. "Let's list it."

I couldn't have known then that we'd end up in the apartment for eighteen months. But even if I had, I wouldn't have done anything different. Because now that I have a real in with Jack, I'm certain this whole excruciating ordeal will have been worth it.

Ian can slam doors and call me names, but he will be at that dinner on Wednesday, bells fucking on. He'll come around, like he always does. We may be in a rough patch now, but he is the most dependable person I've ever known. He gets it from his parents. They've been devoted to each other for over forty years. They'd die if they knew their son called me a bitch. Especially his mom.

Maybe I should make her roast chicken tonight. It might do Ian some good to think about her.

I tap out a text: *Hey Debbie, hope you're having a nice weekend! Can you remind me what type of white wine you use for your chicken?*

*Hi honey!* she writes back. *Usually sauvignon blanc, but anything dry will do. Just call if you need me.*

Now I send another text to our neighbor Natalie to ask if she wants to tag along to the farmers market. Really, I only care about seeing Fritter—her scruffy black-and-white muppet of a rescue dog. Natalie says they're in, so I head down to meet them in the lobby. The communal areas here all have that generic, organic-modern vibe going on—matte black light fixtures, fake fiddle-leaf fig trees—and they always smell vaguely of artificial citrus because the building pumps in a "signature scent." God, I am so sick of living here.

Natalie's apartment is two floors above ours. I met her and Fritter on the roof deck not long after Ian and I moved in. I'd been looking for a quiet place to work on a sunny fall day. She'd been on the phone with her divorce lawyer.

"Hey, Nat. Wow, your hair!"

More platinum highlights. If she goes any brighter, she'll be a traffic hazard. Fritter looks up at me from knee height, with adoring brown eyes. I bend down to give him a deep scratch behind both ears, the way he loves.

"Thanks, girl. I was worried it might be too much, but I think it's growing on me. What's up with you?"

I can't tell her that I found my dream house or that I'm in a fight with Ian about it, so I ramble on about work for a block. Natalie will take over the conversation any second now. It's chilly and lightly misting in that annoying way that isn't helped by an umbrella. I yank the zipper of my North Face up to my chin.

"Have you ever done coke before fucking?" Natalie asks, right on cue, in the same tone you might use to inquire about a colleague's Wordle score. A guy walking past with a toddler on his shoulders does a double take.

"Um, no."

"Color me shocked," she deadpans, rolling her eyes at my lameness.

"Aren't you glad you at least have me around to keep things interesting?"

Natalie got married right out of college—evangelical upbringing and all that nonsense—and ever since the divorce, she's been trying to reclaim her lost youth. She was a recruiter before she started working as a bartender at some ironically divey place in Mount Pleasant. She swears the career switch was her idea, but one time when she was drunk, she let slip that her old boss put her on "probation" for offering Molly to his assistant at a company retreat. I tried to coax more details out of her, but she was too wasted to focus.

Natalie refers to this current chapter as her "freedom era." Most everyone else would call it a midlife crisis, or maybe a third-life crisis since she's only thirty-one. She hooked up with a new guy last night—there's always a new guy, or a new girl—and she's spilling every gory detail like she's dictating stage directions for a low-budget porn.

"We did it four times. And in between, he did this thing with his tongue that's hard to explain, but it was off the charts. Then we did it once more this morning."

"That sounds . . . honestly, painful."

"Oh, it's all about the lube. I can give you some recommendations if you want." She pops her gum. "I'm sure you need it more than anyone, all that health-class diagram *baby-making* you're probably soldiering through."

Natalie may fuck anything with a face now, but she hasn't forgotten the first commandment of her megachurch past: thou shalt make others feel harshly judged whenever the opportunity arises.

"You're being safe, right?" I ask, pivoting away from her dig.

"Oh, come on, give me some credit. Yes, Mom!"

"All right, all right."

Far be it for me to give a shit. It's not like anyone else is lining up to help Natalie. Her lobbyist ex is already engaged again (don't feel too bad—he pays enough alimony to cover all her rent). Her parents are still mad about the divorce, and from the way she talks about her other friends, it sounds like they've all settled happily into their own newlywed routines. I would've cut her loose a long time ago, too, if it wasn't for Fritter. She leaves him alone so often, he's basically half mine.

"You know I'm always happy to take him if you can't make it home," I say, nodding down at him as he eagerly investigates patches of U Street grime. More than once, I reach over and jerk him away from a chicken bone. You'd think Natalie might get the hint and start paying attention.

"I know, girl. You're the best. But we were at my place last night."

Now I feel bad that Fritter probably had to witness all that. I shoot him a sympathetic look.

It's twelve forty-five and the crowd at the farmers market is already starting to thin. Some vendors are packing up. I hustle over to the produce section for carrots and thyme; then I hit up the dairy lady for a container of fresh butter. (The weekend market in Grovemont has a much better selection than this—and it's *so* much cleaner.)

I spot Natalie at the smoothie stand, leaning into the counter just enough to push up her cleavage. The guy working there—he looks barely out of college—crouches to pet Fritter. I wonder if that's why she keeps him around, for the extra attention he attracts. While I wait for her, I rummage for my phone in my crossbody bag. Still no word from Ian.

"Everything okay?" Natalie asks, a heaping acai bowl threatening to drip down the front of her white zip-up.

"Oh yeah, it's nothing." I stash my phone again. "Just an annoying email from a client."

We pick up the pace on the way back since the sky has turned angrier. I remind Natalie that I have a work event this Thursday—one of her late-shift nights—but that I'll still come by to let Fritter out as soon as it's over. We say goodbye on the street, and I detour to Whole Foods for the rest of my dinner ingredients.

...

The lights are off when I get back to the apartment, the whole place cast in the same stormy gray as the clouds outside the floor-to-ceiling window. Part of me expected him to be here by now, parked on the sofa, waiting to apologize—he's almost always the first one of us to say sorry.

Before him, I'd been a magnet for assholes ("daddy issues," any armchair shrink would say). But I could tell right away that Ian was different.

When we first started dating, he lived by himself in Chinatown and I had two roommates in Columbia Heights, so we spent a lot of nights at his place. It didn't matter how little notice I gave him that I was coming over, if it was after dark, he would be there waiting for me at the Metro. And every Sunday, rain or shine, he'd meet me at my place to go grocery shopping. Neither of us had a car back then, and that way, he could help me carry the bags.

Ian shows up. It's just what he does. So where the fuck is he now?

At five o'clock, I give in and send the first text: *Are you coming home for dinner?*

I stare at the screen, willing those three little dots to materialize. Nothing.

I mix myself a Manhattan—drinking cocktails again is one perk of pregnancy purgatory—and put the chicken in the oven. At seven, I text again: *Can you let me know you're okay?*

This time, the three dots do appear, but only for a second before fading away. So he's deliberately ignoring me then. A twinge of fury jabs into my ribs. The apartment smells like Thanksgiving and my stomach sounds like a diesel engine, so you know what? Fuck him. I'm not going to sit here and starve.

I carve into the perfect golden bird and take a plate to the couch, along with a bottle of Malbec. Time to open Pinterest and design our dream home.

The kitchen is almost exactly what I want already, though I'm not sold on the oversize lantern-style pendants over the island. They're a statement, sure, but are they the right one? I pin two alternatives: simple milk-glass globes with brass canopies from Schoolhouse, and a solid brass dome-shaped option from Shades of Light.

Zoe Estelle's Instagram has persuaded me that painting the wainscoting in the dining room a high-gloss deep jewel tone is the only way to go. Then I'll wallpaper the rest of the way up to the ceiling. I peruse the options on Farrow & Ball's website and fall for a muted purple called Brinjal. Anthropologie has a few wallpapers that would really pick up that color well. I order samples of all of them and pour myself another glass.

Even though I couldn't fully see the living room from the back deck, I can imagine it easily enough, and given the location of the house's chimney, it must have a fireplace. What if I go with two of the same sofa, facing each other over a chunky, live-edge coffee table? That feels right. They'd frame the fire nicely. Chesterfields might be too traditional, but I want to keep the space cozy and inviting, so anything too minimal won't work. Ooh, maybe I do a modern shape but in distressed leather? Or something curvy! In velvet. Moss? Hunter green? No, moss. Definitely moss. Crate & Barrel has a few curved sofas that I pin to my board. I top off my glass, then order some fabric swatches so I can be sure about the shade.

The house already has loads of curb appeal. But the one thing I didn't love were the house numbers. I get it, a Colonial can lean stuffy if you don't make the right choices. But those skinny black things are way too sterile for such a charming facade. What I need is a more classic font, in a warmer finish, maybe antique bronze?

I fill my glass and type those descriptors into Google. Here we go—a nice bold serif from Rejuvenation that looks just about perfect. I think the eight-inch numbers will match the scale of the portico and outdoor lanterns better than the standard six-inch. They're made to order. Better buy them now so we'll have them by the time we move in. So exciting! My first real purchase for our new home!

Shit, did I already polish off this whole bottle?

. . .

After the oven's been on all day, the house swaddles me in its warmth. The oak tree in the backyard blazes a deep auburn. There's a girl on the tire swing, her legs barely long enough to dangle through the opening. Is that Penny? I move closer to the French doors, squinting through them. My breath steams the glass as I let out a surprised little puff.

It's me. I'm the girl.

Going by those purple overalls, the same ones I wore for my third-grade photo, I must be about eight. I look so happy, smiling and giggling, even though I'm all by myself.

My older brother—the adult version—doesn't seem to realize I'm there. He and his boys toss around a football in the grass. I can't believe Cheryl let Mitch take the kids on a holiday. It's drizzling, so I'll have to remind them to leave their shoes on the deck before they come inside.

I'm back at the Carrara marble island, apron on, tending to a homemade piecrust. The heft of this rolling pin, the roughness of its handles, affirm that it's my grandmother's. But how did it get here?

Maybe my mom brought it. She's behind me, checking on the turkey roasting inside the Thermador. My dad's voice dances in from the living room. Did I really invite him? Somehow, I don't feel angry that he's here. I don't feel angry about anything anymore. He's telling some story that's obviously bullshit, but Ian's parents and sister are laughing anyway.

Someone's coming down the stairs now. That must be Ian. I catch a glimpse of him through the arched opening into the living room. He cradles a soft little lump against his chest—our baby. I wish he would turn around so I could see her face.

Fritter is curled up at my feet, hoping I'll drop something delicious. Sweet potatoes, their skins crisp from the oven, rest on a baking sheet on the counter. They're cool enough to cut open, so I run a knife through a small one and scoop the fluffy orange middle into a dish for my little muppet. I am so full of love that I can feel it radiating out of me, touching every corner of every room of the house.

I look up when I hear the French doors opening. My eight-year-old self runs through them. Before I can tell her to take off her Keds, her arms are around my waist.

"Margo," she says, beaming up at me, "we did it."

. . .

A key fumbling in the lock drags me back to consciousness. My mouth feels like I ate a glue stick; a sharpness drills into the backs of my eyes.

Am I still on the couch?

More sounds in the doorway. Keys hitting the shelf. Sneakers kicked off. I squint up at the ceiling; then a figure comes into view, lit only by the blue flickering of the television.

Ian.

"You made my mom's chicken?"

# 7

When my alarm goes off, I wish for death.

Ian snores softly next to me, passed out on his stomach. He didn't get home till after three, which means I've been asleep for maybe four hours. He's never done anything like that before. Where the hell was he? Do I even care, as long as he feels bad enough about it to just do what I fucking want?

As soon as I sit up, my head begins to throb. I stumble into the bathroom and inspect the damage in the mirror. My lips and teeth are stained purple—*Brinjal by Farrow & Ball*. I hold my mouth to the tap and guzzle three Advil, then stand still for a minute to make sure I'm not going to be sick.

On mornings like this, I'm grateful my hair is so thick and straight that I couldn't style it any other way even if I had the time to. I check my weather app—no rain, mid sixties. A wrap dress will do. I throw a pair of heels into my work bag and slip on some flats, since I'd have to be clinically insane to take the bus while teetering this close to puking.

Before I leave, I stick a Post-it note to the fridge: *Don't forget to bring some leftover chicken for lunch. XO.*

Subtext: *You owe me.*

On the walk downtown, I cautiously polish off an egg-and-cheese bagel. It seems to do the trick. By the time I swipe in, I can feel my hangover receding.

Our office hasn't been this full in months. But it's all hands on deck this week for the opening party we're throwing Thursday night for a new hotel client—a boutique operator out of Amsterdam called Mythos Group. They've transformed a nineteenth-century church in Penn Quarter into their first stateside property, The Bexley. It has ninety-eight rooms, an art-deco-meets-mid-century design, and a French brasserie in the lobby helmed by a Michelin-starred chef.

So far, Mythos Group has only hired us to handle the marketing around their US debut. But if we do well, they'll put us on a monthly retainer. And with plans to open at least two more hotels in the area, they could turn into one of our most important clients.

About twenty of us file into the fishbowl conference room in the middle of our space. A few of the younger staffers wear masks—a passive-aggressive middle finger about the mandatory in-person meeting. Fucking Gen Z.

Jordana arrives last, towering over the rest of us in black patent-leather Louboutins as glossy as her dark curls. Those shoes could probably cover a third of our rent.

"Nice to see so many bright, shining faces here today," she says, claiming her place at the head of the table. "Hope you all got some rest this weekend, because we have a full week ahead. As you know, I'm personally handling the national design and travel press attending on Thursday. We'll send around the complete list right after this, so you can review it in advance. But in case you forget who's on it, all the VIPs will be wearing black wristbands."

She pauses to let the life-or-death matter of the wristbands sink in.

"Black. Wrist. Bands," she continues, tapping her own, Cartier-clad wrist. "This is very, very important. If you see someone in a black wristband and their cocktail is empty, or they're alone, or they look otherwise unhappy or bored, step in immediately. Our number one job is to make sure they're experiencing the fun and the luxury and the sexiness of The Bexley at all times."

Jordana settles her gaze on a young assistant named Beth. "You're in charge of the gift bag table, just like when we did the Viceroy opening. But this time, the VIPs are all spending the night in comped rooms, so before they go upstairs, they'll also get a morning-themed gift *box* with monogrammed espresso cups and Chef's house-made granola. Are you taking notes?"

Beth nods solemnly.

"Whatever you do, Beth, do not give those boxes to our regular guests. They are VIP only."

Beth nods again, this time while typing furiously on her laptop.

If you'd told me when I moved to DC that I would spend my days thinking about wristbands and which members of the media were worthy of gift bags versus gift boxes, I might've punched you in the face. I came here to be a journalist. And to start fresh—with an entire continent between me and the wreckage of my family's briefly charmed life.

Student loans and waitressing paid most of my way through the University of Washington; my grandparents pitched in a little, too. I only majored in communications because it seemed like a catch-all for someone who hated math. I'd spent a lot of time by myself when I was little, scribbling down stories in my room to pass the hours alone, but I didn't realize that I had a talent for writing until I took an intro to journalism elective my sophomore year. The same semester, I volunteered to cover a war protest for the school paper and felt the rush of reporting for the first time. I was harder-working than nearly all my classmates, obsessive about getting the story. One of my professors was impressed enough that she emailed a former colleague at *The Washington Post* to help me snag the entry-level aide gig. Back then, I would've told you I planned on becoming an editor one day. But when Ian quit the law firm, I had to rethink everything.

The real estate idea came to me first. We were still digging out of the recession, so home prices weren't terrible—at least not by DC standards—and Ian's parents had given us $30,000 to spend on our wedding. If Ian and I (well, mostly Ian) threw in our savings, we'd have a decent down payment for something small. And if we chose the right neighborhood, with the right potential, we could build serious equity in just a few years.

Ian initially hated the idea, but all it took was a little reminder of how horrific weddings can be for the environment. "Just think of all those floral arrangements, all that leftover catering, rotting away in a landfill," I said. "A traditional wedding just feels so off-brand for you."

Not long after, Erika told me about the open position at Buzz. She'd been on the business beat for a year, and Jordana had become a source for stories about the hospitality industry. "She's a total badass," Erika said. "I think you'd love working for her. And after that mess with the councilman, maybe the timing is right for you to make a change."

Every reporter knows the PR option is out there, beckoning with its promise of luxuries like predictable hours and a living wage. I'd been promoted to general-assignment reporting on the local desk by then, but I was still barely cracking $40,000. I figured it wouldn't hurt to at least send Jordana an email inquiring about the details.

When she sent back the ballpark salary, I was convinced I must be hallucinating. I went in for the interview two days later. And look at me now—Our Lady of the Black Wristbands.

Jordana swivels her chair toward our senior vice president of events. "Okay," she says, "I'll turn it over to Taylor, before we get Margo's update on Rivière."

"Thanks, J," Taylor says chummily. Of all of us, she's closest with Jordana. Not that I don't like my boss. I do. Erika was right, she is a badass. But unlike her and Taylor, I can't bring myself to take this stuff too seriously. The work is fun enough—and I do a good job—but it's a paycheck. A means to a lifestyle.

Taylor is the one with the cousin and the off-market house. She told me about him on the Tuesday that offers were due on house number seven. We were eating salads from Sweetgreen together in the conference room, and I was obsessively checking my phone for any updates from Ginny. Watching me sweat it out, Taylor felt compelled to share her opinion that "it's basically impossible to buy a house in DC right now, unless you're paying all cash. You guys aren't paying cash, right?"

"Definitely not," I'd said, faking a laugh.

"Well, the other way is to find something off-market. That's how my cousin and his wife just did it."

"How'd they manage that?"

"They knew the sellers. Their kids all go to Sidwell together," she'd said nonchalantly. "They figured if they put a deal together themselves, they'd save a fortune on the agent commissions."

Of course, I'd heard of this as a possible strategy. But Taylor's cousin was the first tangible proof I'd gotten that it could really work.

Now Taylor launches into a lecture about the step-and-repeat for Thursday night and how critical it is that every guest have their photo taken in front of it. The key to her plan is the coasters. She holds one up—black cardboard embossed with gold lettering. "These will be at all the bars, and on every cocktail table," she says. "They're printed with the QR code to download the step-and-repeat photos, and The Bexley's Instagram handle so everyone knows who to tag when they post." It is our sworn duty, Taylor explains, to point out the coasters to all the reporters and influencers in the room.

Before I deliver my update—a recap of the media plan around the restaurant—I take a sip from my Swell bottle. The water hits my stomach like a glug of battery acid.

At some point after thirty, my hangovers started to do this—lie cold and still long enough to make me think they're dead, only to heat back up just when my defenses are down. I close my eyes and take a shallow breath.

"Margo?" Jordana says. "Are you all right?"

"Yep, all good, let me just find the right file here." I buy some time while I pretend to search my laptop. "Okay, here we go ... we have confirmed RSVPs from all the usual local suspects. The crew from *Washingtonian* magazine, the editor of Eater DC, a couple from *The Washington Post*'s dining team."

I pretend to search for a different file, while beating back another wave of nausea.

"Here we are. Um, on the national side, we're expecting the food writer from *GQ* and a senior writer from *Bon Appétit*." I glance up from my screen. "I believe both of them are black-wristbanders, right, Jordana?"

She nods.

"Great," I choke out, my egg-and-cheese-bagel threatening an encore.

I lean away from my laptop, cold sweat percolating through the back of my dress. Jordana is still looking at me. What else can she possibly want?

"And what about *advanced* coverage, Margo?"

Jesus Christ, I should've made myself puke before I left the apartment.

"Right, just a sec." I fumble around some more on my computer. Jordana sighs loudly.

"As far as advanced coverage goes, I gave the exclusive first look at the restaurant design to *Washingtonian*. They're sending a reporter and a photographer tomorrow at noon, and they'll publish online Wednesday. And the *Post* is running their Q&A with Chef online first thing Thursday morning, then in print in the Weekend section."

Shockingly, Jordana gives a little golf clap. "Thank you, Margo. Not sure why that was such a struggle, but it all sounds excellent."

I manage a weak smile. As soon as the meeting wraps, I beeline to the bathroom.

The rest of the day gets easier. Jordana goes to lunch with a client at noon, and by three, she's still not back so I take that as a green light to leave early. When I get to the apartment, I see my Post-it note is gone, and that Ian did, in fact, take most of the leftover chicken to work.

He texts around six: *Heading home. Hope we can talk.*

I've spent the afternoon devising a PR strategy for myself. I've decided that anger should be a last resort—it'll be more effective to play the victim.

When he walks in, red bike helmet still on, I'm on my laptop on the sofa, braless in one of his old UVA T-shirts.

"Hey," I say softly, eyes still on my screen. I want to make him come to me.

He sighs and hangs up his helmet. "Will you please look at me?"

I do as he asks, summoning the right memory. I think of those bitches sophomore year who made my life hell after my dad's ridiculous business tanked and the bank took our house. A stinging spreads through my chest. My vision blurs, then clears up as the tears break free down my face. Works every time.

"Jesus." Ian rushes to my side, drapes an arm around my shoulders while he waits for me to calm down.

"I was really worried about you," I say through ragged breaths. "Where were you last night?"

"I know, I should've called." I notice him check out my boobs. "I was at Brant's."

Figures. Brent with an A, the last bachelor standing of our original DC friend group. Our token sleaze.

"You were at Brant's until three in the morning?"

"It was stupid. We weren't even doing anything, really. We went to a bar for a while and watched the Nats, then we just kept drinking at his place and I passed out on the couch."

"But I don't get why you couldn't even bother to text me back. How was I supposed to know you weren't dead somewhere? Or in the hospital?"

"I know. I wasn't thinking."

I stare into the distance out the window, before turning back to him. "You can't do that to me again, Ian." I let my eyes burrow into his. "I love you, and you scared the hell out of me."

I rehearsed that last bit before he got home, tested out a few different versions—"I *fucking* love you" (too dramatic), "You scared the *shit* out of me" (starts to sound gross when you say it over and over). I felt pretty confident about where I landed, but I didn't expect this—his eyes are damp. He's fully crying by the time he pulls me in for a hug.

"I love you, too," he says. "I'm so sorry. I feel terrible about those things I said. I shouldn't have called you . . . that."

I mean, it's not like he used the C word, but fine. More than fine! I pull back from him. This is the hard part, but I remind myself it's for a greater cause: "I'm really sorry, too, Ian."

He tucks a strand of hair behind my ear and kisses me.

"We have to talk about the house, though," I say, gently steering us toward the point.

He sighs and wipes his eyes.

"I didn't lie, Ian. It's true that we've had trouble conceiving, and who knows? We might want to adopt one day. Please, just come with me on Wednesday night—you'll really like Jack, I promise, and Penny is so cute. It's really not that big a deal."

He shakes his head adamantly. "I'm just not comfortable with this."

"But why? People write sappy letters with their offers all the time. We'll just get to make our case in person. And if they say no, I will let it go."

"I'm sorry," he says, standing up and heading into the kitchen, "this just feels way over the line."

Maybe it would've been better if he *had* used the C-word.

"Ian, the whole market is over the line," I say. "People are doing all sorts of crazy shit. I saw a woman on TikTok who offered to let a seller name her baby!"

He smirks—progress. "That can't be real," he says.

"Well, either way, at least I'm not that nuts."

He laughs!

"Seriously," he says, smile fading, "I don't think this is healthy. You know all this stress isn't good for you."

"Right, and this could finally be a way to put an end to it! You said yourself that you loved that house, Ian. It's perfect for us. You can't deny that."

He leans against the fridge, arms crossed, staring at the floor.

"You heard what Heath said the other night," I add, wondering how I didn't think to leverage that asshole sooner. "He couldn't believe *how lucky* he and Erika got. Well, maybe it's our turn to finally get lucky. I mean, if anyone deserves a break, it's you, not him."

Another long sigh snakes out of him. When he finally meets my gaze, I hold my breath.

"Fine," he says, after an eternity. "But if this doesn't work, we're waiting for it to come on the market just like everybody else."

I spring from the sofa and run to give him a hug. "Absolutely," I say, "that'll be the only thing left to do."

# 8

It has been five days since I first saw the house. Every day since, I've talked myself out of coming back here. It would've obviously been too risky. How many more times could I possibly explain away bumping into Jack out of sheer coincidence? But I haven't stopped thinking about it. It's like a middle-school crush. All I've wanted to do is study every inch of this place and imagine what it'll be like when it's mine.

Now I finally get my chance.

Someone has planted the window boxes since last week—they explode orange and violet and fuchsia. I follow Ian's stare up to a plump cardinal singing from the big maple in the front left corner of the yard. He was silent the whole car ride here. "You're sure you still wanna go through with this?" he asked when we woke up this morning. But I can feel him mellowing as he absorbs this scene, dreamy and golden in the faded early-evening sun.

We make our way up to the stoop, where I give the brass door knocker a couple raps. Jack's muffled voice floats through from somewhere on the other side—"Penny, they're here!"—then small footsteps patter down that gorgeous wide-plank floor.

Here we go. The beginning of the rest of our lives.

The door is flung open. "Hi, Margo!"

"Hi, Penny! Oh my gosh, your dress is so cool." It has navy blue and white stripes on top, with a navy tulle skirt.

"Thank you! Your shirt is my favorite color."

"Pink?"

She makes a confused face. "No. Coral."

This kid is such a trip. Jack comes up behind her, looking like a movie star in meticulously pressed chinos and a lightweight cream sweater.

"Hey, guys," he says. "You must be Ian."

If Ian's still nervous, he doesn't let on. "Great to meet you, man," he says, grabbing hold of Jack's hand, then passing him the bottle of prosecco I picked up earlier. "I hear you and Curt have a lot to toast these days."

Jack thanks him, then turns to hug me. I hand him the plate of oatmeal cookies I spent the afternoon baking. "I know you said not to bring anything, but these freeze beautifully so you can have them anytime."

"I'm making out like a bandit here," Jack says. Ian and I both laugh, maybe a touch too hard. "Well, come on in. Curt's this way."

And just like that, I'm inside the house. My senses feel reborn—like they were dead before this and now they're alive and starving for every last detail. It smells expensive in here. Leather mixed with some type of fancy candle. Sandalwood maybe? A flush-mount fixture, tasteful and classic, illuminates the foyer, its milky shade turning the light gauzy and soft. The handrail of the staircase that leads to the second floor is stained ebony, the curve of it so polished that it could be liquid.

I have to find a way to get up there.

Before we follow Jack through the archway into the kitchen, I size up the living room, off to the left. It has a fireplace where I expected it to be, with a Carrara marble surround that matches the kitchen countertops. They've laid it out just the way I imagined—it's like the house has been talking to me—with a pair of sofas facing each other in front of the hearth.

To the right, behind a set of glass doors, I spy a more casual den with a plush-looking sectional. Floor-to-ceiling built-ins full of books flank a wall-mounted flat-screen. I can't think of anything I'd do differently. These rooms announce the second you walk in that their owners are classy and smart and stylish. It would be impossible not to be happy here.

"There they are!" Curt, shirt sleeves rolled up under a chambray apron, stands in front of the range—which, I can now confirm, is indeed a Thermador. "Margo, wonderful to see you again." He wipes his hands on the front of the apron before extending one across the island: "And you must be Ian." A wooden board, two feet long, is heaped with charcuterie and cheeses.

"What are we drinking?" Curt asks. "I have a pitcher of gin martinis ready to go, or if you're wine people, we also have some very nice Sancerre chilling in the fridge."

"I would love a martini," I say. "This is such an impressive spread. And your house! My God, it's impeccable."

"Oh, well, it doesn't always look quite this perfect," Jack chimes in. "Your timing couldn't have been better. We just had the place shot today, for the listing. I was chasing the photographer around until a couple hours ago."

My stomach drops. It's not a shock, of course, that they'd take pictures to sell the home. But the thought of these immaculate rooms on display for the greedy hordes floods me with panic.

Ian clears his throat.

"How exciting!" I say, powering through. "When are you putting it on the market?"

"Two weeks from tomorrow. I still can't believe it," says Jack. "Feels like yesterday Penny was in a booster seat at that island."

Two weeks. Two fucking weeks.

"Well, I'm sure people will be lining up for it," I say calmly. "It's stunning."

"Yeah, this market is absolutely bonkers," Curt says as he pours Ian a martini. "Our agent told us a couple weeks ago that someone was already sniffing around about it. I mean, how would they even know? Can you believe that?"

Ian and I both shake our heads, martini glasses pressed to our mouths.

"But we don't need to tell you how ridiculous the market has gotten, do we?" Curt continues. "I hear you've been through quite the house-hunting ordeal yourselves."

My breath catches. I'm not ready to go there yet—we haven't even made it past the appetizers.

"Daddy?" Penny interrupts. "Can I please have some Manchego on a date crisp?"

I exhale.

"Sure, sweetie." Jack gets to work assembling the cracker.

"Gosh, what a sophisticated palate you have," I say, seizing on the change of subject.

"We went to Barcelona last year for spring break and I ate a lot of Manchego there," says Penny.

Everyone laughs. That's exactly the kind of thing I want my kid to be able to say one day.

"Has anyone ever told you that you have an old soul?" Ian asks Penny.

"Papa says I'm mature for my age because I'm around a lot of adults."

Curt chuckles. "It's true, I do say that. We've always let Penny come to our dinner parties and spend time with our friends. I really don't understand why more parents don't do it that way."

"Oh, Penny, that reminds me, I brought something for you. But maybe you're too grown-up to want it?" I tease.

She giggles. "I don't think I'm too grown-up."

I fetch the surprise from my purse. I wisely chose an "adult" coloring book with much more intricate drawings of London landmarks than your typical kids' fare.

"Thought you could do this on the plane ride over."

Her tiny round face stretches into a smile as she flips through it. "Thanks, Margo. I love it."

Her dads are glowing.

"Have you been to London before?" I ask her.

"Once, but I was too little to remember. I have some pictures of it in my room, though. Do you want to see?"

A ticket to the second floor.

"That sounds like fun," I say, turning to Jack and Curt. "If you guys wouldn't mind?"

"Not at all, go right ahead," says Jack. "In fact, why don't we all go? I'll give you a tour."

Hell yes.

"I'll stay and get the salmon ready to put in," says Curt, "but here, let me top you off before you head up."

He comes around the island with the martini pitcher. I hold my hand over my glass: "I'm a lightweight," I say, smiling, attuned to the subtle fizziness already spreading through my limbs. I need to stay sharp.

The rest of us follow Jack back to the front of the house, where he points out the den. "Those built-ins were one of the first things we had done when we moved in," he says. "And this is the more formal living space over here."

"I love the fireplace," I say. "Is it wood-burning?"

"Yeah, it's original from 1948." He leans over to adjust a knit throw draped over the back of the sofa closest to us. "It's one of my favorite parts of the house, especially around the holidays. We put the tree right over there, in that corner by the window."

I lock eyes with Ian. He has to be thinking the same thing—this is meant to be.

The first time I met his parents was over Christmas, the year we started dating. I'd never been serious enough with a boyfriend to spend the holidays together, so I was a nervous wreck trying to figure out what to pack, what types of gifts would come across as thoughtful but not trying too hard. His dad picked us up at the airport. I let him and Ian catch up in front while I rode in back, silently coaching myself on the things I might say when we got to the house—*Your home is lovely! Thank you so much for having me!*

When we pulled up, I felt like I'd landed inside the Hallmark Channel. It was creamy brick, like the outside of this house, with red-bowed wreaths in each window, and ivy climbing up one side. It's not that it was anything ostentatious—Indiana real estate is obviously a lot cheaper than here. Before they retired, Ian's mom taught high-school English and his dad was a pharmacist. But it just looked so . . . what's the right word? Solid. Like it was built to last. The polar opposite of the vulgar, vinyl-clad McMansion that my parents opted for in a new-money (or, in our case, imaginary-money) subdivision.

Ian's mom and his sister Brooke took turns enveloping me in long hugs. "We've all been dying to meet you!" his mom said. She took the shopping bag full of gifts off my hands, and showed me over to the tree—past the fireplace, in a corner of the living room, right by a window.

Exactly the same way we'll do it here.

After she finished stacking my presents beneath it, she pointed out the ornaments that Ian made as a kid: Popsicle-stick snowflakes, salt-dough candy canes and snowmen. She and Brooke enlisted me to help with the Christmas cookies. They even shared the secret family shortbread recipe.

We stayed a whole week. By the end of it, I felt like I'd gained an entire family.

. . .

Jack invites us to follow him upstairs. Penny runs ahead. "My room's this way," she says when we reach the top, taking my hand and tugging me down the hall.

When she pushes open her door, I see that her walls are almost the precise shade of my blouse. "I told you coral was my favorite," she says, flopping onto a white four-poster bed in the center of the space.

Her ceiling is wallpapered in an oversize floral print. A low antique dresser sits beneath the window. But I bet a changing table was there first. This must've been the cutest nursery. Am I getting emotional? I blink away the tears before anyone can notice and redirect my focus to a photo in a gold frame on Penny's desk.

"Is this Suni Lee?" I say, picking it up. Of course they wouldn't let her Scotch-tape some tacky sports poster to the wall in here.

Penny and Jack both gasp. Ian, still in the doorway, lifts his eyebrows so that only I see.

"You know about her?" Penny asks, springing up from her bed to join me.

"Suni Lee is Penny's idol," says Jack, smiling.

"Heck yes, I know about Suni!" I say. "I was obsessed with her during the Olympics last summer. Did you see her stick the landing on the vault, even with her bad ankle?" (I've been doing some Wikipedia research on the women's gymnastics team. Figured it couldn't hurt.)

Penny's eyes widen. "Yes! That was so cool!"

"Do you think *you* want to go to the Olympics one day?"

"I don't know. My coach says I can if I keep working really hard. But there might be other things I want to do, too, once we move to London."

"That's very reasonable," I say.

"You can see why we're so proud of her," says Jack, grinning.

"Didn't you wanna show me your pictures of London?" I ask, remembering why we came up here in the first place.

"Oh yeah." Penny retrieves a photo album from her bookcase.

"Daddy made this for me after Papa told us he got the new job." She pages through, showing me all the sights she doesn't remember seeing as a toddler.

"Oh, look, the London Bridge." I point to a photo of her atop Curt's shoulders in front of it.

"That's the *Tower* Bridge," she corrects me. "I thought you'd been to London?"

"Remember your tone, please," Jack interjects.

I laugh and wave him off. "Penny, you're just too smart for me." Ian shoots me a look.

"Why don't we go see Daddy and Papa's room real quick before we go back down?" says Jack, ushering us back into the hall.

We pass a guest bedroom on the way. Jack leans in and flips on the light to offer us a look. The walls are a pale taupe. The space easily fits a queen, with nightstands on both sides. More than enough room for Ian's parents.

Jack motions to a closed door across the hall: "That's Curt's study. Nothing very exciting in there." But I'm doing the math, and including the primary, that'll make four bedrooms, just as Ginny said. The perfect size.

Then we come to the grand finale. "When we built the addition, we spent even more time and money in here than we did on the kitchen, if you can believe that," says Jack, pushing open the door for the big reveal.

It's like we've been transported to a luxury hotel. The walls, trim, and ceiling are all the same dusky blue. A black canopy bed that I recognize from the Room & Board catalog sits between a matching pair of walnut dressers, almost certainly vintage. Generous windows frame a sky turned the color of sherbet by the setting sun. There's a sitting area at one end, with a leather Eames lounger and a matching ottoman.

This has to be the biggest primary suite we've seen in the neighborhood. Here comes the panic again—if this place makes it to the open market, we are dead in the fucking water.

"This is really something," says Ian.

"Thank you, we've been spoiled here," says Jack. "I doubt we'll find anywhere in London that can fit a king-size. But I might miss our bathroom even more."

He opens an adjoining door, and I have to remind myself to breathe. It must be almost half the size of our apartment. The double vanities are a buttery oak; the amount of storage in them could save any marriage, maybe end wars. They've kept the finishes classic, with white marble on the floors and in the shower. A soaking tub sits beneath a window.

"Why would you ever leave this place?" I blurt out.

Jack laughs. "I know, right? I'm sure I'll be a mess when the day comes."

I spot another door. It has to be the closet. I have to get in there.

"And where does that lead?" I nudge.

"Oh, feel free," Jack says, gesturing to go ahead.

I cross the marble, and turn the sleek, brass handle. I feel for the light switch. When I find it, the world momentarily halts. This must be heaven. My soul must have departed my body. What other explanation could there be for a closet that looks like this?

The perimeter is lined with custom storage, painted the same moody blue as the bedroom. Each compartment of hanging clothes is lit from within, like in a high-end boutique. One wall is reserved for shoes, tucked into perfectly sized shelves, and cubbies of folded items in crisp stacks arranged by color. Like macarons in a pastry shop. In the center, there's an island full of drawers and topped with Carrara. A miniature version of what's in the kitchen.

I'd be euphoric if I wasn't terrified. If we can't have this place, I will literally lie down and fucking die.

Ian comes up behind me in the doorway, places a hand on my

shoulder. I hear him suck in a breath. "Holy shit," he says, before remembering Penny.

"Shoot." He turns back to Jack. "Sorry, man."

"No sweat—I probably should've prepared you." Jack laughs. "Shall we head back down before Curt finishes all the martinis?"

On the way, I lean into Ian. "This is it," I whisper. "It has to be."

It's a spectacular evening, almost cloudless and still in the high sixties. Penny takes me by the hand again, guiding me to the backyard. She does cartwheels across the lawn and I pretend to be impressed. But my focus is on the tire swing.

Once she's done showing me her splits, I point toward it. "Did your dads put that up for you?"

She shakes her head. "It's always been there."

I think back to the tax records I dug up for this place. The owners before Jack and Curt had lived here since the seventies. Which means the swing has probably been here my whole life, maybe longer. All those mornings and afternoons, walking to and from my bus stop, staring pathetically at the tire swing that hung in the Satos' front yard, I was wishing for the wrong one.

Alyssa Sato was a grade older, so even though we rode the same bus for all of elementary school, we weren't really friends. Her dad sold cars—every few months, they'd have a new one in the driveway—and her mom stayed home. Unless it was raining, in which case Alyssa got a ride all the way to school, her mom would walk with her to the bus. In the afternoons, she'd be there with a Capri-Sun, the straw already punched into its tiny hole, ready for Alyssa to enjoy.

Some of the other kids made fun of this, but I was transfixed. I couldn't fathom what it must feel like to be the center of an adult's universe like that. I made a point of sitting behind Alyssa on the bus so I could disembark after her and trail a half block or so behind on the sidewalk. From there, I could pick out bits and pieces of conversation—her mom asking about such-and-such friend or how Alyssa did on the spelling test. Whether she remembered to turn in her homework. The sorts of mundane things that my parents never brought up.

The Satos' house was on the block before the town-house complex where I lived. It was the same street, but their stretch was greener and shadier, all single-family homes. By the time I reached their place, Alyssa was usually clambering up onto that tire swing, her mom watching from the porch.

Their life looked idyllic and I wanted badly to be a part of it, so one morning, when I was in third grade and Alyssa was in fourth, I worked up the courage to sit next to her on the bus. I'd decided to invite her to come over to my house after school, figuring she'd have to return the invitation, maybe as soon as the next day.

Instead, she went quiet for several long seconds, before finally admitting she didn't think she'd be allowed to—"because your parents are never there, right?"

I'd had no idea that other people knew this about me, let alone that the topic had apparently been discussed inside the perfect Sato home. My whole body flushed with shame at the realization that something about me wasn't good enough.

But finally, after all these years, I can let that go. Because now I know *this* tire swing, behind a house far more perfect than the Satos' ever was, has been waiting for me all along.

I take a few steps toward it. "Do you want me to push you on it for a bit?" I ask Penny.

"Nah, let me show you something cooler," she says, running back toward the deck.

I have no choice but to follow. Around the side of it, she points out a short flight of stairs leading to a basement.

"One time, our neighbors' cat Lunchbox got stuck down there," she says. "He was trapped in our basement until almost bedtime when I heard him crying."

"Really? But how did he get in?" I ask.

"Come look, I'll show you."

I follow her down the concrete steps.

"See?" With hardly any effort, she pushes open the top half of the door at the bottom.

"Oh, it's a Dutch door?"

"Yeah. The top part doesn't latch right," she says. "Papa was supposed to have it fixed, but he never got around to it, and now he says there's no point because we're moving."

Curt's right. Nobody in this market would care about such a small repair, especially not in a neighborhood as safe as this one.

"Daddy says I can have my own cat once we're in London," Penny says.

"That's exciting! When Ian and I find our new house, I think we'll get a dog."

"Hey, Margo?" Ian, calling from up above. "Are you two down there?"

"Guess it's time for dinner," I tell Penny.

The long table on the deck is set with linen placemats and two low vases of white hydrangeas. Curt insists that we all take a seat while he brings out the food on his own. He passes it off as politeness. "No, no, you're our guests," he tells us. But I suspect he just likes the spotlight.

He makes a show of bringing out the main event—a roasted salmon, which, frankly, just about anyone with an oven timer could pull off. "Voilà!" he says, setting the platter down dramatically. Ian and I both instinctively clap. I catch Jack rolling his eyes.

Everyone except me and Penny has had at least two rounds of martinis. And now Curt is pouring the Sancerre. "Just a splash for me," I say. "Someone has to drive us home!"

Once Curt takes his place at the head of the table, he raises his glass. "A toast to Margo and Ian, and their adoption journey," he says.

I'm sure Ian wishes he could sink into the floor, but this is the time to lean in. I try to tap into the emotion that I felt in Penny's room.

"Thank you so much," I say. "But it should be us toasting you three. What a lovely surprise this has all been, getting to know you, and being welcomed into your gorgeous home. I only wish we could've had more time together before your move."

"Maybe you can come stay with us in London," says Penny, in between sips of pamplemousse LaCroix.

"Of course she can, honey," says Jack. "And we can see her and Ian when we come back to visit DC, too."

"Maybe we'll have a baby of our own the next time you're here," I say. Ian shifts uncomfortably beside me; the weathered wood of his chair groans. "I've been meaning to tell you," I turn to Jack, "I just called Hope Springs on Monday. We have an appointment with them next week."

He brings his hands to his mouth. "Oh my gosh, that is so great!" he says. "We had such an awesome experience with them."

"We really did," says Curt, nodding. "You know, I have a tendency to go overboard on research—a hazard of academia, I suppose." He chuckles and thrusts a thumb in Jack's direction. "It can drive this guy a little mad. Penny told you we were in Barcelona last year? They practically had to drag me out of the Sagrada Familia, kicking and screaming. I could've read every single plaque."

He chuckles to himself some more. I wonder when he'll arrive at his point. After a sip of wine, he starts up again: "All that to say, I treated the adoption process just as I would any academic pursuit. I really dug into it." He balls up a fist. "And I can tell you with complete confidence that Hope Springs is the best private domestic agency in the region. No question."

"It sure seems that way," I say. "I was really encouraged to read about the level of care they take with the birth parents—all the counseling and support they offer to make sure they're really ready to place their children with another family."

Ian pushes his fingers back through his hair, drains the rest of his glass.

"That part was important to us, too," says Jack, before subtly shifting his eyes toward Penny. "We can talk more after bedtime."

I nod, taking the hint, mouthing, "Thank you."

Ian visibly relaxes once he's certain we've moved on from the adoption chatter. He and Curt are hitting it off—swapping self-congratulatory stories about their heroic career paths. Ian explains how he never felt like "I was living up to my potential" at the law firm, but now every day is "a gift" because he gets to make a difference with his work. Curt nods along vigorously. "It was the same for me at the hedge fund," he says. "I tried to follow in the old man's footsteps, I really did, but I just felt called to education."

Jack and I look at each other and burst out laughing. This is going even better than I'd hoped—we have genuinely connected.

Time to go in for the kill.

"You know what? I'm just gonna say it and cross my fingers that I don't make things awkward." I aim for an endearingly nervous smile. "We want to make an offer on your house. It's everything we could ever want, and this neighborhood is amazing."

Ian goes rigid. Beneath the table, I see that he's gripping the edges of his chair. But Jack and Curt both laugh. The knot in my stomach loosens.

"Well, you're already ahead of the game," says Curt. "You won't need to come for a showing."

"I'm sorry to be crass," says Jack, "but what did you say your budget was again?"

My pulse picks up. "Um, one-point-three."

"You're in the ballpark," Jack says. "We're planning to list just under that, at one-two-fifty."

"Is Margo going to live in our house?" Penny asks, bouncing in her chair.

"But you know how this market is," Curt quickly interjects, ignoring his daughter. "Theresa, our agent, expects it'll go for *much* higher."

Jack throws his husband a pointed look, then refocuses on me. "That doesn't mean you shouldn't give it a try," he says. "I would love to know we were selling to a family as deserving as you guys. I mean, we've put so much work into this place, it's going to be really tough letting it go."

"Well, if we end up here, maybe you wouldn't have to, at least not fully," I say, palms sweaty against the linen napkin in my lap. "We could finish the basement and build a whole guest suite down there for you."

Ian presses a hand into my thigh—not a gesture of affection; he's telling me to rein it in. But he knew this was what he signed up for. And this is not the time to puss out.

I laugh and lean away from the table. "I'm sorry if I'm getting ahead of myself."

Jack smiles. "That's okay, it's a tempting idea."

"I like that idea!" Penny adds.

"Let's leave the negotiating to the agents," Curt says with a wink. "Don't wanna ruin a fun evening with business."

"Exactly," says Ian. He gives my leg a final pat before removing his hand, apparently convinced that's the end of my pitch.

But I can't stop now. We're at their dinner table, for chrissake! When will we ever have an opportunity like this again? Sure, we could write some interesting perks into an offer—let them design their own guest suite, commit to letting them use it any time they want. But in the end, the only thing that ever really matters is the money. Whatever it takes, I cannot let this place wind up in a bidding war.

I clear my throat. "No, no, absolutely, you're right, Curt," I say. "I'm sorry to have brought it up. I think I've just been so preoccupied with the adoption research, and the thought of still being stuck in that apartment for the home study has really started to freak me out."

"Margo, we don't need to get into that," Ian says, the pressure of his hand back on my thigh.

"I just want to explain myself," I say, smiling at him reassuringly, then turning my attention back to our hosts. "What I mean to say is the house hunt has just started to feel even more urgent. And then, only this morning, a colleague was telling me how her cousin recently bought off market, from some friends. Since they put the deal together themselves, they didn't have to use agents, and they saved a ton on the commission. Your home is just so stunning, I guess I've started to wonder if maybe there was any possibility that we could make something like that work *here*, for all of us—a win-win, you know?" I pause to cringe at myself. "If I'm being inappropriate, I'm so sorry!"

Ian is squeezing now, almost hard enough that it hurts. Curt and Jack look at each other, wordlessly, over one of the vases of hydrangeas.

"That's an interesting proposition," Jack says finally. "I think you've just caught us a little off guard."

Curt chuckles uncomfortably. "Why don't we take a break for dessert?" He pushes away from the table. "Jack, can you help?"

Once they're inside, Ian leans in. "Margo, that is enough," he says through clenched teeth.

I ignore him, keeping my eyes on Penny, still seated across from me. "So, have you told all your friends about London by now?" I ask cheerily.

She perks up. "Yeah, they're going to have a party for me at gymnastics!"

As she unpacks the details—pizza, a tumbling contest, siblings are invited, too—her dads return with a chocolate torte, a pile of raspberries in the center. "Penny, would you like to help Papa?" Curt asks. She nods and climbs down from her chair.

As he plates each piece, Penny passes them around. But I've lost my appetite. We're barely even talking now. Are they just going to pretend I never brought it up? I need to get us back on track.

"Mmmm," I say, forcing myself to eat my slice. "Curt, you're a serious talent. This reminds me of something the pastry chef at Causa just put on the menu." She would die before serving something so pedestrian, but I'm desperate to change the vibe.

"That's right!" Jack says, looking grateful for a benign topic. "Curt, I forgot to tell you, Causa is one of Margo's clients."

"Wow," Curt says, "that's a tough reservation."

"We'll all have to go before you move!" I say. "Penny, too, of course, since she has such grown-up taste. My treat."

Jack and Curt exchange a look that I can't quite read. But I think that might've worked. I think they're coming back around.

"That sounds great," says Jack.

But the silence descends again. We all keep eating, forks scraping against plates, the only sound piercing the excruciating nothingness.

"So, about the house," Jack finally breaks in.

The air goes completely still. My heartbeat roars in my head.

"We'll certainly be rooting for you when we list it," he continues. "But we had a quick chat inside, and we're just not comfortable committing to anything . . . unorthodox."

My stomach plummets. This can't be happening. This isn't how it's supposed to go.

Ian says something beside me, but he sounds muted somehow. Like I'm listening to him from underwater. Like I'm drowning.

"Completely understood," I think I hear him say. "Ginny would've killed us for doing a deal without her anyway."

*Ginny.*

The night slingshots back into focus. Her name is the corkscrew resting by the wine bottle, twisting into my gut. It is the one word I told Ian we absolutely could not say. The one word that could blow our cover.

Jack narrows his eyes. Terror slithers around my insides.

"Ginny Gunther?" he asks.

Ian's shoulders slump as he realizes what he's done.

"*Jenny*," I say immediately. "He said *Jenny*. Our agent is Jenny."

But Jack remains frozen, chiseled jawline set, dark eyes accusing.

"Ginny Gunther's sister-in-law does yoga with me at Power + Grace," he says to Curt. "Zelda Gunther. You've met her. She's been to the house."

Curt cocks his head in confusion. "I'm not sure I follow . . ."

"What aren't you getting?" Jack snaps, the alarm intensifying his features. "One of my closest friends at yoga is *their agent's* sister-in-law. Zelda was in class with me the morning we decided to sell. She was one of the first people I told we were going to list." Keeping his eyes on Curt, he jabs a finger toward me and Ian. "Zelda must've told Ginny who told *them*."

Curt knits his brow.

"The exact same morning, Margo just happens to show up in front of our house." Now Jack fixes his glare on me. "You weren't really lost that day, were you?"

"I . . . I . . . what?"

"Oh my God." His mouth goes slack, a look of recognition falling over his face. "You guys aren't really adopting, are you?"

"I . . . what? Jack, I . . . I don't know what you're talking about."

"Margo, cut the shit," he says. I hear Penny draw in a little gasp.

"Please . . ." My throat feels like it's closing up. I can barely get the words out. "I think there's been a misunderstanding here."

Curt, now grasping what's going on, rises to his feet. "Okay, party's over."

He waits for me and Ian to get up. When we do, he comes around to our side of the table and places a hand on the small of both our backs. He guides us inside, away from the tire swing, back through the flawless kitchen, through the living room where we were supposed to celebrate our next Christmas, out onto the front porch, into the glow of the handsome brass lanterns.

Now, with Penny well out of earshot, he leans in so close that I can feel the humidity of his breath, smell the acid of the wine. "You two are fucking sick." His voice is unnervingly calm. "If you ever come near my family again, I will call the fucking cops, do you understand?"

"I'm ... Curt, I'm ..." My body is on fire.

"Get the fuck off my property. Right fucking now."

Then he slams the gorgeous, glossy-black front door.

# 9

"Margo, are you there? Where the hell are you?"

I pry open one heavy, swollen eyelid. Through the blur, I see my phone lying next to me—the screen informing me that it's past one o'clock in the afternoon. And that I have thirteen missed calls. Ian holds his own phone to the side of my head. Jordana is screaming out of it.

"Jordana? Um, hi."

"We have been trying you all day, Margo! I was about to send someone to your apartment, but then Beth had the idea to get Ian's number from HR. What the fuck are you doing?"

It's a good question.

I lift my other eyelid and the entire nightmare comes hurtling back into focus. The door in my face. Pulling over to get sick on the car ride home. Making Ian sleep on the couch for ruining everything. Scrounging up three Xanax from an old prescription bottle in the back of the bathroom drawer.

So, what the fuck am I doing? I am lying on the bedroom floor for some reason, curled around a pillow, a sweaty sheet pulled down from the mattress above.

"Jordana, I'm so sorry. I think I had some bad shellfish last night."

"Well, figure your shit out, Margo. I already heard from both *Bon Appétit* and *GQ*. Their writers arrived at Union Station a half hour ago. Neither could find the black cars you were supposed to send."

"Oh, um . . ."

"That is your last fuckup today, do you hear me? I need you at The Bexley by three."

She hangs up before I can respond.

I pass Ian's phone back, my growing rage eclipsing my grogginess. "What the hell, Ian? Why didn't you wake me up?"

"I didn't know you were still in here," he says, holding his hands up. "I've been on back-to-back conference calls in one of the co-working suites upstairs."

I bury my face into the pillow and scream as loud as I can.

. . .

When I get to the hotel, the lobby is already a swirl of event staff. A crew is setting up the step-and-repeat. Several of the assistants from my office are carting in rented cocktail tables and boxes full of plastic champagne flutes from the loading dock. Beth is arranging dozens of black gift bags, "The Bexley" embossed on them in gold lettering, on a table by the front entrance.

I hear Jordana coming before I see her. She rounds the corner in a magenta tuxedo that's stunning against her brown skin, and a pair of leopard-print stilettos that collide like bullets with the black marble floor. The sound echoes around the vaulted ceiling, a sculptural brass chandelier the size of a Fiat suspended from its sixty-foot peak.

I really do love a brass light fixture.

"Margo, feeling better?"

She sizes up my long-sleeved emerald sheath, my sturdiest pair of Spanx giving it their all underneath.

"Yes, much," I say, hoping that I've caked on enough foundation and concealer to hide the puffiness beneath my eyes. "I am so sorry again, Jordana. I was completely out of it. But don't worry, the bad shellfish wasn't from a client!"

I force a laugh. Her airbrushed face doesn't move.

"Your friends from *Bon Appétit* and *GQ* are all checked in. Why don't you see if Serina can arrange something special for them, to make up for the incident with the cars?"

"That is a fantastic idea. Thank you. I'll check in with her now."

"Oh, and Margo, you can take these up to their rooms." Jordana holds out her hand like she's proffering the key to another dimension. Two black rubber wristbands rest in her palm.

I find Serina, the hotel's beverage director, in Rivière's cocktail lounge, just off the lobby, organizing bottles behind the bar. Her reflection—chestnut shag, nose ring, red lipstick—bounces off the mirrored shelving. For tonight, this space will be off-limits to the guests, so it can serve as a staging area to restock the four bars set up around the lobby.

"Why don't I put together a mini tasting for them?" Serina suggests, after I explain my earlier fuckup. "I could do some of the signature cocktails that we'll have once we're fully open, like a little sneak preview."

"Oh my God, Serina, that would be a dream. Can I bring them down like forty-five minutes before the party starts?"

"Yeah, perfect."

Okay, this is going fine now. I can do this. This party couldn't have come at a better time. It will force me to forget about the house for a few hours and just focus on work. I head up to the ninth-floor suites and deliver the wristbands to their rightful VIP owners. They both seem genuinely excited about the private cocktail tasting. See? Like I said, everything is fine.

By six o'clock, the team from Rivière is starting to set up food stations around the sprawling lobby. I've confirmed with Chef that the kitchen is on schedule and let him know that I might bring a few VIPs back to say hello once service is winding down. The whole place looks epic. Jordana must be thrilled.

Taylor must be, too. Her step-and-repeat is all set up—"The Bexley"–branded backdrop looking very Insta-worthy, with a strip of red carpet in front beckoning guests to strike a pose. Here she comes now, in a strapless black jumpsuit, strawberry waves grazing her freckled shoulders.

"Hey, Taylor, congrats! Everything looks awesome." My smile does not summon one from her.

"Thanks, Margo, glad you're feeling better. Do you have the coasters?"

The coasters.

Oh my God.

I shut my eyes, the panic closing in. Four boxes of custom coasters—emblazoned with the QR code and Instagram handles that are pretty much the linchpin of the entire social media strategy around the event—are in the back of the Prius. I picked them up from the office yesterday, when we were all divvying up tasks for tonight, and agreed to bring them here.

But I took a Lyft.

"Margo?" Her voice is more hiss than whisper.

"Taylor, I am so sorry. I forgot they were in my car."

Now her face does contort into something closer to a smile—but there's violence behind it.

"Margo! What the fuck!"

"I'll call Ian right now," I say, fumbling around in my clutch for my phone. "I'm sure he can run them over. It won't even take ten minutes."

She glares at me while I dial, my skin getting hotter with every ring.

The call goes to voicemail.

"Hey, babe, it's me. Listen, I was such an idiot and I forgot I have something really important for tonight in the back of the car.

I need you to run it down here. Please call me back. Party starts at seven, so it's an emergency!"

Taylor has stopped blinking, her false eyelashes lending a bug-like quality to her face.

"I'll text him," I say. "If he doesn't respond, I can go back for them myself. It's going to be okay."

I tap out: *EMERGENCY!! Check your voicemail. Need you to bring me the car NOW.*

Relief washes over me as the three dots appear. I glance up at Taylor: "He's typing! Just a sec."

But then his message comes back: *Just got to Pittsburgh. Told you I have depositions here for the river dumping case, starting early morning.*

Taylor's face darkens as she reads mine.

I swallow hard, my throat like sandpaper, trying to think of something—anything—to say that will cushion this news. I'm coming up empty.

"He . . . um . . . he took the car," I whisper. "To Pittsburgh."

For a split second, I think she might hit me. Instead, she whips around, fists clenched, and marches all the way across the lobby, straight to Jordana, who's huddled in a corner with the hotel's general manager. When Taylor reaches her, Jordana's face snaps up and hunts me down like a sniper rifle.

I look toward the elevator bank to avoid her glare, and I see them there, like a mirage at the end of the world. My charges from *Bon Appétit* and *GQ*. Jordana can't flay me while I'm entertaining VIPs. I rush over to escort them to the roped-off cocktail lounge.

. . .

By the time we reemerge, the place is packed, a steady thrum of chatter and clinking glasses barely audible over the bass from the DJ. I circulate like everything is normal, taking care to surround myself with black wristbanders. Human shields in case I bump into Jordana. They all have some gushing piece of feedback to share—"My suite has such a killer view!" "The steak tartare is better than anything I've had in Paris!" "Holy shit, who designed that chandelier?"—and a full cocktail in hand, per our marching orders.

Except for one.

I spy the older gentleman through an opening in the crowd, a strip of black peeking out from his cuff. He's holding a highball glass containing only a few melting ice cubes—but he's standing with Jordana. How has she possibly let that slide? Maybe it's the multiple flutes of champagne that I've downed, but a jolt of confidence surges through me. This is my chance to prove that I am not totally worthless.

I squeeze my way through to them. "Hey, Jordana, how's your evening going?"

She looks surprised at first but plays along. "Fabulous. Let me introduce you to Marshall Chandler, editor-in-chief of *Travel & Luxury*. Marshall, this is one of our vice presidents, Margo Miyake."

"Such a pleasure to meet you, Marshall." I shake his hand. "You know, I think the director of The Bexley's cocktail program has something special for you. Pardon me for just a moment."

Jordana arches an expertly sculpted eyebrow. "How thoughtful, Margo. Thank you."

I weave back through the mob to the cocktail lounge, where I find Serina and three of her staff quartering lemons and limes.

"Hey, I know you're probably slammed, but I need another favor," I tell her. "Could you possibly whip up one of those Tom Collins riffs from the tasting that we all loved? The one with the yuzu?"

"I could," she says, looking up from her cutting board, "but we're supposed to stick to the approved cocktail list for the party."

"It's for a mega VIP. Trust me, no one will mind."

She shrugs. "Whatever you say." She dumps the ingredients into a shaker. As soon as she's finished adding the garnishes, I whisk the drink across the party, over to Jordana and Marshall, still huddled where I left them. I hand him the fizzing creation, topped with a paper-thin slice of pear and a spiral of lime peel.

"It's exquisite," Marshall says, inspecting Serina's work. "How special to see a cocktail program take such care with a nonalcoholic offering."

Before I fully process what he's said, he brings the glass to his mouth and drinks. He pauses for a beat, glancing at Jordana, then spits the mouthful of clear liquid back into the glass.

"There seems to have been a misunderstanding here," he says coolly, passing the cocktail back to me. "Excuse me, Jordana, I need to find some water."

As soon as he turns his back, Jordana has me by the arm and we're tearing through the room at a speed that seems inconceivable for a woman in nearly five-inch heels. She pulls me into a secluded space behind a black marble column.

"Marshall has been sober for twenty-three years, Margo!" She struggles through clenched teeth to keep her voice down. "He wrote a fucking *memoir* about it, for chrissake! Which you would've known if you'd read the notes on the fucking VIP list."

I flash back to last night. Jordana's same look of utter annihilation coming from Jack, and then Curt. The same all-consuming humiliation burning through my body. I can't think of anything to say.

"Margo, you have to leave." Jordana takes a step back. "I don't know what's been going on with you this week, but I think you need to take some time off."

"Jordana, what? Are you letting me ... "

She holds up a hand. "Margo, this isn't the place for that conversation. I'll be in touch next week to figure out what's next."

...

Every inch of me feels numb on the Lyft ride home. The tears only come once I unlock the door to Natalie's apartment and find Fritter lying on the sofa. At the sight of me, he thumps his tail loudly on the cushion, then rolls over to show off his belly and ask for a rub. I snuggle in next to him and burrow into his wiry fur, the injustices of the last twenty-four hours pouring out of my face.

"Thanks, Fritter." I scratch behind his ears as he studies me with bottomless brown eyes. "Time for a walk. You're sleeping at my place tonight."

I snap on his harness and lock up Natalie's apartment behind us.

# 10

Monday.

And no work.

I haven't told Ian that I may not have a job anymore, which is probably the most Dad-like thing I've ever done. My sophomore year of high school, he spent weeks setting his alarm—showering and shaving—pretending he still had an office to go to. He must've known long before then that we weren't going to be able to keep the house.

We could all tell something was wrong. For one thing, he'd started smoking again. On the nights he was home for dinner, he would sit at the table like a zombie, wordlessly shoveling food into his mouth, never looking up from his plate. The afternoon that Mitch and I got home from school and found the foreclosure notice in his nightstand was almost a relief. At least we understood what had been going on.

My situation isn't anything close to that, of course. I'm not lying to Ian—just withholding some details. I have been loyal to Jordana for over a decade. She knows we're trying to buy a house and start a family. She isn't heartless.

But until I hear from her, the day blinks back at me like the cursor in an empty search bar.

I'm at my desk, where I'd been pretending to respond to work emails before Ian left for the office. Now I'm mindlessly scrolling Twitter. Oh, look, here's a nice little nugget from CNBC: "30-year fixed mortgage rates inch past 5 percent." Fuck me.

Now we really can't go a dollar above one-three. Though higher rates *might* weed out some of the competition. Wonder what Ginny thinks. I've put off calling her long enough, and this is as good an excuse as any. I'll wade in with some interest-rate chatter, then ease into my "It's not you, it's us" breakup speech. Obviously, we can't use her to bid on the dream house if we want to keep our offer anonymous, but I'll just say we want a fresh start after so many losses.

I get my phone from the charger in the kitchen. But her number doesn't even ring—it cuts straight to voicemail: "This is Ginny Gunther, it's a great day to make a deal! Leave a message and I'll get back to you as soon as I can."

Did she screen my call? I send her a text: *Can you let me know when you have a sec to talk? I have a couple things to discuss. Thanks.*

I stare at my phone, trying to conjure a response. I guess I could work out to pass the time. I really have no excuse not to today.

At ten thirty on a Monday morning, I'm the only one in the fitness center. I reluctantly climb onto a Peloton, the forty-five-minute ride feeling even more like some kind of elaborate yuppie torture thanks to my stubbornly silent phone. It only chimes once I'm back upstairs, getting out of the shower.

Ginny, finally: *I'm sorry, but I can't work with you and Ian any longer. Good luck.*

*She's* breaking up with *us*? The steam in the bathroom suddenly feels suffocating. Jack must've ratted us out to Ginny's sister-in-law. He has the perfect house and he looks like he stepped out of a goddamn Renaissance painting, but he still feels the need to pile on? Or maybe Curt made him do it. I bet that's what happened. That smug asshole.

I take a deep inhale to steady my breathing, then type out a response: *Thanks a ton, kiddo. It's a great day to go fuck yourself.*

My thumb hovers over the send button. But I can't do it. Taking this out on Ginny feels misdirected. Who knows what blown-out-of-proportion version she got of how things went down? And she's not the one who treated us like criminals.

Curt's words ricochet around in my head.

*If you ever come near my family again . . .*

As if Ian and I are perverts or something!

*Get the fuck off my property . . .*

Is that *all* that house is to him? A piece of property?

Still in my bathrobe, I go to my desk and tug open the top drawer. I pull out my copy of Curt's book, most of which I read last week when I probably should've been reviewing the VIP notes for the party. I flip through it, searching for what, exactly, I'm not sure. I skim the acknowledgments again. He thanks the usual suspects: His "unflappable" agent, "who assured me from the jump that this idea was a winner." His "esteemed colleagues" at Georgetown for "indulging my passionate ramblings over many a cafeteria lunch as I was putting this tome to bed." And "Jack and Penny, the loves of my life, the center of my universe."

Something about this guy doesn't sit right. That's at least one thing I learned from being around my dad—to be skeptical of people who seem to be trying just a little too hard.

It's been long enough since *Falling Apart* came out that I'm sure no one is paying attention to the ratings anymore. Except for Curt. I bet he monitors them religiously. A new anonymous one-star review could really be a day-ruiner.

I pull up the book on Amazon and click on the ratings—still 239 of them, with an average of 3.5 stars. Before I write my own, let's see if any of the other one-star pans can provide some inspiration.

Here's a write-up titled "Patronizing and dull" from a user called

Tom S.: *Bradshaw weighs down chapter after chapter with oversimplified anecdotes about the complex mechanisms of the global supply chain. You'd think he'd assume some basic level of intelligence from his readers, but instead he relentlessly talks down to us, deviating from his patronizing tone only for an occasional, unsuccessful attempt at a joke. The result? Flabby, sophomoric, obnoxious.*

Damn, Tom S.

There are a few others, generally in the same vein, though not quite as devastating. A user named GenieLee says the book is *repetitive and obvious*. Someone called PrincetonProf deems it *pseudo-intellectual*.

But then I scroll to the review that stops me cold. It's dated January 17, 2019—only a couple days after the book was released. It's five words long, all caps:

DO NOT TRUST CURTIS BRADSHAW.

Whoever left it identifies themself only as "…"

As in, just an ellipsis. Three dots. No initials or numbers or special characters. Essentially, a blank space.

I read it over and over:

…

DO NOT TRUST CURTIS BRADSHAW.

A chill prickles my neck beneath my still-wet hair. It's not really a review at all. It seems more like a message.

But from who?

# 11

I really did try to do this the nice way—tried to be a friend to Curt and Jack, truly wanted to be a role model for Penny. I wasn't even bullshitting about building them a guest suite in the basement. We could've been one big, happy, transatlantic family—if only they hadn't freaked the fuck out.

Now I'm left with no choice. I have to find another path to the house. And Amazon may have just supplied one possible route: Blackmail. (Guess Bezos didn't call it the Everything Store for nothing.)

*DO NOT TRUST CURTIS BRADSHAW.*

The one-star review that could lead to my five-star life. Because if Curt really is hiding something, and it's juicy enough, I might be able to use it to pressure him into selling the dream home to me and Ian.

So, I spend the rest of the afternoon Googling varying combinations of his name with possible misdeeds.

*"Curtis Bradshaw harassment"*

*"Curtis Bradshaw cheating"*

*"Curtis Bradshaw fraud"*

*"Curtis Bradshaw theft"*

*"Curtis Bradshaw disorderly conduct"*
*"Curtis Bradshaw disorderly conduct Sagrada Familia"*
*"Curtis Bradshaw pretentious dickhead"*

I run his name through PACER, the electronic database of federal court records. I try in every jurisdiction where I know he has a connection: Connecticut, where he grew up; New York, where he worked at his dad's hedge fund; Maryland, where he lives now; DC, where he lived previously and where his employer, Georgetown University, is located; and New Hampshire and Pennsylvania because he has degrees from Dartmouth and Penn.

Then I do the same thing with the local courts in all those places—both county and state level.

But after hours of digging, the only hit that comes up is a twenty-year-old civil suit against his dad, Curtis Bradshaw, Sr. According to the complaint, an analyst at his hedge fund accused him of forcing his tongue down her throat in the office one night, then withholding a promotion after she rejected him. Curtis Senior settled with her for an undisclosed amount before the case got to trial.

Imagine being so rich that you could throw money at a problem like that and make it vanish.

This is embarrassing—and gross. But I need something that incriminates Curt, not his dad. Something damning enough that he'd sooner sell to us than have it come out. And so far, I can't even find a lousy DUI.

By the time I hear Ian's key in the door, it's after six thirty and my eyes feel like sandpaper. I'm also starving. Did I ever break for lunch?

I peer over my shoulder at him from my desk. "Hey, let's go out to eat tonight. Maybe the Royal?"

He inspects me from the doorway, probably debating whether I'm setting a trap. It's true we haven't been speaking much. But if we're still going to find a way to make a run at the house, I need to coax him back onto my team.

"Okay..." He sets his brown leather backpack on the floor and puts his keys on the shelf. "Are you, um, doing all right?"

I look down and take in that I'm still in my robe. Only when he flips the switch in the kitchen do I realize that the apartment had been nearly dark.

I've always been like this. In college, and later, when I was trying to prove myself at the *Post*, I'd get so wrapped up in a story that I could lose hours and hours tracking down a single phone number. Last year, when I was deep into researching fertility options, Ian came home from a work trip to find me glued to my computer screen, barely having eaten in two days.

"Yep, I'm all good," I say, standing from my desk. "Just hungry." But my legs betray me. They nearly give out, both asleep.

"Whoa, careful." Ian hurries over, grabbing hold of my elbow. The gesture startles me. It's the first time he's touched me on purpose since the night of the dinner.

"I'm fine. Really." A warm buzzing fills them now. "I had a break this afternoon so I worked out downstairs. I just haven't had a chance to get dressed since I showered."

He eyes me warily, rakes a hand back through his hair. "When do you want to leave, then?"

"Just give me twenty."

I pat on some tinted moisturizer and pull on some jeans and a top, and we're out the door. The sky is cloudless, and the air bites now that the sun is disappearing. Late commuters and other people in search of dinner snake around each other, everyone well rehearsed in the clipped choreography of the after-work rush.

The Royal, a neighborhood spot with great coffee during the day and even better cocktails at night, is only three blocks from our building. But this walk seems to grind on forever—Ian staring at the ground as he cuts down my attempts at a conversation.

"How was the office today?" I ask.

"Fine."

"Anything new in the river dumping case?"

"No."

Even on a Monday, the restaurant is nearly full. The whole bar and a long communal table up front are occupied by happy-hour holdovers. I've tried more than once to convince the owners here to sign with Buzz, but they're probably right that they don't need any help with publicity. There's a couple vacating a table toward the back, so I hastily pull Ian behind me to claim it. He discards my hand as soon as we get close.

He didn't come home from Pittsburgh until Saturday morning. Then I took Fritter on a hike along the Potomac that afternoon since Natalie had a day shift and I needed to clear my head. Ian spent Sunday at the Nats game with work friends. Somehow, we've managed to successfully avoid a real conversation since last week's disaster, which was fine with me because I was still figuring out what I wanted to say. But now I'm ready to explain the other possibility I've been working on, and a public venue makes for safer territory than the apartment.

"So, I broke up with Ginny today," I say, after the server sets down our cocktails and we've both finished ordering food through the QR code on the table.

"What?" He looks up from his phone, no longer able to ignore me. "Why would you do that?"

"Well, I've been thinking—and please just hear me out for a minute—I think we should still make an offer on the house, and obviously we can't use Ginny for that."

He throws his head back in exasperation. I knew he'd react like this, but I just need to keep him from walking out.

"Listen to me, Ian. There has to be a way to do it anonymously, right? People buy houses with LLCs all the time—that stands for 'limited liability corporation.' You can use them to hide your identity."

"Yeah, I know what an LLC is."

"Well, the rules about them are different everywhere, but it looks like you can set one up pretty easily in DC, right online—it only takes a few days. Or, another option could be designating our new agent as a trustee who could sign the paperwork for us. Have you heard of those, too? It seems like either way might work, but I was hoping you could help sort out the details, since you're the lawyer."

He sighs and crosses his arms. "Margo, I'm worried about you."

So, Condescending Ian has arrived.

He leans forward, his gaze flitting to the table next to us to make sure they're not eavesdropping. "This is not normal behavior," he whispers. "You must know that."

I resist rolling my eyes and remind myself that I need his help.

"Babe, I know it sounds like a lot of extra trouble. But haven't you noticed that not a single decent house in our price range has even come on the market in the last two months? It's not like we're drowning in options. And if we get started tomorrow, I think we can have the legalities of it all squared away by the time Jack and Curt list it next Thursday. They probably won't even take offers until after the weekend, which gives us even more time." I pause for a sip of my daiquiri. "I thought we might ask Erika and Heath to refer us to their agent."

Ian pinches the bridge of his nose. "Is this what you worked on all day, sitting there in your robe, in the dark?"

No, honey, I researched this yesterday. Today, I combed through court records looking for blackmail material, just to cover all our bases.

"Not *all* day," I say placidly.

"All right, let's put aside the fact that there are many, *many* legal and financial reasons this would never work, and walk through the hypothetical." He swallows the rest of his negroni. "We submit this brilliant, anonymous offer, and then what? You think after everything we put those guys through, Jack and Curt are just going to look at it and say, 'Oh, gee, nothing weird about this! We'll just consider it right along with the other nineteen bids in the pile'?"

"Oh, well, that's another thing—I don't think they're going to get nineteen bids, Ian. Did you see the news about rates today? They're past five percent! That has to cut down on the competition, don't you think?"

He buries his face in his hands, just as the server arrives with our food. She sets down Ian's burger and my fish, then starts to ask if we need anything else, but upon assessing the scene opts to flee instead.

When Ian lifts his face, his eyes are wet. I can't tell if that's a good or bad sign.

"I blame myself. I think I've really failed you."

I tilt my head. Is he apologizing? He's usually much easier to read than this.

"I never should've agreed to go to that dinner with you. I knew we were crossing a line, and I still let it happen. I should've seen that you were struggling and stepped in."

Okay, so these are bad tears, then. I need to course-correct.

I smile and rest my hand on his. "Ian, I'm fine. I am not struggling. Forget I said anything. Let's just enjoy our dinner."

He takes my hand in both of his and kisses it. I feel myself flush. Public affection has never been easy for me.

"I just want you to be happy. I want *us* to be happy." Another line of dampness threatens to breach his lower lids. "Let's hit pause on the house hunt, okay? We need a break. I need my wife back."

He needs his wife back? I didn't realize I was a thing he could loan out.

I force myself to keep smiling.

"I get it, I really do. This has been a lot. I know it has. But now I'm just worried about interest rates. They only seem to be getting higher, and we might get totally priced out if we don't make a move pretty soon here."

There. A perfectly reasonable point, made by a person who is not struggling.

"That's a risk I'm willing to take." He lets go of my hand and picks up his burger. "I'm sorry, babe, even if we could, I wouldn't make an offer on that house with you. We need a breather, just for a little while."

He takes a hulking bite. A blob of orange cheese sauce plops onto his plate, gleaming and fatty. Is he really chewing that audibly? Or am I so disgusted by him that I'm imagining the most unflattering soundtrack possible? Something vicious stirs within me. The space behind my eyes begins to throb. The scattered twinkling of the string lights overhead fuses into a single, searing beam. I want to scream in his face. To grab him by the collar and shake until he understands that we can't go on like this. How is it fucking possible that he doesn't grasp the urgency? But instead, I keep the smile fixed in place. I blink slowly a couple of times to clear the spots dappling my vision. Pushing this idea any more will only hurt me. Blackmail it is.

"Okay, fine, enough house talk," I say, as I swipe a fry off his plate. "You can have your wife back now."

## 12

I'm wearing real pants and pouring the remains of our French press into a travel mug because Ian says this is what I need.

He rolled over in bed this morning, after the alarm went off, and declared in his most concerned tone: "I think it would be really good for you to go in today. You know, see other people, socialize a little?"

He said it like a question, but it wasn't one. I'd already been awake for hours, the fury cresting and crashing inside my chest like a boiling wave, while Ian snored softly beside me—the unbothered slumber of a man whose wife carries his stress for him. I thought of how satisfying it would be to throw the lamp on my nightstand against the wall on his side of the bed. The collision, and maybe the sting of a few shards, tearing him from the quiet.

But I need Ian to believe that I have truly moved on. So, when the alarm sounded and he looked at me like I was more breakable than that bedside lamp, all I said back was "You're right. I'll go in."

He's working from home today, so I can't fake it. I have to pack up my laptop and kiss him goodbye. Now I head out the door like a white-collar nomad, wandering the city, on the hunt for a coffee shop with free Wi-Fi where I won't run into anyone from my office or, worse, Ian on a break from the apartment. I walk all the way to Dupont Circle—that's almost a mile and a half, and in ankle boots, not sneakers—and take the Red Line north to Woodley Park.

Late in the morning on a Tuesday, the Starbucks across from the zoo is sparsely populated by a couple of tourists waiting for their drinks, and a woman who looks barely out of college trying to sweet-talk a toddler into eating grapes from a plastic cup. The nanny.

I order a cappuccino and install myself in a quiet back corner, next to an outlet. I refreshed my work email every ninety seconds the whole ride here, but it's still the first thing I check once my computer is plugged in and open. I drum my fingers on the table while the Wi-Fi connects. Six new messages appear, one after the other. Most are from clients—they'll get my vague out-of-office reply: *I'm away at the moment, but looking forward to connecting upon my return!*

None of the emails are from Jordana.

A knot tightens in my stomach. I can't take much more of the not knowing. All the blackmail material in the world won't do me any good if I don't have the salary to pay for the house.

But at least this gives me more time to dig. I open my bookmarks bar and click on the Amazon page for *Falling Apart*. I stare at the one-star review from Ellipsis, my nickname for the mystery author.

*DO NOT TRUST CURTIS BRADSHAW.*

Simultaneously, the most exhilarating and frustrating five words I have ever read.

One rabbit hole I didn't have time to dive down yesterday was the press around the book. Maybe the clue I need is hidden in plain sight—in some interview that Curt gave somewhere—not buried in decades of old court records. Maybe I've been overthinking things.

I do a simple news search for Curt's name and the title of the book. The Squawk Box interview with Andrew Ross Sorkin comes back as a top result. I put in my earbuds and listen to it again, but nothing stands out. It just sounds like a lot of bloviating.

Curt also did a TV interview with Fox Business. But it's more of the same—almost verbatim. When the Fox interviewer asks how he got the idea for the book, he gives nearly the same aw-shucks humblebrag response that he gave on Squawk Box: "Frankly, somebody should have beaten me to the punch writing it. All I did was explore a question that every single one of us has probably considered..."

*Bloomberg* and *Business Insider* both ran short pieces, too, though neither outlet seems to have interviewed him. Both articles include the same pair of canned quotes, which I can only assume were written by somebody like me for the press release announcing the book, and not ever really spoken by Curt himself.

A story from *The Washington Post*, dated January 26, 2019, appears lower down in the results. Since Curt is local, maybe someone there actually bothered to pick up the phone and talk to him. When I click on it, the byline explodes off the screen: Erika Ortiz.

I skim quickly to make sure there are real quotes, and of course there are. Erika would never turn in some boilerplate bullshit. Then I start from the beginning and read the whole thing. It doesn't take long, since the article can't be more than six hundred or seven hundred words. And, honestly, it's a snooze. Erika must've been desperate for copy that week.

I pick up my phone and search for the same story. I include the link with my text: *Hey, do you remember anything about this guy?*

Erika's response comes back right away: *Not really. He was a little arrogant but that's about it. Why?*

I have my cover story ready to go: *He's an investor in a restaurant that we might sign. Just doing some due diligence.*

*Gotcha. Which restaurant?*

*Doesn't have a name yet.*

*I only talked to him on the phone/pretty sure he's gay so he didn't #MeToo me or anything if that's what you're asking.*

*LOL thanks.*

Damn. I scroll back through Erika's story one more time, trying to unearth some deeper meaning.

Another order of business occurs to me: *While I have you, would you mind connecting me with your real estate agent? Please don't mention to Heath, tho. Still trying to convince Ian it's time to dump ours.*

*Ofc! I'll shoot you both an email in just a min.*

I remember my auto-reply: *Thanks! Use my gmail.*

A chime through my earbuds—I never took them out—pulls my attention back to my laptop.

A new work email. From Jordana. Subject line: *Let's chat.*

*Margo,*
*Call me tomorrow at 11a.*

*Thanks,*
*J.*

It's not much, but it's typical of Jordana to keep it brief. And if the news was bad, surely I would've heard from HR instead. This feels like progress.

*Great!* I write back.

I look up from my screen just in time to see a mom battling to get through the door. She pushes a double-decker UPPababy stroller with one hand and drags a little boy—maybe three years old—behind her with the other. He clutches a stuffed tiger.

The customer by the entrance is too engrossed in his phone to notice, so I rush over to help. "Thank you," she says, her face a mixture of exhaustion and gratitude. "It's been a morning—I didn't think it was possible to feel resentful toward pandas." She laughs at her own joke, and I almost miss the cue to join in because I'm transfixed by the baby sleeping in the stroller's upper tier. Her cheeks are smooth and plump like mochi. She has a full head of fluffy brown hair. I wish I could bury my nose in it and inhale.

"She's really perfect," I tell her mom.

The woman laughs again—"At least when she's napping"—then she hustles up to the register, oblivious to the fact that she has everything. A dull throbbing begins to pulse behind my eyes.

*No house, no baby.*

*No house, no life.*

This is no time to second-guess myself. Back at my corner table, I pop two Advil and do the thing that I hesitated to do yesterday: Pull up the number for Curt's dad's hedge fund.

Curtis Bradshaw, Sr. must be pushing eighty, but he's still listed there as chairman. I wait for the boy with the tiger to stop whining at his mom for a cake pop, then put my earbuds back in and dial star-67 to block my number from showing up on the other end of the call. A receptionist answers.

"Bradshaw Capital Management, how may I assist you?"

She sounds young. I hope Curt's dad hasn't tried anything with her.

"Yes, hello, is Mr. Bradshaw available?"

"He is in today, yes . . ." I hear the clacking of her keyboard. "I don't see that he's expecting a call right now, though. Does he know what this is about?"

"No, he doesn't. My name is Lisa Waters. I'm a reporter at *The Chronicle of Higher Education*." Lisa Waters is a real byline there, just in case anyone bothers to Google me. "I wondered if he'd be willing to give an interview for a short profile I'm writing about his son, Curtis. You might've heard he was recently appointed to a senior faculty position at King's College in London, and I'm doing a series on American professors who go abroad."

"Oh! No, I just started, so I don't know anything about that. Sounds awesome, though. Let me just put you on a quick hold."

I endure almost a minute of smooth jazz before I hear the click that announces her return.

"Um, Lisa?"

"Yes, I'm still here," I say.

"I'm sorry, but Mr. Bradshaw says he's not interested in speaking with you."

The energy has drained from her voice.

"Really?" I assumed he'd be happy to brag about his kid for a puff piece—and in the process, maybe drop a lead or two about where I should snoop for dirt next. "I could call back at a more convenient time. It's a very positive story, I'm just hoping to gather some color."

"Yeah, I explained it to him, but he said if it's about his son, he's not interested." She pauses. "Please don't write that part, though."

"Okay, sure, but did he say anything—"

She cuts me off before I can finish. "I'm sorry, I really have to go," she says. "But good luck!"

She hangs up.

Have Curt and his dad had some sort of falling-out then?

Apple's ringtone fills my ears, followed by Siri's sedate voice: "Call from Erika Oritz. Answer it?"

"Uh, yes." The line connects. "Hey, Erika."

"Hey, sorry to call, but this would be hard to explain over text."

"No problem. What's up?'

"So, I ran that guy's name through my inbox for you, you know, just to see what came back, and an old reader email popped up."

"Okay . . ." I straighten in my chair.

"All it says is 'Do not trust Curtis Bradshaw. He is a liar'—that's it—and it came from an anonymous address. It looks like I did try to respond to it, but I got a bounce-back that the account had already been deactivated."

"Oh, um, wow." I feel light-headed. "And you forgot about this?"

She laughs. "It's not like I have any shortage of wack jobs emailing me on the regular. And who remembers *anything* that happened before the pandemic?"

"Yeah, true." I push out a laugh.

"I have to run," Erika says, "but I can forward it to you if you want."

"That would be great." My heart is racing. "Oh, personal Gmail again, please. Our office email has been down all morning."

"Cool. Talk to you later," Erika says, then hangs up.

I open my Gmail and find two unread messages from her—the introduction to her agent, and the forwarded email that could hold the break I need.

The sender's address is nobody.noone97@hotmail.com. It's dated January 27, 2019—the day after Erika's story ran. And the note is just as Erika said: *DO NOT TRUST CURTIS BRADSHAW. HE IS A LIAR*. All caps, like the Amazon review, and even more aggressive.

I copy and paste the email address into a new message, subject line: *Curtis Bradshaw*.

*Hi there. I think we can help each other. Curtis Bradshaw hurt me, too. Please call me or let me know how to reach you.*

I add my cell number and press send.

"Please, please, please," I whisper to myself. I hold my breath and refresh the page.

An automatic bounce-back, identical to the one Erika got, populates at the top of my inbox, letting me know the account no longer exists.

But there is at least one more thing I can try.

I text Erika again: *Hey, thanks so much for that email. Any chance your IT dept can trace the IP address?*

Some IP addresses are impossible to track, but I know for a fact that the *Post*'s IT desk can at least attempt this. I had them do it for me once, not long after I'd been promoted to reporter. There'd been a kidnapping in northern Virginia that was all over the news, and

I'd gotten a tip from someone claiming they'd seen the little boy that very morning, playing in a front yard in rural North Carolina. It could've been the story of a lifetime. But the IP address showed the email was a hoax—it had come from Honolulu.

Erika's response lights up my phone: *I guess . . . this is really only about a restaurant?*

*Yes, long story. You would be doing me a huge favor. I'll owe you big time.*

The three dots materialize, fade away, then appear again. She can't figure out what to type.

Finally, she sends: *Don't worry about it. I'll let you know what they say.*

I reply: *THANK YOU!*

# 13

Natalie is twenty minutes late, not that I have anywhere else to rush off to.

I'm perched on one of the last two available barstools at Jane Jane. My work bag reserves the one next to me—pretty obviously, I think, but three people have asked if the seat is taken. I'm dying to hear back from Erika, which is why my stomach lurches at the sound of my phone vibrating on the bar.

But it's only Ian. *Hey babe, are we eating together?*

Translation: *Are you making dinner?*

*I think we're eating here*, I text back. *Order whatever takeout you want.*

For all the worried looks and prolonged hugs he gave me before I left this morning, I barely heard from my Very Concerned Husband all day. I took myself to the movies as a distraction while I waited for word from Erika—some arty mess that's getting Oscar buzz. The movie wasn't the point anyway. I mainly wanted to disappear into the cold, black void of an empty theater, and stuff my face with fake-buttered popcorn and Junior Mints.

It was after five o'clock by the time the movie ended, so I figured I was in the clear to go home. But then Natalie texted about getting drinks, and even she sounds like a better hang than Ian right now so I told him I was going to happy hour with work people. (*Good for you!* he replied.)

I see her by the door and wave her over. She's wearing those leggings that look like leather from far away, but up close, they're really just shiny black spandex.

"Hey, girl!" She leans in to hug me. "Nice job getting a spot."

She surveys the room while she peels off her jean jacket—no doubt hoping to catch someone checking her out.

"Yeah, I got lucky and grabbed the last two." (We made these plans too last-minute for me to call in a favor for a table.) "What's up?"

"Oh, not a lot. Sorry I'm late, I was all the way in Southwest, down on the waterfront, and it took forever to get an Uber."

I'm pretty sure I know the answer but I ask the question anyway: "What was in Southwest?"

She giggles. Here we go.

"Just a girl I met at the bar last night. Very little chill—she texted me first thing this morning."

"Ah, something new and different for you."

She laughs, loudly enough that a few heads turn our way, definitely the goal. The bartender also notices and comes over to take our order. The spicy mezcal thing is on the menu now, so we get a round of those.

"Want any food?" I ask Natalie.

"Oh, no, I'm stuffed. She lives at the Wharf so we ate a late lunch down there."

I make a face at the mention of DC's douchiest neighborhood. "She's not some self-loathing head case, is she?"

"Hell no, you know I draw the line at Republicans," says Natalie. "She just wanted the water view. I mean, her condo *is* really nice."

"You saw her place, then?"

She laughs again. "Yeah, we went upstairs afterwards."

As the bartender delivers our drinks, it hits me: "Wait a minute, you were at the bar last night? You don't usually work Mondays."

"It was a last-minute thing. I had to cover for someone."

"When did you get home?"

"A little after one."

"Natalie! Why didn't you tell me? Fritter was alone that whole time? And now you've been out practically all day?"

"Oh my God, Margo. Fritter is fine. He's only a dog. He sleeps the whole time I'm gone."

*Only a dog.*

The rage that I've suppressed since Ian called off our house hunt last night simmers dangerously close to the surface. I imagine crushing my cocktail glass against the side of her dumb, blindingly blond head. Instead, I take a healthy slug from it and will the pitch of my voice to stay even.

"But wouldn't you feel better knowing he was with someone?" I ask. "Eating his dinner on time, and not feeling like his bladder might explode?"

Is she a fucking sociopath?

She rolls her eyes. "You're always wound so tight, Margo. Didn't your doctor say that's why you can't get pregnant?"

Isn't that rich—a medical opinion from someone who counts uppers and downers as separate food groups. The rage is in a full-on tantrum now, thrashing and scratching to be let out. But before I can unleash it, my mind skips to a future where Natalie has taken back her key and revoked my Fritter privileges, where all I can do is pace around my shoebox on the nights I know she's working, convinced I can hear him crying two floors above.

Leaving him behind is the only thing I'm dreading about finally breaking out of that hellhole. But I'll offer to watch him at our new place, on the weekends at least, so he can experience a real backyard.

I take another long drink.

"I don't mean to overstep," I say. "I just love that dog, so please, just tell me when you'll be gone and I'll hang out with him. I'm always happy to do it."

She sighs. "I know you are, it just slipped my mind to text you last night." She pauses to scroll through her phone. When she looks back up, she tilts her head. "If you love Fritter so much, why don't you guys get your own dog?"

"I would love to, but we're waiting to find a house first."

"You really have a whole checklist, don't you? House. Baby. Dog." She holds up a finger as she counts off each item. Then, smirking, adds: "Menopause. Death."

"I guess so," I say, smiling, refusing to give her the satisfaction of getting under my skin.

"Well, I do appreciate how great you are with him. You're a natural," she says. "You really didn't have dogs growing up?"

"No, not really."

"What does that mean?" she asks.

My chest tightens.

...

I was nine when I found Blossom by the dumpsters behind our townhouse. It was summer and Mitch was supposed to be watching me, but he'd gone to the neighbor's to play Nintendo. I'd been riding my bike around the parking lot, the July sun blasting down, then radiating back up from the blacktop. I was drenched in sweat by the time I heard it—a small but forceful bark. She only did it once.

I threw down my kickstand and ran over to the two smelly green bins. She was between them, a matted dark-gray mop that reminded me of Toto from *The Wizard of Oz*. A crow was eyeing the Burger King wrapper she held beneath her front paws. I shooed away the bird and squatted down, instantly recognizing something of myself in those uneasy eyes.

"Come on, it's okay," I whispered, holding out a hand. She gave it a lick, then let me scoop her up. I bathed her with dish soap—we'd learned in school that they sometimes did that for animals who'd been in oil spills—and fed her leftover chicken from a Tupperware in the fridge. We fell asleep together in my bed and didn't wake up again until my mom got home from work. Blossom (yes, like the TV show) started barking as soon as she heard the door.

"Margo?" My mom raced into my room, wearing the frantic expression I'd last seen when my dad caught her hiding T.J. Maxx bags in my closet. "Oh my God, Margo. Where did you get that?"

I told her the whole story, then made the strongest case I could think of: "Mitch never hangs out with me when you go to work, even though you tell him he has to. And I never know when Dad will be here or not. A dog would keep me company."

Blossom had done her part, snuggling against my mom when she sat on the edge of my bed, the khaki pants she wore for her hotel front desk job so heavily starched they barely creased. She mindlessly began to stroke Blossom's fur, extra soft from the bath.

"Margo, you know we aren't allowed to have pets here," she told me gently. I remember feeling surprised by how sad she looked. "Plus," she added, "who would take care of her during the day once you go back to school?"

I was not a kid who cried very often, but in that moment, a dam broke. I could hardly form words between my snotty, heaving sobs. I was such a pathetic mess that my mom started crying, too.

She watched me for a minute, chewing her rosy bottom lip. "All right, Margo, we don't have to decide right now." She wiped the tears from the underside of her chin with the back of a hand. "When your dad gets home, let's say a friend from school had to go on a trip, and her family asked us to take care of Blossom while they're away. I'll explain it, and you just agree with me, okay?"

I'd never loved her more.

. . .

"Margo, are you okay?" Natalie frowns at me from her barstool.

"Yeah, fine." I clear my throat. "I just mean that I never had a dog of my own when I was a kid. I took care of one for a while, though. For a friend."

The bartender comes over to ask if we'd like another round. Natalie starts to order, then catches my disapproving look. She rolls her eyes. "Sorry, never mind," she tells the bartender. "I have to get home to let the dog out."

She's frosty on the walk back to the apartment, so when I spy the Prius parked down a side street, I'm glad for the out. "You know what, Nat, I have a quick errand to run, and my car's right there." I gesture toward it. "I'll see you later."

There's only one place I can think to go. I know I shouldn't, but I can't stay away forever. That house is a part of me now. And I only need to see it for a second. Just to know that it's still as perfect as I remember.

Traffic is a mess, so the sun is nearly gone by the time I make it to Grovemont. When the house is in view, I slow to a crawl, debating whether I should risk pulling over. But the front windows are dark. They're probably still cleaning up dinner. They'll never notice me from all the way back there.

I park across the street, shutting the car door as softly as I can. From the sidewalk, beneath the canopy of the big maple, I can see through the window just to the left of the front door. I can make out the curve of the arched opening into the kitchen, backlit by the happy routine taking place just beyond it. A slender figure—Jack—glides past the island. A softness swells inside of me as I imagine a high chair pulled up to it, squishy little hands leaving fingerprints behind on smooth marble.

Wonder what they ate tonight. Did they use the breakfast nook or the deck table? Did they take turns sharing the highs and lows of their days? I've always wanted to do that with my own family. It'll be our dinnertime ritual.

I wonder if they talked about me and Ian. Have they explained to Penny what happened with us?

A rustling overhead draws my attention upward—only a squirrel. But as I follow its dark outline around the branches, my heart nearly stops. The light in one of the windows on the second floor, Curt's office judging by the location, has blinked on. A lone eye watching the street.

How long has it been like that?

I lower my face toward the ground and turn back to the Prius. In a few fast strides, I'm behind the wheel. When I sneak a look toward the house, the light is off again. But I have no way of knowing if someone is on the other side of the blackness.

. . .

I don't hear the text arrive at first because the vibrating of my Sonicare fills my whole head. But once I switch it off and spit out the toothpaste, my phone dings again.

It's Erika.

*Sorry, the day got away from me. The IP address came from 20057. Georgetown.*

Georgetown? I thought Georgetown's zip code was 20007. I run a quick Google search and feel my breath catch.

"Oh my God," I say aloud.

"What, babe?" Ian calls from the bedroom, where the *SportsCenter* theme is starting up.

"Nothing," I reply. "Just a dumb email from a client."

It's after eleven o'clock, but I'm suddenly wide awake. Erika didn't mean Georgetown, the neighborhood. She meant Georgetown University. The school has its own zip code.

Ellipsis must have been another faculty member. Or a student. I can work with this.

# 14

The Toyota Camry bumps along Georgetown's ancient cobblestone streets, the rough ride conspiring with the faint smell of cigarettes in the backseat to raise a gurgling from my stomach.

"Here we are," says the driver, slowing to a stop in front of an intricate wrought-iron gate, its sides swung open like outstretched arms.

"Thanks so much." I gulp in the fresh air as I clamber out.

All these years in DC, and this will be my first time on the Georgetown University campus. I check the map on my phone. I'm at the O Street entrance, so the Lauinger Library—where the archives are housed—should be impossible to miss.

It's almost nine thirty on Wednesday morning. Eight days to go till the house is listed. As in, one week, one day. As in, I'd better dig up a fucking lead about Curt here or I'm about to lose everything.

Students crisscross the sprawling green in front of me like lines of ants in Doc Martens and backpacks. None of them look old enough to me to be in college, which means I must look prehistoric. The overcast sky makes the Gothic building looming just beyond the grass seem especially dreary. According to my map, that's Healy Hall. Why do expensive private schools always look so haunted?

The library is off to the left, as I anticipated, and nothing like the architecture around it—a brutalist 1970s fortress plunked conspicuously among Victorian spires and stonework. I head straight for it.

Inside the special-collections wing on the fifth floor—where the archives are kept—a girl with an eyebrow ring sits at the front desk, reading a bent-up copy of *A Room of One's Own*.

"Hey there," I say, smiling. "I'm hoping to see an old university yearbook."

She lifts her eyes—but not her face. "Domesday book" is the only thing she says.

"Excuse me?"

"That's what they're called here. Not yearbooks."

Right. Some kind of weird old-money bullshit.

"Sure, that's what I meant," I say, the smile still in place. "I'd like to see the Domesday book from 2019, please."

She nods and scribbles something on a yellow slip of paper. "The reading room is that way," she says, gesturing around her desk. "You can wait in there."

I walk down the hall till I reach a glass door, leading to an empty room with a long table in the center. The space is brightly lit and sterile-feeling. More hospital than Hogwarts—not at all how I imagined the Georgetown archives would look while I lay awake in bed last night, puzzling together this plan. I envisioned being led into a two-hundred-year-old candlelit cavern with millions of leather-bound volumes stacked all the way to the ceiling. (Omnipresent Harry Potter references are the cross I bear as a geriatric millennial.)

The yearbook idea occurred to me right after I got into bed. Ian was already passed out and I'd just switched off the TV. He snored next to me while I reread the email from nobody.noone97. The most promising clue I had, other than the location of the IP address, seemed to be those two digits at the end of the account name. I figured it could be a birth year, so I opened the calculator on my phone and did the math. Someone born in 1997 would have been a college senior in 2019.

It only took a few more minutes of sleuthing to confirm that Georgetown does, in fact, have yearbooks—I found an online order form for this year's edition, which included a blurb with the stat that they've been published since 1908. Within a half hour, I'd figured out that every edition is kept in the campus archives, which, with the exception of the rarest items, are open to the public for research.

The longer I lay there considering it, the more likely it seemed that a young person, and not some crusty professor, would be emotional enough to fire off anonymous vitriol not once, but twice. And it's safer to start with ex-students anyway. If I snoop around the wrong faculty member—someone who's loyal to Curt—they'll surely rat me out to him. I'll take that risk if I have to. But not before trying this.

The girl appears, holding a thick book with a watercolor image on the cover that I recognize as Healy Hall. The words "Ye Domesday Booke 2019" are printed across it in an elaborate Old English font.

"Thanks," I say, as she places it on the table in front of me. "Can I make copies of the pages somewhere?"

She offers a one-word reply—"No"—then turns to go.

"Uh, why not?" My question elicits an annoyed sigh.

"We don't allow copies of archived materials. It can deteriorate them."

Jesus Christ, it's a three-year-old yearbook, not a first fucking edition. This is going to take way longer than I expected. As she leaves, I consider just stuffing the thing in my bag and walking out with it. But a fancy-ass school like this is probably wired to the tits with security cameras.

The yearbook is front-loaded with collages of student life. I flip quickly through basketball and field hockey games, kids huddled in self-serious-looking discussions, students lounging on the lawn on nice days. In short: images of freedom. Not that these kids likely had very much to be liberated from. Maybe an overbearing cello instructor. But that's what I remember most about those glorious early days of college—the clean slate of it all, the feeling that I could finally make my own luck now that I was on my own.

In back, I find pages filled with thumbnail-size individual portraits, arranged by class. Judging by the student population numbers I saw online, there should be about fifteen hundred seniors. Unsurprisingly, not all of them sat for photos; some of the thumbnails are just gray placeholder boxes.

But the important details are all here. Beneath each one, whether it's empty or filled with an eager face, both the student's name and area of study are listed. The first of the lot that I'm interested in appears right away: Peter Abdo, Economics. He's out of central casting for a future master-of-the-universe type—blond, broad-shouldered, blue-and-white gingham button-up. I jot his name down as fast as I can in my notepad, and wonder briefly about the acts of terrorism he and his frat bros probably committed.

In a little over an hour, having read every entry twice, I'm satisfied that I haven't missed anyone. I have twenty-eight names on my list of economics majors who graduated in the year 2019—if I start today, and I eat in front of my computer, I should be able to track them all down well before the weekend.

I'm tucking my notepad back into my bag when my alarm blasts from inside of it, making me jump. I retrieve my phone from the side pocket, struggling to remember why I set it for 10:55, when a calendar notification displays the reason: *Call Jordana!!*

Right. How could I forget? I'm only supposed to save my job in five minutes.

I shut the yearbook and throw my bag over my shoulder. I speed-walk back down the hall and out of the special-collections wing; then I jog down the stairs because they're a surer bet than waiting for the elevator. Outside, it's begun to lightly drizzle. I glance at my phone, still in my hand, just as it flips to 10:58. Plenty of time.

There's a bench that's sheltered from the rain, right here in the entrance. I take a seat and run through the talking points in my head: I am very sorry. I have not been myself lately. Yes, I had food poisoning. But also, the fertility issues are really starting to take a toll. (As cold as she can seem, Jordana has two kids, and she will, I think, sympathize with this.) But it's not an excuse—that part's important. And I will do better. Did I mention I am very sorry?

I take a deep breath and put in my earbuds. I tap Jordana's name in my contacts.

"Hi, Margo." She answers on the second ring, her tone giving away nothing.

"Hi, Jordana, thanks for making the time to talk."

"Of course. How are you? I mean, *really?*"

Her concern takes me aback.

"Doing much better, thank you."

"That's good to hear, Margo. You know, I do genuinely care about you, which is why your behavior lately has been so concer . . ."

I don't catch what comes next. A man in jeans and a brown blazer has stopped, halfway across the green, in the middle of the brick path that leads to where I'm sitting. He wears glasses with thick black frames. He's bald.

He's Curt.

He cocks his head, pinning his gaze to me, trying, I'm sure, to decide if I am who he thinks. I look down at my phone, letting my hair fall around my face, and rise slowly from the bench.

"Jordana, I'm so sorry, I have to call you back," I whisper.

"Margo, what? Are you seri—"

I hang up and turn sharply to the left, down another brick walkway. The green is nearly deserted now; it's fully raining and classes must've started at eleven. I allow myself a half-glance back over my shoulder in time to see Curt pick up speed. My heart bangs against my rib cage.

Keeping my eyes straight ahead, I walk as briskly as I can. If I run, it'll erase any doubt he might still have about who I am, though I can't even know for sure if he's still behind me. I'm too afraid to turn around and risk him getting a closer view of my face. I see movement out of the corner of my eye—a student exiting through a side door from Healy Hall. It's my best option. I hurry over and slip inside before the door can close.

A vacant corridor of repeating brick archways stretches before me, possibly even more haunted-looking than the exterior. It doesn't help that my own footsteps follow me like a ghost's, echoing off the checkerboard tile floor. Doors, presumably classrooms, line the wall to my left, every one of them closed.

I come to a turnoff, another brick passageway that will funnel me deeper into the core of the building. I scramble down it just as a sharp, metallic sound cracks the silence behind me—the push-bar releasing on the exterior door. Someone else has come inside.

Leather-soled footsteps approach, hitting louder and harder than the ones my sneakers made. He'll reach the turn any second. I crouch behind the base of the nearest archway, tucking my knees to my chest to make myself into a ball.

The footsteps stop. All I hear is my own rapid breathing.

Then two drawn-out syllables singsong down the corridor: "Maaaaar-gohhhh."

# 15

Curt's voice, eerily calm like it was on his front porch a week ago, sends a chill across my skin. If I stay put, he'll find me. If I get up and run, he'll follow.

A third choice—the only real choice—floats into my head, blotting out everything else around it: I am not the one who should be cowering here as if I did something wrong. Even if I were, I don't have time for this bullshit. I just need to face him.

I push a hand into the rough brick and hoist myself up. The main corridor is only two or three steps away. I take them swiftly, and when I reach the turn, I walk out into the open without hesitation. He's a few yards down the hall, his stance wide.

"Hi, Curt," I say nonchalantly.

He narrows his eyes and takes fast, sweeping strides to meet me. "What the fuck are you doing here?" he hisses.

"Jesus, don't be so dramatic. It's an open campus. Shouldn't a tenured professor know that?"

He shoves a finger into my face. "Don't you fuck with me, you little psychopath. I saw you last night. Outside the house. I know it was you, and I called the cops, just like I said I would."

I frown at him. "To tell them what, exactly? That you think you maybe, possibly, saw a woman outside on the public sidewalk, who might have, at one point, been interested in buying your house?" I laugh. "I'm sure they rushed right over."

"You need to listen to me, Margo." His voice trembles. Is he afraid of me? "If you don't leave us alone, you'll regret it—that's a promise."

Wonder what he'll do if I give him just one more tiny push.

"You sound unwell, Curt. If your father still spoke to you, I bet he'd be *very* concerned, too."

It was a shot in the dark, but I hit my target. Curt's nostrils flare as he snatches my wrist.

"What the fuck did you just say?" he growls, his bony fingers digging in.

"Professor Bradshaw!" I shout as loud as I can. "What are you doing?"

The door closest to us swings open. A sixtyish woman with a brown bob steps out, looking alarmed. "Curtis!" she gasps. "What on earth is going on out here? Take your hands off that woman!"

I peek behind her and see rows of students, arranged in tiers like an amphitheater. There must be almost a hundred people in there, all witnesses to Curt coming unhinged.

Curt drops my wrist and backs away. "Elizabeth!" He clears his throat and smiles wanly. "I didn't realize our discussion had gotten so heated." He chuckles and looks to me to join in. I do not. "We'll take this elsewhere. My apologies."

Elizabeth looks at me. "Are you all right, dear?"

"Um, yes," I say, lowering my eyes to my Nikes. "I think I'll just go now. So sorry to have interrupted your class."

I brush past Curt and hurry down the hallway. Once I make it through the side door where I first came in, I half walk, half jog the rest of the way to the wrought-iron gate at the edge of campus, out into the neighborhood beyond.

I fly down O Street, past historic pastel-hued row houses,

around trash bins blocking the narrow sidewalk, till I reach the main drag of Wisconsin Avenue. As usual, it bustles with people. I melt into the stream of tourists and students and head toward M Street, dropping a pin for a Lyft on the corner.

By the time I get there, the car is only a minute away. I hold my leather tote tightly against my body while I wait, the list of twenty-eight names nestled safely inside.

...

Ian will be at the office the rest of the day, and I have never been more grateful to have the apartment to myself. I dump the remains of this morning's French press into a glass—no time to brew a fresh batch—and gulp it down cold as I settle in on the sofa with my laptop.

Twenty-eight names—all of them graduates of a prominent university, which means they've almost certainly gone on to the kinds of lives and careers that will make them eminently findable online. I start from the top, with Peter Abdo—the frat bro—and enjoy a literal LOL when I see that he's a mortgage broker working for his mom in Tennessee. All that money on a private education and the guy processes loans in a subdivision outside Nashville.

But the good thing about people in real estate is they usually list their cell numbers on their websites. Peter picks up right away and I toss him the bait: "I'm Lisa Waters with *The Chronicle of Higher Education*. I'm looking into a troubling tip about a Professor Curtis Bradshaw in the economics department at Georgetown, and I wondered if you might've known him when you were a student there. I would be happy to keep this conversation off the record if that makes it easier for you to talk."

It's just enough, I hope, to convince him that I know something—and that he should help me fill in the blanks.

Peter doesn't hang up, a small victory. He says he took a class with Curt junior year. "Off the record? He was a dick for sure. Extremely full of himself," he tells me. "But I don't know about anything illegal or, like, sexual, if that's what you're driving at. Maybe it would help if you tell me more about the tip you got?"

"Unfortunately, I can't disclose anything further until I get independent corroboration from additional sources," I explain. "It's very sensitive—the type of behavior you would remember if you'd known about it. But thank you so much for your time."

Back when I was a reporter, a lot of my colleagues complained about the cold-calling. Inevitably, people hang up on you. Sometimes there's an asshole who tells you to fuck off. I get why people think it's uncomfortable. But I always found it thrilling. Dialing each number always felt like jumping off a mini cliff, not knowing where I'd land. Until now, I didn't realize how much I'd missed it.

The tricky part about *these* cold calls is that I want to do everything I can to avoid leaving a voicemail. I need to catch people in the moment—gauge their honest reactions, then keep them talking.

I mark an "X" next to the name of each person who doesn't pick up, a signal to try them again later. By mid-afternoon, I've managed to have a dozen real live conversations. One perk of the pandemic, I'm learning, is that a lot more people list their personal numbers on their work bios or set up their office phones to connect directly to their cells. I get hold of consultants at McKinsey, researchers at think tanks, financial analysts at defense contractors, all working from their couches on a Wednesday like me.

Many echo Peter Abdo's assessment: Curt is "an egomaniac." He "loves the sound of his own voice." He "probably hoped we'd get the answers wrong when he called on us, so he could explain them himself." A few say they didn't know him, or that they have nothing to share, and quickly end the call.

A couple are downright chatty. One woman with a thick southern drawl, Charlotte Boone, barely remembers Curt but happens to have just started a side hustle selling a skincare line that's all the rage on Instagram. She'd like to mail me some samples and give me a new-customer discount code. I hang up on her mid-sentence.

When I'm done, I have thirteen names with an "X" next to them, and three people who I haven't been able to track down yet: Kirk McAvoy, Dorothy Ross, and Eric Thorson. They're probably the "finding myself" types. You know the ones. They backpack around Southeast Asia and fuck in the mud at Burning Man, all without a worry in the world because Daddy's credit card is connected to their Apple Pay.

I'll circle back to them if I can't turn up any other leads. They all have to be on the internet somewhere—it'll just take persistence. And first thing tomorrow, I'll try again with the thirteen who didn't pick up (it would look weird to call them back any sooner).

All that coffee on an empty stomach is only making me more anxious. I really wish I'd found something more today. But I have to believe this will work. One of these kids has to have the damning intel I need to make the dream house mine. This is my destiny—I'm so close, I can feel it.

I could use a distraction, and it's after five which means Natalie has left for work by now. I scarf down a granola bar, throw my hoodie and sneakers back on, and head upstairs to get Fritter. He greets me as usual, with his thumping tail and request for a belly scratch. I snap on his harness and take him outside into a pleasant spring evening, the sun tinting the few remaining rain clouds pinkish-purple.

Fritter leads us south, away from the hum of U Street, into the neighborhood. We pass century-old row houses that are a lot like the one Ian and I used to own—small, but tidy, with roommates sharing beers on the stoop, or young families out front, playing in postage-stamp yards. Fritter is great with little kids. A couple of them run up to their low, wrought-iron fences and stick their hands through. He sniffs at them gently—the very best boy.

When we reach the corner, he takes me to the right. This street feels grander. The row houses are a story taller and Victorian in style, with bay windows and fancy trim work. One of these would cost about the same as the dream house, which makes absolutely no sense to me. Why would anyone spend that much to share walls with their neighbors and get woken up by ambulances in the middle of the night?

As if to make my point, Fritter noses a partially eaten sandwich, bloated in a dingy rain puddle. "Leave it," I tell him, and of course he does. But this wouldn't be a problem in Grovemont, where the sidewalks are perfect and the dogs mostly run free in their own backyards anyway.

Fritter and I weave back to our building. I can tell he's hungry for dinner because he barely pauses to sniff anything on the way. When we walk into the apartment, I dry his wet paws with the towel I store for him in a basket by the door. I grab the bag of kibble from under the sink and set up his food and water bowls in the kitchen. He's munching happily when Ian walks in.

"Hey, babe." He leans down to kiss me, then lights up when he sees Fritter. "Hey, buddy! You hanging with us tonight?"

Ian squats down to give him a scratch. I expect Fritter to ignore him because usually nothing can get between him and a meal. But he stops chewing and looks up. He pulls away slightly, so he can sniff Ian's hand, then he sniffs further up Ian's arm and moves frantically to his leg. He repeats the same frenzied investigation on the other side. "Whoa, bud," Ian says, ruffling the top of Fritter's head.

"That's weird. Did you sit on an extra gross bus seat or something?" I remember that Ian didn't ride his bike today since rain was in the forecast.

"No idea," he says, extracting an open bottle of wine from the fridge and pouring us both a glass. Fritter returns to his chomping. "How was work?"

"Oh, fine, nothing too exciting," I say, trying to think of some detail to layer in that'll make the lie more believable. "Actually, one cool thing did happen. We had a follow-up call this afternoon with the team at Mythos Group—you know, the company that owns The Bexley?—and they couldn't stop raving about all the press that came from the party. Jordana's pretty sure they're going to sign a monthly retainer."

Jordana.

Shit.

I never called her back.

"That's incredible. Congrats!" Ian clinks his glass against mine. "See? Maybe you'll get promoted again, and then we'll be able to buy an even nicer house than Curt and Jack's."

Or maybe I'll lose my job and we'll be prisoners here forever.

I take a generous swallow of my wine, heat rising through me like mercury in a thermometer.

"Yeah," I say, "I'm sure it'll all work out just like it's supposed to."

# 16

One week to go. Every second counts. And here I am, wasting far too fucking many of them trying to figure out what someone is supposed to wear to save their career.

I flip through the hangers on my side of the ridiculously small bedroom closet. More than half my stuff is in a storage unit across town. Whenever I get to unpack it, maybe it'll all feel new again.

I think this leopard sheath dress could work. It's only from Ann Taylor, but it's probably the most stylish office outfit that I own, and Jordana loves an animal print. I'll pair it with a black blazer.

When I emerge from the bedroom, Ian is on the couch, still in his gym shorts and the same goddamn UVA Law sweatshirt that he wears after working out almost every single day. Fritter is curled up next to him. "Wow," Ian says, eyes skimming over me. "Big day?"

"Kind of. We have a lunch at the Viceroy, to meet the new chef there, and try some of the menu he's planning to roll out later this month."

That was a real thing I had on my calendar for Monday, but I saw in Outlook that Jordana took me off the meeting and added Beth in my place. Wonder what excuse they gave for my absence. Wonder if anyone missed me.

"Your job is so sweet," Ian says, his gaze hovering at my chest. "You know, I'd love to get you out of that dress later."

The lump of fury in my gut stretches out like some feral creature. Yep, that's what I do in a nutshell. All parties and food and fun for me, while Ian toils away saving Mother Earth. Never mind that I manage most of our life. I dig my nails into my palms and try to focus on how adorable Fritter looks when he's asleep. A tiny puff of air escapes his lips, displacing a piece of fringe on the throw blanket beneath him.

"Sure, babe," I say, checking my watch, blood pressure spiking. "Natalie should be coming by to get Fritter in a couple hours. I really need to get going."

Ian stands up to hug me goodbye. He squeezes my ass as he does, and his boner jabs me through the front of his gym shorts. I think I can hear my vagina vacuum-sealing itself shut.

"Okay!" I force a laugh and push him away. "I really have to run!"

I bend down to kiss Fritter on the top of his head and rush out the door.

...

When the elevator opens on Buzz's floor, I don't hesitate or stop to think. I propel myself forward, through the entrance to our suite, past the fishbowl conference room and the mostly empty workstations, past my office, then Taylor's—her red waves jostling as she does a double-take—directly to the all-glass corner kingdom occupied by Jordana.

Her chair is turned away from the closed door so that she faces out the window. Even so, the way she's motioning tells me she's on the phone. But I can't just wait out here like a little kid who got sent to the principal's office. I need her to see me as confident and capable—mostly, as indispensable.

I knock on the glass.

She spins around and purses her glossy lips. Her collarbone lifts then falls; she holds up a burgundy-manicured hand and waves me in.

"I'm sorry, sweetie, I have to jump. But we'll get a release drafted for you before the weekend, okay?" Jordana nods toward one of the ivory leather chairs in front of her desk and I sit. "All righty, thanks much. Ciao for now."

She removes her earbuds and holds me in an icy stare. "Go on then. Tell me what you're doing here."

I cross my legs and straighten my back, self-doubt suddenly pinballing around in my chest. "I mean, I, um, came here to apologize to you, face-to-face. Over the phone didn't feel like enough." I clear my throat, hoping my tone has hit the right balance of contrite and assertive. Veering too far into the groveling end of the spectrum will only annoy her. "I'm embarrassed that I let you down at The Bexley, and I know you're too smart to buy that it was only because of food poisoning," I continue, my voice steadier. "I won't bore you with the details, but our fertility issues have become a bit of a distraction lately. Which is not an excuse, Jordana. I know that. I just want you to have some of the context."

It's subtle, but I think I see her face soften.

"I'm sorry to hear that, Margo."

"Thank you, I appreciate it. But I don't want to dwell on that. I really, sincerely just want to tell you that I'm sorry, and that I hope we can move beyond this. We have so much history together, Jordana, and I've learned so much from you over the years. It would be a real shame, in my opinion, to throw that all away." I pause to let that last bit breathe. "Of course, I respect that the final decision is entirely up to you."

Jordana's never easy to read, but I think I sound pretty convincing. She rocks back in her chair and crosses her arms.

"I agree, Margo. That would be a shame."

A spark of relief catches inside me.

"But what happened to you yesterday?" she continues. "You practically hung up on me."

"Right. That." I sigh, offering just a hint of an exhausted smile. "I was driving, and about to pull over so I could give you my full attention, when I got rear-ended. The guy was a huge jerk about it, and by the time I was off the phone with the insurance company, I just felt like it would be much better to come in today and talk to you in person, when I was in the right headspace."

Jordana appraises me, twin creases appearing between her perfectly gelled brows. I fold my hands in my lap so she doesn't see them shaking.

"I would recommend at least sending a text next time," she says finally. "Not that there can *be* a next time."

I give a small laugh. "Of course not."

"I do have some good news for you, though," she says. "Mythos Group signed a retainer on Tuesday, and they were adamant that you be a part of The Bexley's ongoing representation."

I'm not sure I heard her correctly. For some reason, I look over my shoulder. Maybe I'm expecting a camera crew, like I'm being punked?

"Um, wow" is all I can get out.

"Chef was thrilled about his little feature in the *Post*, and Serina was flattered that you asked her to show off for those reporters before the event," Jordana says. "Fortunately for you, I'm working on generosity with my life coach this month. So I resisted telling her that the cocktail tasting was my idea."

"Thank you, Jordana, that's amazing."

"It is, isn't it? Chef wants to do a seated media dinner soon, so you'll need to start putting together an invite list and figuring out possible dates. We'll need to book a photographer, too."

I nod eagerly. "Absolutely, no problem."

"Okay, well, congratulations," she says. "Time to get back to work, I guess."

She opens her laptop, my signal to leave. As I walk back to my office, it occurs to me that my job hasn't been in jeopardy since Tuesday. Jordana let me sweat it out—for what? Her own amusement?

The lump stirs.

Taylor glares through the glass as I pass her again. I know she thinks she's better than me. She always has. But I can't get sidetracked with that nonsense now. I'm almost an hour behind schedule.

Tucked into my own office, I pull the list of Georgetown names from my work bag. I get up once more to double-check that my door is completely closed, and create a spreadsheet titled "Rivière Media Dinner" so I have something to click over to if Jordana drops by. Then I begin to dial.

I get lucky on the first call. Hunter Bennet works at a hedge fund in Connecticut. He answers from a treadmill in the company gym.

"Yeah, I took a couple classes with Professor Bradshaw," he says, panting. "A lot of people thought he was kind of an asshole. Maybe your tipster is just bent out of shape over a bad grade or something."

"Could be, but I really don't think that's it," I say. "What about you? Did you think he was an asshole?"

"Nah. I liked the guy. He had some swagger, you know?"

"Right. And what do you mean by that, exactly?"

"He was just confident, had a lot of presence." Hunter pauses. I hear the whir of the treadmill slow as he takes a gulp of water. "It made him easier to listen to when he was teaching."

"Okay, I get that. Anything else specific that you remember about him?"

"Well, his dad's a pretty big deal, but you probably already know that."

"I do know a bit about his dad, yes. He's in your same line of work, right?"

"Yeah, Professor Bradshaw got me an interview with him for an internship," Hunter says. This revelation makes me sit up straighter. "It didn't work out," Hunter continues, "but I guess that's another reason I liked the guy. He did me that solid, you know?"

"Uh-huh, and do you remember when that was?"

"Let's see, that would've been second semester my junior year. So, spring 2018 sometime."

I'm typing rapidly now to keep up.

"Great. And you interviewed directly with Curtis Bradshaw Senior?"

"Yeah, he was down in DC visiting his son, so we just met for coffee on campus."

"Professor Bradshaw's father was in DC?"

"Yeah, um, I'm sorry, is this really relevant to your story?"

"Oh, no, not really," I say, dialing back the eagerness in my voice. "I'd just heard a rumor that they'd had a falling-out, that's all. So it's a little surprising to me."

"Well, if that's true, it must've happened more recently."

"Yeah, must've," I say. "Well, thanks so much for your time. You've been a big help."

"Sure," says Hunter. "All off the record, though, right?"

"Yep. Thanks again."

When I hang up, I scan my notes, taking stock of this new intel. It's not much, but it's also not nothing. Now I know that the rift between Curt and his father is fresh. If Curtis Senior was hanging out with his son on campus in the spring of 2018, their falling-out could have happened around the same time that Ellipsis wrote the anonymous messages. What if Curt's dad found out about the lie? What if it's something so bad that it made him cut off his own kid?

That would almost certainly make it damning enough to deploy as effective blackmail. I stare at the names on my notepad. *Which one of you knows the truth?*

The next half-dozen calls all go to voicemail, but I'm getting closer to something—I can feel it. I mark those names with a second "X."

The call after that—to the eighth of the thirteen people who didn't answer yesterday—picks up. Chloe Nelson is back in school, at the University of Maryland, getting a master's in education. She also manages the greenhouse at a local nursery, which is where I've reached her.

"I do remember Professor Bradshaw," she tells me, "but not because I was close with him myself. One of my best friends at Georgetown was Dottie Ross. He was sort of a mentor to her."

I scan my list. Dorothy Ross. One of the three students who I haven't been able to find online at all. I scribble a note next to her name: "Goes by Dottie."

"And what's Dottie up to now?" I ask.

"I don't know," says Chloe. "I haven't talked to her since, um, I guess it was March our senior year, right after spring break."

"Oh, I'm sorry to hear that. Can I ask what happened?"

"I wish I could tell you. She just—I don't know—she just kind of disappeared."

"Disappeared?"

My pulse quickens. I turn the volume on my phone up a couple notches.

"Yeah, we woke up one day—me and our other roommates—and she'd packed up and left. We only had a couple months left to go before graduation, it was really bizarre." Chloe sighs on the other end of the line. "Sorry, I know this isn't why you called, it's just no one's asked me about her in a while."

"No, no, if she and Professor Bradshaw were really that close, this could be helpful," I say, struggling to wrap my mind around this new information. "I'm just not sure I totally understand . . ."

"I still don't really understand it myself," says Chloe.

I'm trying to think of an articulate follow-up question, but none of this is making sense.

"So she was just... gone?"

"Yeah."

"Are you sure she left on her own? How do you know something didn't happen to her?"

My head swims. What, exactly, is Curt capable of?

"Oh yeah, we talked about calling the police," says Chloe, "but later that morning, she Venmoed her rent for the rest of the year. We were shocked she had that much cash. She included a message—something about just needing a break. I texted her constantly for weeks afterward, but I never heard back. I was really hurt by it."

"That must've been really hard," I say, as another new email appears at the top of my inbox. That makes an even thirty unread. I close out the window so I'm not distracted. "And you really have no idea why?"

"None. I mean, she'd been acting a little out of character, like, partying harder than she did typically. But we were in the home stretch, you know? I guess I thought she was finally letting herself have some fun. She'd always taken school so seriously."

"Oh yeah?"

"Yeah. She never missed a class, studied harder than anyone, you know the type. I think it had to do with being the first one in her family to go to college."

"That's impressive." (I do know the type.)

"Her plan was to work at the Treasury Department for a couple years, then go back to school for a PhD. I figured she'd be the Fed chair one day."

"Huh," I say. "Seems even weirder, then, that she'd go MIA."

"Right," says Chloe. "I still look for her online sometimes, but I've never found anything. My best guess is she's back in Florida somewhere, since that's where she's from."

"Hm, okay," I say. "But if we could just backtrack a little bit—what did you say her relationship with Professor Bradshaw was like?"

"Oh, they were close. He got her an internship the summer after sophomore year at his dad's firm. He was basically a mentor to her."

"Did you ever talk to Professor Bradshaw about where Dottie might have gone?"

"Now that you mention it, yeah, I did send him an email about it."

My fingers hover over my keyboard, waiting for her to say more. I notice I've been leaving sweaty prints behind as I type.

"And what did he say?" I nudge.

"Just that he didn't know anything, but he'd let me know if she got in touch."

"But that was the last time you heard from him?"

"Yeah."

"How did Dottie and Professor Bradshaw become so close in the first place?"

"Well, like I said, she was just a star. Every class I had with her, she was always the one raising her hand, asking the brilliant questions, debating the professors. We had one class with Bradshaw together, and a lot of us didn't like him much, but she got along great with him. If he wasn't gay, I'm sure we all would've wondered about it, you know? But I think he just thought she had a lot of potential. He just kind of took her under his wing."

"Do you know if they were still that close when she left?"

"I assumed they were, but I guess I don't know that for sure," says Chloe. "You calling does have me wondering if maybe something went wrong between them. I mean, if you're saying you have some kind of dirt on Bradshaw..." Chloe's voice trails off. I resist the impulse to fill the silence. "Do you think Dottie could've known about it? Can you tell me anything else about what it is?"

"I'm sorry, not at this point," I say. "But I'd like to try asking Dottie about it myself. Do you still have her contact info?"

"I can give you what I have, though I doubt any of it will work."

Chloe reads off a cell number and a Gmail address. She asks me to let her know if I have any success. I promise that I will.

Before we hang up, she adds one thing: "If you find out that Bradshaw had something to do with Dottie disappearing, you can put on the record that I always thought he was a prick."

"Thanks," I say. "I'll do that."

My hands tremble with adrenaline. I quickly read back through my notes from this morning's calls. Then I open the email from nobody.noone97 and the screenshot of the Amazon review saved to my desktop. I type up a list of my findings so far:

1. Curt and his dad were on good terms as recently as the spring of 2018, and maybe later.
2. They no longer seem to be speaking.
3. The messages from Ellipsis and nobody.noone are from January 2019.
4. Dottie Ross, one of Curt's favorite students, disappeared in March 2019.

I read through it silently; then I recite it out loud—a trick I sometimes used when I was a reporter to help things make more sense.

"The messages from Ellipsis and nobody, dot, no one..."

"Dottie Ross, one of Curt's favorite students..."

I look at the screenshotted Amazon review:

. . .

*DO NOT TRUST CURTIS BRADSHAW.*

Then I say it out loud for the first time: "Dot, dot, dot. Do not trust Curtis Bradshaw."

An ellipsis read aloud is dot, dot, dot.

Nobody. *Dot.* No one.

Dot.

Dottie.

Dot. Dottie.

Dot means Dottie?

Dot means Dottie! Fuck yes! I knew I could crack this.

Whatever happened between them, she clearly wanted Curt to know it was her sending the messages.

All I have to do now is find Dorothy Ross.

# 17

Chloe was right. Neither of Dottie's old contacts work. The cell number is out of service. The email address bounces back. Googling "Dorothy Ross Florida" returns dozens, maybe hundreds of possibilities, many of them senior citizens. "Dorothy" does kind of sound like an old lady. Maybe it's a family name.

What I need is access to LexisNexis. That's the database of personal information for just about anyone in the whole country, used by places like news organizations and law firms to track people down. It pulls from all kinds of records—court filings, utility bills, addresses on file with the post office—to spit back the details of where someone has lived and how they can be found. Unless someone is long dead or in witness protection, searching for them in Lexis should turn up a result.

I bet Ian has access to it at the EPA, but there's no way I can bring him into this. Everything would be so much easier if he would just get on my goddamn side. *Think, Margo.* This is a solvable problem. And literally everything is on the line.

*No Dottie. No blackmail.*

*No blackmail. No house.*

*No house. I will motherfucking die.*

In an instant, the answer floods my brain like dopamine. I've always performed well under pressure.

I grab my phone off my desk—quickly adding a thumbs-up emoji to a Slack from Jordana with some suggested guests for the media dinner—then fire off a text: *Hey, are you downtown today? Can I buy you lunch to say thank you for helping with the IP address?*

It only takes Erika a minute to write back: *K Street Tavern at 1?*

. . .

The Tavern is a total dive, but it's sentimental. In our twenties, Erika and I spent countless happy hours here that devolved into sloppy all-nighters, especially on karaoke Wednesdays. We'd often be back by noon the next day to soak up our bad decisions with a greasy lunch.

She's already stationed at one of the red vinyl booths, her laptop open, when I arrive. She's striking, even amid these dingy environs. What must it be like, to go through life looking like that?

"Seriously? They have Wi-Fi at the Tavern now?" I say, as I approach. "Is nothing sacred?"

Erika laughs. "You look awesome. Love that dress." She gets up to hug me. "And I know what you mean, but at least the seats are all still cracked and half the light bulbs are out."

"True enough. God, I can't remember the last time we were here together."

"I know, kinda fun, right? My team still does happy hours here sometimes, but it's just not the same. Man, how did we get so old?"

I wish I knew the answer to that one. Time really is a motherfucker—and it has never once been on my side. I have been racing against something, or toward something for as long as I can remember. Racing to grow up and get away. Racing against deadlines. Racing to make enough money. To start a family. To find the house. To feel like I've finally made it. To feel like I can finally just live. Erika and I might be the same age, but she's already won her race. She's been right on time for every single thing.

It's funny, I probably thought I was ahead of her when I started dating Ian. We were here the first time he and Erika met. Wednesday karaoke, but a "celebrity" edition. I came as Britney Spears, in a blond wig and too-tight skirt, and tried way too hard to look sexy for him during my rendition of "Toxic." Erika did a whole retro thing, teased her hair into oblivion to sing "These Boots Are Made for Walkin'" as Nancy Sinatra. It didn't matter how much midriff I was showing, her performance was still way hotter than mine.

Ian didn't seem to notice, though. He was all over me that night. And he was great with my work friends, asking sincere questions about the stories they were pursuing and how they ended up at the *Post*, doing his charming, smiling-from-the-eyes thing. They all loved him, Erika especially. "He's perfect," she'd said, when the two of us made a trip to the bar for a round of Red Bull–and–vodkas. "Does he have any single friends?"

Yeah, that night, I'm sure I thought I was finally winning.

Our server approaches now, with two red plastic baskets of grilled cheese and french fries, our go-to hangover cure from back in the day.

"It's really good to see you without the guys around," Erika says, before taking a bite of melty American between oily white bread. "They can be so competitive with each other. It's ridiculous."

"Oh my God, I know." I pause to dab some grease from the corner of my mouth. "I'm really sorry about Ian the other night. He gets way too defensive. I'm sure Heath thought he was being an ass."

She shakes her head in protest, until she finishes chewing. "You have nothing to apologize for. I let Heath have it on the ride home. He was totally provoking Ian, as if you guys don't have enough to stress about. I still can't believe you haven't found a place yet."

There it is—the pity. It stings, but it's also kind of nice to feel seen. Because she's not wrong.

"Yeah," I sigh. "It's been . . . a lot."

"How are you two doing with it? I think I would kill Heath if we were in a one-bedroom."

I'm too proud to tell her the whole truth—that I don't like my husband right now; in fact, I may hate him. But a little bit of venting won't hurt . . .

"Honestly? He's starting to drive me crazy," I say. "The smell of his aftershave gives me a headache. And this morning, when I came out of the bedroom, he was on the couch in the same fucking gym shorts and ripped-up navy UVA sweatshirt that he wears almost every single day, and I swear to God, for a second? I couldn't even see him. He was just a big navy-blue blob, sweating onto my sofa. I am just so sick of looking at that damn sweatshirt, you know?"

Erika, her eyes wide, nods sympathetically, but I can tell she's trying to suppress a smile. We both lose it at the same time. I'm laughing so hard I can barely breathe. I needed this.

"That sounds awful. Really," she says, wiping away tears. "But at least you have the tight quarters as an excuse. Heath and I live in four thousand square feet and he still annoys the shit out of me half the time."

I don't know if she's only saying that to make me feel better, but it does.

"Don't kill all my hope," I say, still catching my breath. "I'm counting on liking my husband again once we move."

"Oh, you will," she says. "You guys have always been so great together."

She's right. The last year and a half may have been terrible, but every couple has their ups and downs. And we're almost through it—I can feel it. Dottie is the key. And people don't just up and disappear. I know I can find her. I know she can get us into the house. And once that happens, everything will be fine. No one could be unhappy there.

"How's the decorating with Zoe Estelle coming?" I ask, suddenly feeling charitable.

"She's amazing. Seriously, she's so creative, I would never be able to come up with half the stuff she does." Erika pauses to check her phone. "She was just over yesterday showing me some fabric swatches for the drapes in the living room, and you'll never guess the crazy story she told me."

"What?"

"Do you remember the Murder Mansion? From, gosh, it must've been six or seven years ago?"

"Wow, I'd forgotten all about that. But yeah, that was a huge story."

"I know. So huge. She's done a ton of houses in our neighborhood, so I guess I shouldn't have been surprised. But she told me she redid the kitchen there."

"Shut up."

"For real. Right before those poor people got killed. She said they were the nicest clients."

"Ugh, that's so sad. I don't think I realized that happened so close to you."

"Yeah," Erika says, nodding. "They only lived a street over."

We chew in silence for a minute, polishing off our grilled cheeses.

"So," Erika breaks in, "are you going to tell me what the deal was with the IP address stuff?"

"That perfectly normal request?" I say, laughing. "Yeah, it was sort of a big deal that it came from campus, so thank you again. Off the record, we'd already heard a rumor about some possible harassment with a student there."

"Really? That's terrible."

"I'm pretty sure your email came from her, too—Dorothy Ross. We found some other stuff she'd posted under her real name on Reddit, though she didn't identify the professor she was accusing there."

"Wait, Dorothy? Like, a girl?"

"Yeah, a twist, right? Which means it might all be bullshit. Or Bradshaw isn't as gay as you thought."

"Huh. That's so odd. I know he had a husband," she says.

I shrug. "Like I said, it might be nothing. We're just doing our homework."

"But why do you care so much?" Erika presses. "He's just an investor in a restaurant that you may or may not take as a client?"

"I really can't get too far into the details—Jordana would kill me if she knew I was telling any of this at all to a reporter—but we had a disaster with another new client last year. Sank a ton of money into a whole campaign for them, only to find out there was a similar problem with one of their backers and the woman in that case was threatening a lawsuit. We had to take a bath on the campaign and walk away before they even opened. So now we try to be a lot more careful on the front end."

"I guess that makes sense," Erika says slowly.

"My problem now is I can't find Dorothy to confirm any of this," I say, beginning to drop the breadcrumbs that will lead Erika to do what I want. "These guys would be a big get for us—a few of the other partners have some really hot restaurants in other cities that you would probably recognize. So we need to be pretty confident that we're dealing with something real before we throw in the towel, you know?"

"What do you mean you can't find her?"

"It's like she just disappeared," I say. "I can't find any current info for her online. And there are about a million Dorothy Rosses, as it turns out."

"Well, I could run the name for you," Erika offers. "What other details do you have?"

Gratitude wells up inside me. I knew she'd come through. At the *Post*, I always had Erika's back and she always had mine. Even when that idiot councilman called my editor to accuse me of stalking him, she didn't flinch. In fact, it had been her idea to involve our union rep. He made the case that I'd only been doing my job—I needed the interview and that asshole had been ignoring my calls—so wasn't waiting for him outside his house just dogged reporting? The councilman claimed he'd seen me in his backyard, but he had no proof that I'd trespassed. So, that had been that. My editor had to drop it.

I rattle off the other attributes that will make the right Dorothy Ross easier to isolate: "She was born in 1997, so she'd be twenty-four or twenty-five now. And she's lived in both Florida and DC."

"Okay, that should be enough. Just give me a sec."

It takes a while for her to log onto the *Post*'s secure server and bring up LexisNexis. But once she plugs in the few things I know about Dorothy, the top search result appears to be the winner:

*Full name: Ross, Dorothy Lilian.*
*Date of birth: 2/1997 (Age: 25).*

The whole report is five pages—quite short, from what I remember of these. Erika downloads a PDF and emails it to me.

"Is this the real reason you wanted to have lunch?" she asks when she's done.

"No!" I lean away from the table in shock. "Not at all. It didn't even occur to me."

"Mm hmm." She narrows her eyes. "Well, whatever the case, I hope you find what you need."

...

I race the five blocks back to Buzz as fast as I can without looking like a total psycho, ignoring the blisters screaming from my heels.

On the way, I tear through my inbox, most of it non-urgent. But I do respond to an editor at *Imbibe* who wants to interview one of my distillery clients about some new cocktail trend.

When I'm finally enclosed behind the glass of my office, I open the PDF, my heart raging. The defunct cell number and Gmail address that I already have for Dottie are listed first. Then comes a Georgetown University email address that obviously won't do me any good now, and three additional phone numbers, all 850 area codes—the Florida panhandle, the internet tells me.

I lean in closer to my screen, sipping in fast, shallow breaths, and scroll down a little further to her address history. The most recent entry is for the Georgetown apartment that she must've shared with Chloe; earlier, she appears to have lived in a dorm on campus. And before that, she lived at two different addresses in Pensacola. I quickly Google both of them. One belongs to the management office of a trailer park. The other belongs to a small rambler with peeling powder-blue paint.

I make my way to "Potential Relatives"—often a useful section of these reports, in my limited experience, when it comes to finding people who don't want to be found. I see both Pensacola addresses there, too. The trailer park is listed next to *Ross, Jessica Lynn (Age 44)*, and the blue rambler belongs to *Ross, Patricia Dorothy (Age 68)*. Dottie's mother and grandmother, I'm betting. I don't see a father.

The other parts that I thought might hint at Dottie's whereabouts are out of date. The most recent entry under "Employment Locator" is a Mexican restaurant in Georgetown from her college years, and her only voter registration, also from her time in DC, is categorized as inactive.

But there is one thing, toward the very end of the report, that stops me. It's under "Criminal Filings."

In August 2020, Dottie was charged with a misdemeanor for driving with an expired license—in Morgan County, West Virginia.

That was a year and a half ago. But it's the most recent location I have for her.

Jordana approaches right as I'm opening the site for Morgan County's local court. I expand the Rivière media dinner spreadsheet to full screen just in case, giving her a quick smile. When she keeps going, I put in my earbuds so I can pretend I'm on the phone whenever she passes again.

The courthouse website looks like something from the AOL days of the internet; I can practically hear the dial-up sound. I click around a bit to be sure, but the result is what I expect: I can't access digital case files here. This is the kind of place that makes you come in person.

Jordana returns—I pause my fake typing and pretend to laugh at the very witty thing that the fake client on the other end of my fake call has just said; then I give her another smile and a wave. She nods back.

To keep her off my scent, I speed through a little actual work, responding to meeting invites and adding comments to a couple of Slack chats. The *Imbibe* editor has gotten back to me with the list of interview questions I requested. They look easy enough, so I forward them to the client with my recommendation to do it: *Seems like a fun opportunity! Lunch soon?*

That should hold me for a while. Now it's time for some real phone calls. The first of the three 850 numbers is out of service. My guess is it may have been Dottie's cell phone before she moved to DC.

The second one rings a half dozen times, then goes to voicemail: "You've reached the Sunset Dunes Trailer Court. Our lots are full up right now, but if you wanna get on the wait list, leave a message and we'll get back to ya."

Only one number left, then. If it's a dead end, I don't have a plan for what happens next. For the first time since lunch, a creeping doubt starts to dull the adrenaline.

I suck in a deep breath and dial.

The line rings once, then a second time...

"Hello?"

An older woman's voice on the other end, raspy and deep.

"Um, hi," I stammer. "I'm not sure if I have the right number, but I'm trying to reach Dottie Ross."

The line goes quiet, but I can hear the woman breathing. I know she's still there.

"Ma'am?" I press. "Do you know Dottie?"

The woman sighs.

"What do you want with Dottie?" she says finally. My mouth goes dry.

"I'm a classmate of hers from Georgetown. Chloe Nelson," I say, pulse pounding. "We were really close in school, but we lost touch. And I'm getting married soon, so I'd like to invite her to my wedding."

"Oh, yeah. Chloe. She mentioned you once or twice."

Exactly the response I was hoping for.

"She did? That's so nice to hear. I miss her a lot," I say. "She talked about you, too. Her... grandma."

The guess seems safe enough.

"Yeah, well, I always made her call me GiGi. I was too young to be a grandma when she was born."

"Right. GiGi. I remember that now. Very cute. Um, so, do you happen to know how I might reach Dottie? The number I have for her doesn't work anymore."

"I'm sorry, I don't. That girl doesn't wanna be reached." GiGi's voice is the bitter kind of sad, the way my mom's sounded all the time after we lost the house. "She calls here every six months or so, to let me know she's okay. But she hasn't come around in years."

"Gosh, I'm sorry to hear that," I say. "She cut me off before graduation, but I didn't expect she'd do the same to her family. I always thought I must've done something to upset her."

"Oh, no, honey, I don't think it has anything to do with you. She said she was just tired of everything. Just burnt out on, uh, what'd she call it? *The grind.* I think she just wanted to start over, and I can't really blame her for not wanting to come back here. Her mama was never very good to her. I'm sure she told you some of that."

"Um, yeah, I knew they weren't close."

"You say she talked about me, though? Is that how you knew where to find me?"

The hopefulness in her voice breaks my heart a little. The least I can do is throw her a bone.

"Oh yeah, I could always tell she really loved you," I say. "We were roommates for a while, and she gave me your number as an emergency contact. I'd forgotten I still had it. But I've been thinking more about her lately, with the wedding and all."

"That's sweet. Thank you for telling me that," GiGi says. "I'm sorry I can't be more helpful to you, I really am. Only thing I know is she's in West Virginia somewhere."

Jesus, lady, way to skip over the fucking headline.

"That's something!" I say brightly, feeling the adrenaline build again. "But you don't know where in West Virginia?"

"Not for sure, no. She sent a postcard once from Berkeley Springs. Maybe you've heard of it? The front of it said they're famous for being America's first spa."

I type Berkeley Springs into my search bar. It's in Morgan County, same as Dottie's misdemeanor.

"Well, thank you for all your help," I say, desperate to hang up and start gaming out this road trip. "It was really nice to talk to you."

"Sure, I'm glad you called. Would you mind letting me know if you end up getting a hold of her?"

"Yeah, of course, happy to."

"Thanks, hon. Oh, and congratulations."

"I'm sorry?"

"On your wedding."

Ian is in the kitchen, his head in the fridge, when I get home from work. A sturdy-looking cardboard box—about double the size of a shoebox—sits on the counter.

"Hey, babe," he says, backing out, some terrible IPA in his hand. "The mailroom had that for you."

I give him a quick kiss and inspect the box. What did I order from Rejuvenation? When I lift it, something solid slides around inside.

Shit. The house numbers. They're here early.

"What is that?" he asks.

"You know, I can't quite remember . . ."

"Why don't you just open it, then?" He hands me the scissors from the knife block.

"That would be one way to figure it out," I say with a laugh.

I push one of the blades into the taped seam as slowly as I can, trying to think how I can possibly explain this away. Right as it begins to split, I pull back.

"Whoops, you almost got me. I just remembered, this is something for *you*."

"For me?" Ian asks.

"Your birthday isn't that far off, you know."

"Is June that close?"

"I just really liked it and I didn't want to wait," I say, playfully clutching the box to my chest. "Enough questions! Leave me alone while I try to think of somewhere you won't be able to find this in six hundred fucking square feet."

He smiles. "All right. Well, thanks, I guess."

I bring the box into the bedroom and open it with my keys. I take out the numbers—heavy and handsome, like jewelry that'll tell everyone the house belongs to me—and divide them between two purses that I rarely use, shoved into the far reaches of the top closet shelf. (My fabric swatches and wallpaper samples are already hidden there, too.) Then I break down the cardboard so it's flat enough to stuff into our recycling bin, and change into sweats.

Ian frowns when he sees me. "You already took off that smokin' dress?"

"You mean that extremely uncomfortable dress that I've been stuffed into all day?" I settle in next to him on the sofa.

"I would've gotten it off quick enough," he says, grinning. He pulls me onto his lap, so that I'm facing him in a straddle, then he kisses me deeply. Somehow, the roughness of his stubble and the beer on his breath aren't ruining this. Are they making it better? It's because I was at the Tavern today, I realize. This is how it felt—how it tasted—to make out with him when we were first together.

He moves his hand under my T-shirt, then over my stomach and up to my boobs. He has a point that sweat pants aren't as fun as real clothes for these purposes. We both wriggle awkwardly out of ours—none of the sexiness involved in wrestling with zippers or belt buckles.

When we're done, he spoons me on the couch. Erika was right. Ian and I are going to be fine—better than fine, fucking spectacular—just as soon as we get out of this apartment.

I turn to face him. His arm, draped heavily over my waist, feels like a security blanket.

"Hey, I meant to tell you when I got home, I have to go out of town for work for a couple days. We're pitching some wineries out in Virginia."

"Cool, when?"

"Leaving tomorrow, back Sunday morning."

He scrunches his face. "That's short notice."

"I know, I'm sorry," I say. "Beth was supposed to go with Jordana, but she tested positive for Covid this morning, and Jordana doesn't want to do it alone. She only asked me to come this afternoon."

"Huh, okay. No big deal, I guess."

"Really? And you don't mind if I take the car?"

"Yeah, that's fine. Maybe I'll ask Brant if he wants to hang out this weekend."

"Thank you. I really appreciate it," I say, rubbing the back of his neck. "Oh, one other thing—can you take Fritter out for his walk Saturday night? And maybe just let him sleep here? Natalie has a shift."

"Sure." He laughs and tucks a strand of hair behind my ear. "Man, you really love that dog."

I kiss him again, then get up to shower and pack a bag.

# 18

Berkeley Springs, West Virginia, is as old as the United States—seriously, the town was founded in 1776. It has a current population of 755 people. And its claim to fame is its namesake natural hot springs that allegedly have mystical healing powers. Or so Wikipedia informed me this morning.

Given those details, you might expect the courthouse to be a two-hundred-year-old white-columned affair with, like, the ghosts of hanged Confederate soldiers banging around at night. And maybe the old one was like that. But the building that I pull up to just before three o'clock is a hulking beige thing with an asphalt parking lot. Turns out the original burned down.

I got here much later than I'd wanted to. There were a couple of Zoom meetings this morning that I couldn't get out of, so I was basically held hostage in the apartment while the secret to my life's happiness was just languishing out here, waiting for me to come find it. Pushing the Prius over eighty for any significant stretch is dicier than counting on Ian to distinguish the cilantro from the parsley at Whole Foods, but thank God the cranky old bitch made it. Somehow, I still have an hour and a half before the court closes for the weekend, which should be plenty of time to pull a single case file.

I find the clerk's office on the first floor, not far beyond the metal detectors at the entrance. A guy with a buzz cut, about my age, sits behind a plexiglass window, focused on a computer screen. We're the only two here.

"Hi there," I say warmly. (Reporter 101: always be nice to the court clerk.) "Sorry to bug you so late on a Friday, but I'm hoping you can help me access a misdemeanor traffic case from 2020."

He stops pecking at his keyboard and looks up. "You have a case number?"

"I'm sorry, I don't. But I do have a full name and the date of the violation."

He stares at me for a beat, as if either of us wants this interaction to last any longer than it has to. "Go on then," he says finally.

"Oh, okay. Uh, it's Dorothy Lilian Ross. Lilian with one L." I quickly glance at the note I made in my phone. "She was cited for driving with an expired license on August 6, 2020."

The man nods and punches the information into his computer.

"Not much of a case here," he says, his tone a little friendlier. "Looks like she paid a fine and went on her way. Which isn't unusual for a misdemeanor back when the courts were closed during the pandemic."

"Thanks, I'll still take a look at whatever you have."

"All right. You can wait there while I pull the file." He gestures to a row of government-gray chairs.

I install myself in one and scroll through Slack and my work email. It took over two hours to drive here from DC, so I have a backlog of messages to sift through. I told Jordana I had an appointment with my gyno, so she wouldn't wonder why I wasn't responding right away. The most important email is a calendar invite for the kickoff planning meeting with Mythos Group. Now that The Bexley is up and running and they've signed the monthly retainer, we need to strategize a longer-term media plan. It's on Thursday next week—the same day the dream house is scheduled to hit the market. But if this little West Virginia adventure goes the way it's supposed to, I'll have everything locked up well before then. I RSVP yes, wondering what my life will feel like by next Thursday, just as the clerk taps on the plexiglass and waves me back over.

"Here ya go," he says, sliding a thin brown folder through the gap beneath the window. "Like I said, not a whole lot in there."

The folder holds only two pages—a charging document and a filing that confirms payment of a fine. But even among such sparse contents, I see the single, shining prize that will make this entire field trip worthwhile: an address for the offender.

Although on a closer look, I'm worried it might be bogus.

"Thanks," I say. "Can I have a copy of the charging document, please?"

"It's fifty cents a page."

"I think I can swing that."

He smirks.

Back in the Prius, I open Google Maps and plug in the address listed for Dottie. It's in a place called Hidden City, West Virginia, which sounds made up. But I'm relieved to find that it is, in fact, a real destination, and according to the app, I can be there in under two hours.

Unlike the thriving, 755-person metropolis of Berkeley Springs, however, Hidden City appears to be a dot on a lonely highway, on the verge of disappearing into the dense national forest that surrounds it. I went into this not knowing exactly where I'd end up tonight, but Berkeley Springs at least has a couple of hotels to choose from. Hidden City, on the other hand, appears to be a hot destination for getting eaten by a bear, or murdered by a human after turning onto the wrong backroad.

I search it on Airbnb, my only hope, and feel some relief as a smattering of options appear—a few don't look half bad. Must be weekend places owned by DC people. I select an A-frame cabin that rents for $150 a night and send a message to the host to confirm I can stay there on such short notice. I check Slack and my work email once more—at four o'clock on a beautiful spring Friday, I'm not surprised that things seem to be quieting down. Then I pull out of the courthouse lot and direct Google Maps to Dottie's last known address.

. . .

The drive is desolate, all pastures and woods. Deep *Deliverance* territory.

Eventually, I wind through a small town with a half-shuttered main street that's over within a couple choruses of the Taylor Swift song pumping through the Prius's speakers. Then I take a ramp onto a vast, empty highway that careens over a jagged canyon before spitting me out onto another isolated country road.

A couple more turns and I'm carving through a valley lined with farms and rundown churches. Steep cliffs climb up from both sides—the foothills of the Appalachians. The weekend homes must be tucked away somewhere up there, presumably with views impressive enough to make this whole haunted-hayride vibe worth it. But according to my GPS, Dottie's address is down here, on this road.

The map says I'm nearly there, but as far as I can see, there are no houses on this stretch. Maybe she lives on one of these farms? Or the house is up a hidden driveway or something? I creep along, barely breaking ten miles an hour, so I won't miss it.

Around the next bend, there's a tattered-looking building, painted faded red, its front porch cluttered with old furniture. A sign nailed to the side that faces a small parking area reads "Hidden City Antiques." I turn in. Mine is the only car here.

Gravel crunches beneath my sneakers on the way to the entrance. The wooden address numbers over the porch confirm I'm in the right place. But the door is locked. A small sign in the window informs me, "Thurs–Sun 10–4." I look at my phone. Already almost six. Fuck.

I head around back. The air smells like pine needles and the subtle rottenness of damp woods. A set of rickety stairs leads up to a deck littered with more stuff, and another door. I knock on it and wait a minute. Then I pound harder. Not a footstep from inside.

There's nothing else here, just a narrow strip of weedy grass that dead-ends into a wall of thick trees. Could Dottie really have some connection to this place? Or did she give a fake address? I can feel the beginnings of a freak-out kicking around in my gut, the panic starting to tighten around my chest—

*No.*

*Stop it, Margo. There is no time to think like that.*

Dottie has to be here somewhere. I'll just come back tomorrow morning at ten, and I'm sure everything will make perfect sense then. I could use a good night's rest before I meet her, anyway.

Back in the Prius, I open my email for the first time since leaving Berkeley Springs, expecting to find a confirmation from the Airbnb host. But I don't have any new messages. Is that even possible? I swipe down, trying to get my inbox to refresh. The wheel endlessly spins.

My eyes flit to the upper right corner of the screen, and I can no longer hold it off—the avalanche of ice-cold panic descends. No bars. Just a tiny, terrifying "SOS."

Only the GPS must've been working. I don't have cell service here. I don't really even know where "here" is.

...

Okay, so maybe I will actually die out here in the deep-red West Virginia wilderness, trying furiously to turn my dream life into a reality. But you know what? Fucking fine. That would still be better than never having tried at all. During the brief period when I did go to therapy, I at least figured out that much.

I started a few weeks after we got back from that first Christmas at Ian's parents' house. I'd been depressed since we'd come home—

not sleeping, dissolving into tears at random times for no reason. Clearly, the visit had stirred something up. Ian was worried—I wasn't as good at hiding things from him back then—and a colleague at the law firm gave him Dr. Clancy's name. She took my insurance, so I figured why not?

I certainly didn't need a shrink to point out that my childhood wasn't ideal. But it's true I'd never really allowed myself to unpack it.

Until I was thirteen, the four of us—my mom, my dad, Mitch, and I—lived in our shitty townhouse south of Seattle, near the airport. Since I was younger than my brother, I got stuck with the third "bedroom," which didn't have a closet or a window. But according to my dad (an "entrepreneur" in the same way that my "bedroom" was a bedroom), he was always on the cusp of some breakthrough business venture that would finally get us out of there. It's why he refused to sign anything more than a month-to-month lease, even though a longer commitment would've come with a discount on the rent.

My mom met him when she was still in college at Washington State. He was a few years older and, at the time, riding high on an idea having to do with customized scented candles (yes, she'd admit now, it was every bit as asinine as it sounds). But back then, she was naive and twenty-one, and he was nothing if not a convincing salesman. So convincing, in fact, that she wound up pregnant with my brother before she could graduate. A month after the shotgun wedding, my dad went bankrupt.

He'd been working on his comeback ever since, bouncing from one brilliant idea to another, sneaking off to the racetrack between the shifts that my uncle gave him out of pity at his hardware store. At home, he was what you'd expect—the predictable loser cliché haranguing my mom for spending too much on groceries or stuff for me and Mitch, saying anything he could think of to make her feel small.

I fucking hated him. I still do, wherever he is.

But in '97, at the dawn of the internet, things started to turn around for us. One of Dad's friends was launching an e-greeting card company (yes, also ridiculous) and he asked Dad to be his partner. There was enough dumb money swirling around dot-coms back then that those two morons managed to find real investors. I could hardly believe it, but within a year my mom quit her job at the airport hotel and we were packing up the townhouse.

My parents became the proud owners of a buttery-yellow new build with a "Tuscan"-style kitchen on the outskirts of Bellevue, one of the nicest Seattle suburbs. By then, I was too old to inquire about installing a tire swing, though there were plenty of other reasons for a thirteen-year-old to get excited. Namely, my room had a walk-in closet and two windows, and was on an entirely different floor than my parents'.

But whatever thrill I felt living there—and surely, I must've been elated for a while—has been demolished in my memory by the utter humiliation of losing it all when that stupid business inevitably tanked.

We barely made it two years in that house before the bank took everything away.

All four of us moved into an apartment, still in Bellevue so Mitch and I wouldn't have to change schools again. My mom thought she was doing us a favor, but we became the only two losers in the whole place who didn't live in a neighborhood where every other house had a tennis court. Being Asian only made it worse. The other Japanese-American kids had parents who were CPAs and dentists and Microsoft millionaires—quintessential model minorities. Overnight, the cunts who had been my best friends decided I was nothing. You can still find four faint crescent moons on the back of my left arm where one of them broke the skin with her acrylic nails while she held me against my locker and whispered in my ear that I was trash.

That was about when I started to feel angry all the time. The tight mound of rage simply took up residence one day, like a pet that's never left. Mostly, it stays quiet and still enough to ignore. But it's always accessible. And even now that I'm an adult, the right trigger can mutate it into an all-consuming thing. As I explained to Dr. Clancy, it's almost a comfort to feel anchored by something so constant.

We finally left Bellevue the summer before my junior year. When my mom told me we were moving to Spokane to live with my grandparents, I broke down crying. She thought I was upset that she was divorcing my dad, but really, I was just so intensely relieved to go someplace where nobody would know who I was. Mitch had graduated by then and found a job in construction. I finished the rest of high school in blissful anonymity.

All of this was a gold mine for Dr. Clancy. She must've had a blast, but for me, reliving this shit was agony. Fortunately, it only took four sessions to land on the obvious: "Margo," she said, tapping the end of her pen against her notebook, "do you suppose experiencing where Ian came from has finally allowed you to grieve the life that you always wanted, but never had?"

I did, in fact, suppose that.

But where Dr. Clancy and I diverged was on what I should do next. It seemed to me that rather than sit around and grieve that life for fifty minutes each week, I would be much better off using the time to get to work building it for myself.

# 19

A sharp knock on the driver's-side window yanks a scream from the deepest, most primal part of my core. My head snaps up from my useless phone, adrenaline overtaking me. A woman, sixtyish and sturdy, in a fleece jacket and knit beanie, is outside the Prius, holding up her hands, looking stunned.

"Sorry," she says through the glass. "Didn't mean to give you such a scare."

I release a whoosh of breath, my heart rate evening out, as I roll down the window.

"I just wanted to see if you were okay," the woman continues. "We came back after dinner to do some tidying up, didn't expect to find a car in the lot."

"Uh, thanks," I stammer, forcing a weak smile. "Guess I'm a little on edge. I can't seem to get any bars and I'm trying to find my Airbnb."

"Happens all the time out here," she says with a laugh. "Come on in, I'll let you connect to the Wi-Fi."

I'm so grateful I could cry. Who is this angel of Appalachia—and most critically, how fast can she lead me to Dottie?

I follow her into the antique store, a bell over the door jingling as we enter. The place has the musty, dusty scent of an attic. It's a single room, jam-packed in every direction.

Baskets and rusty metal bins form precarious towers atop old farm tables. Stacks of framed artwork fill the seat of a bulging, striped sofa. A collection of taxidermy on high-up shelves—ducks and squirrels, deer and coyotes—encircles the whole space.

"The Wi-Fi is HCAntiques, you should see it now," says the woman, adjusting a spindle-backed chair that hangs from a hook in the ceiling. "Password is mountainair, one word, all lowercase."

I squeeze in next to the junk on the striped sofa, relief surging through me as my phone connects. A text from Ian dings first: *Hey babe, let me know if you made it ok.*

Then my inboxes start to populate, the messages stacking up like chips during a winning hand of poker.

My stomach drops when I see that Jordana has forwarded something from a *New York Times* reporter, who apparently only reached out to her after I didn't respond to him sooner. I spot his original message buried at the bottom of my inbox. They're planning a "36 Hours in DC" and they want to feature Causa.

*I got back to him myself,* Jordana has written, *but why aren't you all over this???*

*So sorry!* I respond. *Somehow he got stuck in my spam filter.*

Shit.

But at least I'll have somewhere to sleep. Among the J.Crew sales and Athleta ads cluttering up my Gmail is the jackpot I was counting on: a response from the Airbnb host.

*Hi Margo,*
*The cabin's ready for you. Address is 1800 Black Bear Dr. The lockbox is to the left of the front door, code is 8409. And yes, it's also available tomorrow night if you need to extend your trip.*
*Thanks!*
*Steve*

"Find what you needed?" the woman asks, as I rise from the sofa.

With the Airbnb squared away, I can finally get back on mission. My pulse picks up.

"Well, partially . . ." I say slowly, the excitement building. "I'm actually in Hidden City because I'm trying to find a young woman named Dorothy Ross. It's kind of hard to explain, but I thought you might know her."

"Huh." The woman sniffs. "Can't say that sounds familiar."

Her confusion seems authentic. But she probably just needs a little time to think—I forge ahead.

"Are you sure?" I press. "Maybe you know her as Dottie?"

She shakes her head. "Sorry, don't think I can help you."

Why is she being so difficult? If she would just take a goddamn minute to mull it over, surely something would come back to her. Is she *trying* to rush me out of here? If she thinks I'm giving up that easily, she's in for a rude fucking awakening.

"Listen," I say, the fury at a low simmer, a faint throbbing behind my eyes, "I really think Dorothy has some connection to this place and if you would only—"

The groan of the back door interrupts. The woman turns toward it: "Ah, come on, Lily," she scolds gently. "You know you need to clean those off better before you bring 'em inside."

I suck in a breath.

Lily.

Dorothy *Lilian* Ross.

Her arms hug two wooden apple crates, one on top of the other, their bottoms caked with dirt. She's about my height, in baggy overalls, with choppy, Pepto-pink hair that falls just below her ears—an aesthetic about an ocean away from "Georgetown economics major."

I clear my throat: "Hey."

Her gaze meets mine. The roundness of her face makes her look younger than twenty-five.

"I was just talking with your boss here about someone I've been trying to find. Maybe you know her?"

Dottie's eyes dart from the older woman back to me.

"Okay," she says, clutching the apple crates like armor.

"Her name is Dorothy Ross. Probably goes by Dottie, though. Does that ring a bell?"

The color deserts her cheeks.

"No." Her voice is soft. "No, I, uh, I don't know that name."

"Hm, okay," I say, feigning disappointment. "That's too bad. I'm a reporter investigating a professor at Georgetown—Curtis Bradshaw, you might've seen him on TV—and I'm pretty sure he did something awful to her. Last anyone heard, she was in the area. Maybe I can leave a number in case one of you happens to run across her?" I take a cautious step closer to Dottie. "I'm just trying to help."

"Lord, you didn't tell me all that," says the older woman. "Sure, you can leave—"

Dottie cuts her off.

"Why don't I put your number in my phone?" she offers. "I have to take these outside first, so you can just follow me."

"Great," I say, rushing over to hold the door for her.

Once it closes behind us, Dottie drops the crates on the back deck and descends the stairs into the grass. She motions, wordlessly, for me to join her.

"Dottie Lilian." I state it as a fact, not a question.

She leans in so her face is only inches from mine. "Who the fuck are you?" she whispers.

"Just let me explain," I say, taking a step back. "I'm here because I think we can help each other. We both know Professor Bradshaw is an asshole. I don't want to let him get away with his bullshit anymore."

This is the tricky part. I have no idea what Curt did to Dottie, so I need to lead her into spilling some hints.

"I am doing everything I can to *forget* about his bullshit!" she rasps. "The last thing I need is to get wrapped up in it again."

She whirls away, putting several paces between us, but if she wanted to leave, she would've done it already. She's thinking. That's good.

"Listen, Dottie, I wouldn't be here if it wasn't really impor—"

She whips back around, brown eyes blazing in the golden early-evening light. "Keep your voice down, I am *Lily* here."

"Got it," I say, holding up my hands. "I just think you should know, Lily, that he's done the same thing to other students."

I'm out on a limb. This will either make sense to her or it won't. But the way her face has aged before my eyes—the intensity in her expression overriding the baby-fat cheeks—makes me think I've hit on something.

She studies me, arms in a knot.

"I guess I shouldn't be surprised," she says finally. "Is their shit in his dumb book, too?"

What the hell is she talking about?

"Um, I don't follow."

She cocks her head in confusion. Shit. I've stopped making sense.

"You mean he plagiarized them somewhere else then? Like, in news articles or something?"

"Oh yeah, exactly," I say, imploring my face to stay neutral as a swell of giddiness consumes me. "I assumed he did the same to you. But you're saying your work is in *Falling Apart*? That's next level."

"I wrote the whole first fucking chapter."

My mouth drops open—I can't help it. I have to instruct myself to breathe.

"Are you serious?" I manage to get out, the ground suddenly unsteady beneath me.

She shrugs her confirmation, as if she hasn't just handed me a career-obliterating bomb and the keys to my dream house all in one spectacular sweep. (I make a mental note to order those moss sofas tonight, since Crate & Barrel says they'll take eight weeks to arrive.)

"That's outrageous," I say, stuffing my hands into the back pockets of my jeans so Dottie can't see them shaking. "But why haven't you called him out?"

She stares at her black Converse. "That's a long story." Then she meets my gaze again and narrows her eyes. "What did you say your name was?"

"Lisa. I'm with *The Chronicle of Higher Education*."

"Lisa what?"

"Waters. Lisa Waters."

"How'd you even find me? I haven't told anyone about this."

"I guess we both have long stories to share," I say. "I can keep yours off the record, if you want."

She chews her chapped bottom lip. "I have to get back inside. Where are you staying?"

"A little ways up the mountain, in a cabin—1800 Black Bear Drive."

Dottie's pretzeled arms heave up and down as she lets out a heavy sigh.

"I get off work tomorrow around four thirty," she says. "I'll come to you."

# 20

The A-frame is an urbanite's take on mountain living—small but stylish, with modern furniture and a minimalist kitchen with dark green cabinets and open shelves stocked with white dishes. Wonder how much rental income it generates each month. Maybe a few years down the line, once Ian and I have built enough equity in the dream house, we can consider buying a second place like this.

The temperature barely reached sixty today, so I followed the meticulous instructions left by the Airbnb host for setting up a fire in the wood-burning stove in the living room. Phoebe Bridgers plays over the Bluetooth speaker system—some of the younger girls in my office just went to her show, and I want to make Dottie feel as comfortable as I can.

The grind of tires on gravel announces her arrival.

I pour myself a glass of Chardonnay to calm my nerves. A car door slams, followed by three solid knocks on the door. I take the wine bottle with me to open it.

"Hey!" I say, with a big smile. "Thank you so much for coming."

Dottie wears nicely fitting jeans and a gray sweater. She's even put on a little makeup. She cares what I think of her.

"Hi," she says, eyeing the wine.

"Come on in! Can I pour you some of this? I have red, too, if you like that better?"

"White's fine."

I head into the kitchen to get her a glass, but she doesn't follow. She waits awkwardly in the entry.

"Seriously, make yourself at home." I wave a hand around. "Take a seat anywhere you want. Or help yourself to some snacks."

I've laid out a whole spread on the kitchen table—chips and salsa, crackers, salami, pretty much every type of cheese the sparse grocery store back in town had available. It's a mish-mash, but of all the excuses Dottie might think of to leave, being hungry won't be among them.

She tentatively makes her way to the sofa. "This is a cute place," she says, her voice sounding steadier.

"It was a lucky find," I say. "The view from the loft is amazing if you want to take a look up there."

She shrugs. "I've been staring at these mountains for three years. Kinda all blends together at some point."

So, she's been here the whole time.

"Listen," I say, coming into the living room with her wine, and taking a seat on the leather sling-back chair by the couch, "I'm really sorry for just showing up like that yesterday. I didn't mean to freak you out."

She doesn't respond, so I keep going.

"But I couldn't figure out how else to get a hold of you. I get that Professor Bradshaw fucked you over, but why are you hiding out like this?"

"You go first," she says, a new edge to her tone. "I'll tell you my story after you tell me who you really are, and how you found me."

"What do you mean?" I scrunch my face in confusion. "I told you, I'm a reporter. Lisa Waters, at *The Chronicle of Higher Education*."

"Lisa Waters is a redhead." Dottie narrows her eyes. I feel my face flush. "We still know how to use Google out here in the backwoods."

"Um... Dottie, I'm..."

I knew this was a possibility, but her directness trips me up. Mercifully, she interrupts.

"I obviously can't judge someone for using a fake name," she says. "But don't insult me. It's time to stop bullshitting now."

I laugh nervously. "I'm sorry, I shouldn't have tried that with you. I heard you were smart—the brightest in the economics department."

Flattery seems like the right move.

"Heard from who?"

"Your friend Chloe."

Dottie's mouth parts.

"Tell me who you are right now," she demands.

"Of course," I say. "My real name is Margo—Margo Tanner." Ian would be thrilled to hear me finally take his last name. "I should've been truthful with you. I only started using the reporter thing because I didn't want to ruin my chances of getting a full-time offer at Georgetown. I was a visiting professor there last semester."

I thought of the new cover story earlier this afternoon, in case I needed a backup. Given all the practice I've had lately, it assembled itself fairly easily.

"One day, a few of us were in the faculty lounge, and Professor Bradshaw had a draft with him of some article he was thinking of submitting, I think to *The Economist*? Or maybe it was *The Wall Street Journal*. That part's not important," I say, hoping she won't whip out her phone and try to Google that, too. "I only glanced at it, but I recognized one of my student's words right away. It was a very particular turn of phrase"—through the window behind Dottie, the same massive tree branch that inspired me earlier sways in the breeze—"about how the supply chain 'snapped like a tree limb in a hundred-year storm' during the pandemic."

Dottie's eyes get wide. She's buying this.

"I assumed my student must've somehow plagiarized Professor Bradshaw, not the other way around, so I asked her about it the next time she was in class. She swore up and down that those were *her* words first—that she'd used the same phrasing in an assignment for Professor Bradshaw, too. Poor thing thought I might be mad at *her* for recycling her own writing."

"Wow," Dottie murmurs.

"Bradshaw has tenure, and I was a nobody. I wasn't sure if anyone would believe me, and the girl from my class didn't want to make a big deal out of it. But it infuriated me, you know?"

She nods.

"Anyway, then I heard about you—the brilliant student who'd vanished."

Her face brightens ever so slightly. "They still talk about me there?" Dottie asks.

"Yeah, for sure." I nod enthusiastically. "I heard you'd been a star in Bradshaw's classes, so I just started to wonder if maybe he'd done the same thing to you."

"Okay . . . but how'd you end up talking to Chloe?"

This part's a bit more delicate. I grab my nearly empty glass from the reclaimed-wood coffee table. "Let me just get a quick refill." This'll buy me a little time to review the details once more in my mind. "You need one?"

Dottie shakes her head.

"So, Chloe," I say, pouring myself a fresh glass in the kitchen, then turning on the sink to rinse my hands. "Since no one knew where you were, I asked around about who you'd been close with." I walk back into the living room. "Another professor, I don't remember who, mentioned Chloe was your best friend."

"Maybe that was Professor Huntington?" Dottie asks, face hopeful. I push away the slightest pang of guilt. Must stay focused.

"Yes, yes, Huntington, that's right. Anyway, unlike you, Chloe was easy to find. I gave her my dumb Lisa Waters reporter story—like I said, the last thing I wanted was for the higher-ups at Georgetown to find out that I was sniffing around about a tenured faculty member."

Dottie nods. I keep going.

"So, I told Chloe I was looking into Bradshaw for an article, and that I'd heard a rumor he'd wronged you in some way. I was just trying to see if it rang true to her."

Dottie leans forward. "And what did she tell you?"

I pause, weighing the gamble I'm about to take. I need to give Dottie a believable reason for why I'd go to the trouble of tracking her down. This still feels like the best option.

"She said she didn't know of anything for sure, but that she saw an email on your laptop a couple months before you left, in an account she didn't recognize. She said it looked like you'd written an anonymous message to someone, saying that Professor Bradshaw had lied about something."

Dottie jerks away, incredulous. "What? How would Chloe have possibly seen that?"

My throat constricts.

"Um, I'm not entirely sure. She didn't want to give me all the details," I say slowly. "She said you'd been acting strangely and that she was worried about you. So I think she might've been snooping in your stuff."

Dottie is silent for what feels like a millennium, squinting in concentration, my blood pressure ticking up with each passing second.

"That's weird," she finally offers. "I really thought I deleted all that as soon as I sent it." She's quiet for another beat as my pulse thunders in my ears. "Well, whatever," she sighs. "Then what?"

I relax into the chair.

"Talking to Chloe convinced me I was right, so I had a friend who really is a reporter run your name through a database that newspapers use to locate people." I decide to skip over my little field trip to the courthouse. "The only contact the database had for you was the address of the antique shop."

Dottie nods again and swallows the rest of her wine. I stand up to fetch the bottle from the kitchen.

"But why do you care so much?" she asks. "Don't tell me you just want to do the right thing."

The Chardonnay glugs into her glass as I pour.

"No, you're right," I say. "I'm not doing this out of the goodness of my heart. Bradshaw has something I want, and I need leverage."

"All right," says Dottie, leaning toward me again, "what's that?"

"A spot on the Georgetown economics faculty. They're not adding any new permanent positions, so the only way I'll get hired is if someone leaves. And if there was ever a good reason to bounce someone with tenure, it's ripping off student work."

"Damn." She finally cracks a smile. "That's pretty badass."

"Thanks." I laugh. "So, will you help me?"

The smile disappears as she looks down at the knotty-pine floor. I stay quiet so she can think.

"I guess it depends what you need," she says, her eyes again meeting mine.

"Why don't you tell me what happened to you, and we can figure it out from there?"

She takes a deep breath, followed by a long swig of Chardonnay. Liquid courage to unfurl the whole story.

# 21

The log in the wood-burning stove pops as Dottie shifts her weight on the sofa, tucking one leg underneath herself.

"It was probably about a month before his book came out," she begins. "Bradshaw sent me an email, asking me to come by during his office hours so he could talk to me about something. That wasn't unusual. I'd had classes with him for years, and I worked for his dad for a summer, so we were pretty close."

I nod, wanting to encourage her to keep going without betraying how ravenous I am for the details.

"So, I went to his office and he had an early copy of the book there, on his desk. He said he wanted to thank me for *helping to inspire*—those were the words he used—the opening chapter, and that he wanted to let me read it right there, in front of him, before the book came out."

God, I'm practically salivating. I wish I could record this without freaking her out.

"Now, looking back," she says, "I know he wanted to see how I'd react—to see whether I was going to be a problem."

"About what?" I prod.

"About him copying a final paper I'd written for him sophomore year, nearly word for word."

"Holy shit." I lean back in the chair, the leather squeaking against my jeans, my mind leaping and twirling like it's starring in a Broadway fucking musical. "The whole paper? That's insane."

"He changed a few things, I guess so it would sound more like him, but yeah, I basically wrote the entire first chapter. The research, the way it's organized, the specific examples—that's all mine."

This is three-Michelin-star delicious. I'm gonna have nothing but fun nailing Curt's ass to the wall with this, watching him squirm like the smug, silver-spoon-fed, born-on-third-base worm that he is.

"Hang on a sec." With so much adrenaline coursing through me, I have to stand up. My work bag hangs from a hook by the front door, so I walk over and retrieve my copy of *Falling Apart* from it. Bringing it along just felt like the right thing to do. But when Dottie sees the bright yellow cover, she grimaces like she's in physical pain.

"Why do you have that garbage?"

"Sorry," I say sheepishly. "I was just curious about it. It was thirty percent off, if that helps."

I flip it open to the first chapter, which, quite cleverly, follows the journey of a dining table destined for Wayfair as a way of introducing the book's overall theme. It moves from the rubber-tree farm in Southeast Asia that supplies the inexpensive wood; to the nearby factory that turns the wood into furniture parts on the cheap; to the shipping container that can hold more tables than ever thanks to the ingenuity of using lightweight materials and flat-packing everything in pieces; to the consumer who buys the finished product for the bargain price of three hundred dollars from the comfort of her couch. It was the most enthralling part of the whole book.

I hold it out for Dottie. "All this is really yours?"

She refuses to take it. "Please don't make me look at it. Yes, it's really mine."

"Sorry," I say, realizing her pained expression wasn't a joke. I reclaim my seat, relieved to see her posture soften when I shove the book under the chair. "So, after you read it in Bradshaw's office, what did you say to him?"

"Nothing. It was like I was numb. I didn't know what to say, or what to do. I don't think I ever even looked up from the pages. I just remember not wanting to look at his face. And then I felt like I might get sick, so I just got up and left."

"Did he follow you?"

"No. But his dad, Curtis Senior, called me the next day."

"What the hell?"

"I knew him because I'd interned at his hedge fund. I was relieved, at first, to hear from him because I thought maybe he wanted to help."

"Why's that?"

"I don't know, maybe because I was panicking and not thinking clearly? He'd just always been really nice to me."

"Okay, but what did he really want?"

Dottie laughs dryly.

"He was calling to cut a deal. I must've freaked out Professor Bradshaw pretty good, because he ran straight to Daddy and asked him to pay me off so I wouldn't tell anyone."

The rage wakes up, unspooling itself in my gut. Curt, you spoiled little bitch. You fucking low-rent Kendall Roy.

"Shit," I say.

"Yeah." Dottie pauses for another long drink of wine. "Curtis Senior said he wasn't sure he could ever forgive his son and that he'd never been more disgusted with anyone, especially since he thought so highly of me." She rolls her eyes at the memory. "I'm sure that was all bullshit. At the end of the day, assholes always protect their own, right?"

"Damn right," I say, seething.

"He said he'd wire me fifty thousand dollars. And on top of that, he'd pay off my student loans. *Curt's fuckup* would be embarrassing for the whole family if it ever got out, he said, and all he wanted was for me to feel like I'd been fairly compensated for my work, so that I could move on."

This would explain the rift between Curt and his dad. That rich old bastard probably thinks he did something noble, but he's just as evil as his son.

"That's a hard offer to turn down," I tell Dottie.

She scours my face. "You think so?"

"Absolutely. You've probably made more off that book than Curt has."

"You don't think I'm awful for taking it?"

It occurs to me that I'm the first person she's ever told about this. She's been carrying it alone for three years. The fury retreats a bit and some sadness creeps in.

"I really don't," I say gently. "I would've taken it, too."

She looks down at her sneakers. "I don't come from very much," she says. "It was a lot of money to me."

"Seriously, you don't have to justify it." I reach over and pat her knee, hoping I'm not overstepping. "But I still don't get what made you come all the way out here."

She lets out a long sigh, and tops off her own wineglass with the remainder of the Chardonnay.

"I started to scare myself," she begins slowly. "I felt okay for a little while, you know, after I took the money. I still had a class with Bradshaw, and it was too late in the semester to drop it, so I had to keep going. I just sat in the back and stopped asking questions. But then the book came out, and it was like I just broke. They had a big display for it, in the window of the campus bookstore, and all the fucking press Bradshaw was doing kept getting retweeted into my timeline. It was just everywhere. And I felt this rage like I'd never felt before."

I want to tell her she's not alone. That sometimes, it's like my own rage is threatening to burn right through my skin and incinerate everything.

"That must've been terrible," I say, giving Dottie a sympathetic look.

"It was," she says. "I didn't recognize myself. And then I did the dumbest thing. I left a review for it on Amazon, warning people not to trust Bradshaw. I made my username three dots—you know, like an ellipsis?—but I knew Bradshaw would understand that it meant Dottie. I just wanted to get in his head, you know? Make him feel some of what I was feeling?"

I nod.

"I was sure he'd react in some way," she says. "He must've been paying attention to his Amazon ratings. But I didn't hear anything from him, which only made me angrier." The wine has started to sand the corners off her words. "So then I sent an anonymous email to a reporter who'd written about the book. I assumed she'd have to forward it to him."

I keep nodding, doing my best to absorb every detail. The fire pops again.

"That was the email Chloe told you about. I'm so embarrassed she found it."

"Oh, don't worry about that. Chloe thinks the world of you. She said she thought you'd be the Fed chair one day."

This makes Dottie laugh, which makes me feel better about forcing her to relive all this.

"Well, anyway," she says, a faint smile lingering, then vanishing. "I was spiraling, and at some point, I started drinking before Professor Bradshaw's lectures to make them easier to sit through, which helped a lot. So then I started drinking more, just generally all the time, and going to more parties and stuff with my roommates. I was never really into any of that before, but it was kind of becoming, like, a self-preservation thing."

"Understandable," I say.

"Then one night . . ." She hesitates, her eyes drifting toward the fire. "One night, I went to a party alone." She toys nervously with a silver ring on her thumb. "There were these guys who sat in my section at the Mexican restaurant where I worked. They got me to do a couple shots with them when my manager wasn't looking and asked me to come to their frat after my shift."

I remember how humiliating it could be to wait on my classmates in college—bringing them round after round of Jägerbombs, only so they'd be so shit-faced that everyone found it hilarious to duck out without tipping. The rage heats back up to a rolling boil.

"It was after midnight by the time I got off," Dottie continues, "and it was only Tuesday, so my roommates were already in bed. But I wasn't tired, and the last thing I wanted was to go home and just lie there thinking about everything, you know?"

I nod.

"The party was, like, crazy packed. Just, like, wall-to-wall bodies. But somehow I found one of the guys in the basement pretty much right away—or maybe he found me, I'm not totally sure. He handed me some kind of punch, gave me a big hug and all that, but I don't think he ever even told me his name."

My stomach turns, as it becomes impossible to deny where this story is headed.

Dottie takes a deep breath, another sip of her wine.

"You don't have to tell me anything else." I whisper it, even though I want to scream.

Her eyes well as they meet mine. "I don't really remember anything else anyway," she says. "Just a strobe light, and the way my shoes kept sticking to the dance floor. And then it was just—the next day. And I was squeezed in next to him in a bottom bunk." Her voice catches. "I was sore," she says, composing herself, "and I tasted blood. I don't know if I fell, or if it was something he did to me, but my lip was busted."

"Dottie, I'm so sorry."

"I found my clothes on his floor," she continues, "and snuck out before he could wake up."

"Do you think he drugged you?"

"Definitely. But I was also wasted, so who would've believed me? And now I had two men on campus who I couldn't bear to look at, you know? I felt like that place was eating me alive."

Acid crawls up my throat.

"I made it about a week longer," she says, "before the anxiety was too crushing. All I wanted was to leave, just for a little while. I chose this place because it was literally called Hidden City. It sounded like paradise."

She pauses for more wine, wipes the corner of her mouth with the side of her thumb, the silver ring catching the light. "I didn't think I'd still be here. I always planned to go back and graduate, maybe finish up my credits over the summer when most people weren't around. But I just kind of fell into a rhythm out here. I didn't realize before how burned out I was, you know? I'd been working since I was fourteen, saving up for college. I waited tables the entire time I was at Georgetown and I still had a three-point-eight. It was fucking exhausting." She takes another drink. The fire crackles. "But being here is easy. Linda, that's who you met at the shop yesterday, rents me her guest cottage for next to nothing. I could make that fifty thousand last forever."

"But you had a whole future planned," I say, voice calm even though I want to throw open the doors of that wood stove and let the whole world burn to the ground. "Don't you ever wonder about it?"

Dottie shrugs. "Sometimes."

"But aren't you angry that Curt"—I correct myself—"that Professor Bradshaw got to change the direction of your whole life?"

She shrugs again, then laughs. "Sometimes."

"I don't believe you."

"I'm serious," she insists. "Maybe I'll still have that life one day, but it also might make me miserable. This life is simple. It's a little boring, but it's peaceful. I mean, look at you, doing all this crazy shit to get ahead. Can you honestly say you're happy?"

Whoa. What the fuck? *Crazy?* Is that what she thinks of me? What does a twenty-five-year-old know about happiness anyway?

I bite the inside of my cheek to keep from saying something regrettable, then steal a glance at my phone for the first time in . . . more than two hours. It's after seven. I have three texts from Ian.

"Sorry, Dottie, I need to check this."

*Hey babe, hope you're having a good day. Just letting you know I'm going upstairs to get Fritter like you asked.*

The next two messages are selfies of them together. Both of them look adorable, even though Fritter clearly needs a bath (if only you could call Child Protective Services on a dog mom). It's true what they say about distance, though. I miss Ian. Maybe when we have a house with multiple floors, I'll be able to miss him every day. Something flutters inside me, a reminder that it's time to get back to business. I didn't come here so Dottie and I could braid each other's hair.

*Love you guys*, I write. *See you two tomorrow.*

I look back up at Dottie. "Do you want to stay for dinner? I didn't realize how late it was. I have all the ingredients for pasta puttanesca."

She hesitates for a second. "If you're sure it's not too much trouble," she says. "I probably shouldn't drive for a little while."

"No trouble at all."

Especially since I have more work to do.

I dig a pot out of one of the cupboards and fill it with water. Once it's on the stove, I ask the question that's been flashing in my head: "So, do you still have it?"

Dottie looks confused. "Have what?"

"The paper that he copied."

"Oh..."

She chews her bottom lip. I press the flat side of my knife against a garlic clove and feel the satisfying split of its skin.

"Yeah," she says finally. "I have the email, too, from when I turned it in. That's what proves my paper came before the book."

A whole fireworks display is going off in my mind, but I keep my face neutral while I slice the garlic. I don't want to scare her off.

"Would you be willing to share it?" I ask coolly, my eyes focused on the blade.

She's silent again as I open a can of olives and pour off the liquid. Then I scoop two tablespoons of capers from a jar and dump them onto my cutting board. My knife hitting wood and Haim on the speakers—another favorite among the youths in my office—are the only sounds.

"I guess I still need to think about it." Dottie's voice wavers. "I'm not sure it would be good for me to get dragged back into all that."

"I get that." I check the burner under the pot to make sure it's turned all the way up. "I'm sure I could keep your name out of it, though. Just the existence of the paper, and the fact that someone other than Professor Bradshaw wrote it, would probably be enough."

I pull a second bottle of wine from the fridge. Another half glass should be enough to wash away the guilt that's started to nag at me, one more asshole taking advantage of Dottie. I wish I could tell her the truth, I really do. But she'd never understand.

I rinse off a bunch of parsley and set it down on a paper towel. Then I scroll through Ian's selfies again, to remind myself why this is all worth it.

*No house, no baby. No house, no family. No house, no life.*

I'm here to protect my dream. Nothing is more important.

## 22

I see it the second I walk in the door.

Small. Smooth. Black.

A foreign object on the kitchen counter. A thing that doesn't belong.

I put my keys on the shelf and drop my bags in the entryway, my eyes never leaving it. Two steps more and the word comes into view: *Nokia*.

It's a flip phone. Did it time-travel here from 2003?

"Ian?" I call out.

No response. I got on the road early enough that I thought he still might be asleep, but the bedroom door is wide open and the apartment is quiet. He must already be out with Fritter on a morning walk.

I hold the phone in my palm. I don't think I've seen one like this since college. When I flip it open, the screen reveals itself, no passcode required. A piece of technology from a simpler time.

There's one unread text message. I tap on it before remembering that's not how these work. When I finally access it, I realize this isn't a phone after all.

It's a fucking grenade.

*Wish you were still in this bed. Loved meeting Fritter. XO.*

It's from a phone number only—no name attached. It arrived at 8:29 a.m. Fourteen minutes ago.

The phone clatters against the quartz. A sound like microphone feedback fills my head; my hands shake uncontrollably, the epicenter of an earthquake that's now rolling through the rest of my body. I crouch down on the vinyl plank floors, my breathing fast and shallow. Is this how it feels to hyperventilate? Am I having a panic attack? I force myself to focus on the fake wood grain. Ripples and lines, ripples and lines. A plasticky imitation of nature.

I really do hate these cheap fucking floors.

But they're helping me now. As I count how many times the grain pattern repeats on each board, the high-pitched ringing dulls, the shaking starts to subside, my breathing steadies.

I tentatively rise to my feet, holding onto the edge of the counter for support. I stare—and stare, and stare—at the phone. What am I supposed to do with it now? It's a tumor, possibly lethal. But I don't think I can resist the urge to prod at it and see what kind of ugliness oozes out, no matter how much it might hurt.

Before I can make up my mind, I hear footsteps, human and canine, pounding down the hallway outside. I hear the jingle of Fritter's dog tags, then Ian's key in our door.

Then nothing.

The deadbolt was no longer locked. I can sense him, just on the other side, letting that sink in. Steeling himself for the fact that I am already here.

Does he remember where he left the phone? Or does he just know that he doesn't have it with him?

As the handle starts to turn, I snatch it off the counter and shove it into the waistband of my jeans, concealing it beneath my flannel button-up. Fritter's scruffy face appears first. He pushes through the door, beelining for me. I bend down to shower him with kisses—and to avoid seeing Ian for a few more precious seconds. I know he won't look the same, that he never will again. I'll delay that tragedy for as long as I can.

"Who's my best boy?" I grab hold of both sides of Fritter's face, kiss his shiny black nose. His happy tail smacks against the fridge, as I blink away the stinging in my eyes.

I make myself get up.

"Hi!" I say brightly.

In an instant, the rigid angles of Ian's jawline mellow. The crease in his brow irons itself out. The transformation happens so fast that I would've missed it if I didn't already know he had something to hide. His smile—the way it turns down the corners of his eyes and makes the green in them sparkle a little—rips me apart. When I lean into him for a hug, I feel the rest of the tension leave his body.

He thinks he's gotten away with it.

"You're home early." He kisses my forehead. It turns my stomach, the ringing in my head dialing back up. "Couldn't stand being around Jordana any longer?"

*Ian has made a joke*, I tell myself. *Laugh at the joke.*

I laugh.

"Actually, it was nice to spend some time with her outside the office. I woke up at the crack of dawn and couldn't fall back asleep, so I figured I might as well beat traffic." I hear myself speaking, but I'm not totally convinced the words are coming from me. "I would've texted, but I didn't want to wake you."

"Well, lucky us, getting you back so soon." His eyes shift to the countertop, then swerve past me, searching the apartment. "Now you'll get to have some Fritter time before Natalie comes down to get him."

"You guys got an early start, too." I gather my bags from the entry and head into the bedroom, pausing in the doorway. "Wow, you even made the bed!"

Ian never makes the bed. That is the same made bed that I left behind on Friday. He hasn't slept here all weekend. This lying motherfucker.

"Uh, yeah. I guess I must've really missed you."

"I missed you, too." It's physically painful to say it.

"Are you hungry? I can make pancakes."

"Sure, that sounds great. I'm just going to take a quick shower."

Fritter follows me through the bedroom, into the bathroom. I close the door behind us and turn on the water. I sit on the edge of the tub, Fritter's chin resting on my knees. The volume of my tears surprises me. There have been so many times since we moved in here when I felt like I hated Ian. I mean, really hated him. But if I ever doubted that I still loved him, the way I feel right now—completely ruined—is my validation.

Fritter whines softly, the worry in his eyes compelling me to get my shit together. "It's okay," I reassure him. "Everything's fine."

I peel off my clothes and hide the phone in a box of tampons under the sink, in case Ian comes in while I'm showering. When I'm done, I take the box and shove it inside one of the purses holding my contraband house numbers, in the top corner of the closet.

. . .

"So, what did you get up to last night?" I ask, pushing gluey, underdone pancake around my plate, already nauseated from the couple of bites I managed to force down.

When I reemerged from the bathroom, Ian was putting the seat cushions back on the couch—looking for the TV remote, he said. Fritter hasn't left my side; now he lies on top of my feet under the table. I think he understands. He was apparently with Ian, after all. Wherever he was.

"Oh, not a whole lot," Ian says. "I took Fritter on a long walk after I went upstairs to get him, then Brant came by for a while, and we ordered a pizza and had a few beers. What about you?"

He doesn't skip a goddamn beat. Why has it never occurred to me that Ian might be just as good a liar as I am? Maybe he's even better.

"We had a pretty lowkey night, too. Cooked some pasta, drank some wine. Went to bed early." I take a sip of coffee. "How's Brant doing? I can't remember the last time I saw him."

Ian laughs. "Well, yeah, he's not really your favorite, right?"

"That's true."

Which, I now realize, is exactly what makes him a safe alibi. I'm hardly ever around him, so he'll likely never have a chance to blow Ian's cover. I pick through my memory for any other times recently that Ian claimed to be hanging out with Brant. He said he was with him the night I made his mom's chicken, when he didn't come home till three in the morning. Something clicks inside, like I'm finally shifting gears. And there it is, thick and scalding, the fury surging past the shock, beginning to burn away the heartache.

Ian keeps talking while he chews. "You know, he's the same old Brant." His fork screeches through a puddle of syrup. I see pancake mush on his tongue. "He has a new girlfriend, but she sounds way too good for him, so who knows how long she'll stick around."

"Oh yeah? What's her name?"

"Alex."

He says it too quickly. It was right there, already formed on his lips. So, that's her then. That's who's on the other end of that fucking phone.

Just then, my own phone vibrates, rattling the knife on the edge of my plate.

It's a text from Dottie. I'd forgotten I was still waiting to hear from her—that she'd left the cabin last night without committing to an answer. That until approximately forty-five minutes ago, getting hold of her paper was my biggest concern.

*You're nowhere on the Georgetown website,* it reads. *I'm not giving you shit, whoever you are.*

"Anything interesting?" Ian asks.

I choke down my rage, along with another gluey bite.

"Just spam."

## 23

Ian fucks his side piece in a shabby brick apartment building surrounded by much grander-looking row houses—the kind that sell for millions to senators and lobbyists—on a narrow, leafy street on Capitol Hill.

I know that now because I am parked across from it, a coiled snake waiting and watching for two disgusting rats.

The affair started seven weeks ago. Or at least that's when Ian started using a burner phone like he's on the fucking *Wire*. He sent the first text from it on February 22: *Can't stop thinking about earlier. When can I see you again?*

Her response: *Another lunch? When's your next day in the office?*

It goes on like this, week to week, them arranging dates in the middle of workdays. They met at the W the first few times, near Ian's office. But then he started to get nervous:

*Worried we'll run into someone from work. What about your place?*

So she texted her address.

After their first rendezvous here, in apartment 201, she sent him a photo of herself in a full-length mirror, naked and pubeless, tousled dark-brown hair, making the pouty duck face of a billion

Kardashian selfies. She looked like a teenager—tiny enough that I could crush her like an engorged mosquito.

Along with the photo, she'd included a note: *Cum back soon. XO.*

The next poet fucking laureate.

After reading that Sunday afternoon—while Ian was allegedly out for a run, giving me my first moment alone with the phone since discovering it—I wasn't sure I'd be able to sleep next to him. At least not without waking up in the middle of the night to hold a pillow over his face. But then I realized what had happened: the rage had fully taken over, shutting out the despair. Basking in the anger, I was perfectly comfortable sitting there on our bedroom floor, on the sisal rug that we picked out together a lifetime ago at West Elm, excavating his betrayal.

So, that's just what I'm doing now: leaning hard into the rage, at least until I figure out how I want to play this.

Now it's a little past twelve thirty on Tuesday, a time when they almost always meet. (Not to mention TWO FUCKING DAYS till the dream house is supposed to hit the market.) As a tan Lexus comes to a stop in front of the apartment building, I sink down lower in the driver's side of the Prius. I'm parallel parked between two cars; Ian will never notice me over here, a rare benefit of driving something so unremarkable. The curbside rear door of the Lexus swings open. Out steps my husband, in the same blue button-up and khakis that he wore to the office this morning, a sight thoroughly familiar and alien all at once. He ascends the front steps to a buzzer by the entrance. Punches something in, says something into the intercom. A second later, he lets himself into the building. Alex must be waiting upstairs.

My mind wanders to the vile things they're probably doing up there. They were here together the day we saw the dream house for the first time, too. That morning, right before Ian told me he had to be at the office for "a lunch meeting," she'd sent him a shot of her ass. That was it. Just the ass. Ian, thank God, hasn't texted her any visuals in return. At least that's one way his aversion to risk has worked in my favor.

It's after one o'clock now. Only when I begin to lose feeling in my hands do I realize I'm squeezing the steering wheel so hard my knuckles are white. I breathe in deep and remind myself about their more recent text messages—the way a disconnect seems to be emerging between them.

*Why don't we go out for lunch today?* Alex texted Ian last Wednesday, the day before I had sex with him on our sofa. *We can still come back to my place after.*

*You know we can't do that*, he wrote back. *I hate it when you make me into the bad guy.*

The week before that, she'd begged to go with him to Pittsburgh. (Yes, he really was out of town with those goddamn coasters in the back of the car. Otherwise, I would've smothered him with my pillow already.)

*It's a business trip. Don't be ridiculous*, he'd responded.

When she wouldn't relent, he came up with a compromise: *Fine. I'll come to your place when I get home Friday night and tell Margo I'm in Pittsburgh till Saturday morning.*

Seeing him use my name with her had momentarily paralyzed me. I sat there unmoving on the bedroom floor before an overwhelming urge to break everything started pumping through me like venom. I wanted to punch through the walls, smash all the furniture. Instead, I tore furiously through Ian's nightstand until I found the maroon velvet box holding his great-grandfather's watch, the one Ian had worn at our little nothing courthouse wedding— the family heirloom that he dreamed of one day giving to his own son. I snatched it from the case and ran full speed from our apartment all the way to the trash chute at the opposite end of our floor. I lobbed it with such force into that dark, metallic abyss that there's no chance it survived the impact with the dumpsters below.

That had done the trick. The rage subsided to its comforting, rolling boil; my head cleared enough that I could focus on the silver lining—that Ian was sounding increasingly annoyed by Alex.

A light rain has started to fall now, pattering on my windshield. While I wait, I confirm tomorrow's Zoom interview between the *New York Times* reporter and Causa's general manager, and follow up with the Rivière team about settling on a date for the media dinner. The street is quiet. Hardly any cars have driven by since I've been here, but now a white Hyundai pulls up and idles at the curb. Ian walks out of the building a minute later.

Alex trails him.

This is why I'm here. I needed to see them together for myself. She is impossibly young, not more than a year or two out of college, in tight black workout shorts and a white tank top, dark hair falling in disheveled layers around offensively buoyant tits. She's so thin, it would take no effort at all to shove her to the ground, to kick in that pretty face.

Especially if I took a running start from this side of the street. I press the button to unlock the car, let my fingers curl around the door handle.

She stops Ian at the bottom of the steps, standing on tiptoes to wrap her arms around his neck. But he pushes her away, looking anxiously over his shoulder. Even from all the way over here, I recognize the aggravation in his eyes and the desperation in hers.

I loosen my grip on the door handle—it would be dumb to interrupt them now, and I didn't come here for a confrontation.

She's saying something, but he waves her off. Before he gets into the back of the Hyundai, he rakes a hand through his hair. They must've had an argument upstairs.

If you bother to watch closely enough, even a fleeting, wordless interaction like this one can be incredibly revealing. When I saw Ian with the other girlfriend—the one he was with back when I met him—I could tell that he was different from the other assholes I'd dated.

A couple of days after he first kissed me in that bar, I waited for them outside the law firm (she was an associate there, too). I was tucked into a bus shelter on the median so they wouldn't see me, but I had a clear view of them. She was willowy like a ballerina, nearly as tall as Ian in her kitten heels, auburn hair pulled into a ponytail. I didn't love that she was so beautiful. But at least she wasn't Asian. I wasn't interested in wasting my time on some creep with a fetish.

I liked the way Ian held the door for her—propping it open, then lightly placing his hand on the small of her back once she was through it. As they made their way down the sidewalk, he offered to take her laptop bag. The entire sequence was passionless—she looked about as fun as a pap smear, I could see easily why Ian was ready to end it—but it was all so considerate. He followed this exact same routine the next night, and the night after that. Ian was a good guy.

I'm not sure he's a good guy anymore, of course. In fact, I'm fairly certain I could kill him. But based on the display I just witnessed, whatever he has with Alex won't last.

And I can't turn my frozen eggs into a baby on my own. I can't, at my age, tear everything down and start from scratch. Not if I still expect to get the life I've been working so fucking hard to build.

I can't keep Ian's family—the perfect holidays together, the sweet check-ins from his mom, the advice from his dad about how to fix literally anything—if I throw Ian away.

Once we're in the dream house, especially once I'm pregnant, this will all get much easier to compartmentalize. I don't have to like Ian. I just need him to be there.

After the Hyundai drives away with my piece-of-shit husband in the backseat, I find the number for Erika's real estate agent in my email.

It rings once. "This is Derrick."

"Hey, Derrick, it's Margo Miyake. Erika Ortiz connected us last week?"

"Oh, right. It's nice to hear from you."

"I'm sorry, I meant to call sooner, but life got a little crazy."

"No problem at all. What can I help you with?"

"The easiest sale of your career, I hope."

He laughs. "All right, you have my attention."

"There's only one house that I want. It's supposed to hit the market in two days, but I think we can get it sooner. I don't need to tour it or anything. I just need you to help my husband and me submit the offer."

# 24

Curt is such a cliché—like a guy playing a professor on TV—that his office at Georgetown is almost exactly how I envisioned it. He has a hulking antique desk, piled with papers and leaning stacks of folders and books, and a burgundy Chesterfield sofa, the leather worn to a faded pink in the spots where legions of students have sat over the years, captive to his bluster.

A whole shelf of his bookcase, positioned perfectly for Zoom appearances, is solid yellow with *Falling Apart*, one copy turned so its cover faces outward. He has precisely two dozen of them here—I've had ample time to count while I wait for him in this visitor's chair in front of his desk. I bet he replenishes the supply each time he hands one out, no doubt offering to autograph it first.

I drove straight here from that whore's apartment, and some kids lounging on the campus green were nice enough to point me the rest of the way. I was pleasantly surprised to find Curt's door unlocked. It'll make for a more dramatic opening, that's for sure. He's apparently in the midst of a lecture, which has given me forty-five minutes to pretend to care deeply about a Slack debate with Jordana and Taylor over which influencers should get comped overnight stays at The Bexley.

I left the office door open so I'd be able to hear Curt before he arrives. And I'm pretty sure that's him coming down the corridor now, leather-bottomed dress shoes on high-polished hardwood, just like that day in Healy Hall. They get louder and louder, then stop.

"Oh, hello. I'm sorry, am I late for an appointment?"

My back is to the door, so he doesn't realize it's me yet. Like I said—dramatic.

I stand and turn to face him.

"What the fuck?" He staggers backward, looking frantically left to right. He's thinking of yelling, or maybe running away. It's hilarious.

"Calm down, Curt. You're going to want to hear what I have to tell you—about Dottie Ross."

Saying her name aloud in here sends a pleasant shiver up my spine. Curt goes sheet-white. He freezes, mouth gaping, considering his next move.

I help him along: "You should sit."

His Adam's apple bobs above the V-neck of his black sweater as he swallows. He slowly closes the door behind him and moves around me to the other side of his desk, lowering himself into the swivel chair. He stares straight ahead, waiting for me to speak.

"You should know I have the paper," I say, sitting back down. "The one you plagiarized for the first chapter of your book."

When I left West Virginia without it, I knew it was possible, even probable, that Dottie would never come through. But I'd siphoned enough details out of her to feel like I could still make this work. And judging by how Curt looks now—like he's about to vomit all over his keyboard—I was right.

"Dottie gave it to me on the condition I don't tell you where she is, or how to find her. She's doing really well, by the way, considering how royally you fucked up her life."

Curt's eyes jump from my face to the exit behind me. As it dawns on him that he's trapped himself, I flash him a smile.

He lets some silence settle between us, before clearing his throat.

"I don't know what you're playing at, Margo, or what this *Dottie* has told you, but I have no idea what paper you're referring to."

Ballsy choice.

"Really? You're sure about that?"

He rests a hand atop the landline phone on his desk. "I'm calling campus security if you don't leave immediately," he says. His voice is calm, but I can see that his fingers are trembling.

"Go ahead, if that's what you want to do." I lean back in my chair, as if taking a little break from a scrumptious twelve-course prix fixe. "But I'm trying to do you a favor. I mean, if the wrong person got a hold of this information, it could really ruin things for you. For Jack and Penny, too."

He lifts the receiver.

"The wire transfer from your dad is the part that'll really fuck you, I think. I also have a copy of that."

Curt sets the receiver back down. His gaze flits briefly to the door again.

"Paying someone off with fifty thousand bucks sure seems like bribery," I continue, really hamming it up now, "but I guess I'm not a lawyer . . ."

He raises a hand, signaling that he's heard enough. "You've made your point," he says, squeezing his eyes shut, probably wishing he was anywhere else in the world. "I just, I don't understand . . . How do you possibly know all this?"

"I already explained that. Dottie told me."

He puts his elbows on the desk and cradles his face in his hands, massaging his temples.

I don't think I've ever had this much fun.

"What do you want, then?" he asks, looking back up.

I scoff.

"Have I not made that obvious? Come on, all these diplomas on the wall?" I sweep my hand toward the frames hanging off-kilter above the Chesterfield. "I thought you were a smart guy."

"I know you want the house. I just want to understand, specifically, what you're asking."

"Well, I'm not really asking. I already tried that, remember?" I scoot to the edge of my seat. "I'm telling you, Curt—sell me your house, or I tank your career."

He looks stunned.

"Why are you doing this?"

"Because you gave me no choice! But I'm nice enough to give you a very easy one. Sell me the house, for the very generous price of one point three million dollars, and this all goes away. It's not like I'm stealing from you, Curt. I'm trying to give you almost all of our money."

He lets out a sigh. "Give me a second," he says, taking off his glasses and pinching the bridge of his nose. "I'm just trying to think this through. How exactly do you envision this working?"

"The way things are *supposed* to work. Our agent sends you a contract—*today*—and you accept it. Easy. Simple. No bullshit bidding wars."

Curt shakes his head, the panic beginning to show through on his face. "That's impossible. What am I supposed to tell Jack? He doesn't know anything about Dottie." Curt's eyes start to well. "If he knew what I did to her . . . if Penny ever found out . . ."

"That part sounds a lot like your problem," I say, rising from my chair.

"No, no, wait," says Curt, standing to meet me. "Please. Just give me some time to figure this out."

"Why would I do that?"

"Think about it, Margo. You need me to handle this carefully. Obviously Jack won't want to sell the house to you. I'll figure out a way to convince him, I promise I will, I just need to take a breath and wrap my head around all this."

I shift my weight, considering him.

"Just give me until Thursday, when we list, to figure out how to explain this to Jack," he continues. "You can make your offer the minute it goes up—we're posting the house at nine a.m.—and we'll accept it then." His eyes drill into mine. "Margo, please. I promise."

Annoyance stabs into my rib cage. I hate having to concede anything to this daddy's boy dipshit, but I'm not seeing another option.

"Fine," I say finally. "But if I don't get the house, no one does. Fuck this up, and I'll send everything I have straight to King's College. London will be over for you. You'll have no reason to sell the house at all."

Curt nods. "I understand."

I turn and walk out.

# 25

I'm mixing a batch of Manhattans when Ian gets home. His blue button-up looks particularly rumpled, but maybe I'm only imagining that.

Has he showered since this afternoon? I force down a wave of nausea.

When he bends to kiss me on the cheek, I inhale deeply, an airport security dog trying to detect the deception. All I pick up is Old Spice—he must've reapplied. It's almost impressive, the lengths he's gone to cover his tracks. I underestimated him.

"How was your day?" I ask, calm and casual, giving the lid that's been holding in all my hurt and disgust a few more turns.

"I've had better," he says, taking one of the cocktails from me. "There's just a lot going on right now."

"With the river case?"

"Yeah." He takes a healthy gulp. "It's turned into a real monster."

He has to be talking about her.

I stroke Ian's arm with one hand and pick up my coupe glass with the other. "I'm sorry to hear that. Why don't we have these on the couch and unwind a little?"

I snuggle in, curling my feet under my butt and angling toward him. I could hoist myself over his lap right now—he'd love it at first—but then I'd squeeze my hands around his throat while I straddled him. I'd watch his excitement turn to confusion, and then horror.

He rubs my thigh and clicks on the TV.

"Actually"—I gently take the remote and mute the volume—"there's something I need to ask you about."

He goes rigid beside me. Good. Let him fear the worst.

Once I was done reading through the burner phone, before Ian got back from his run on Sunday, I deleted the most recent text (since he surely would've noticed it had been opened—and not by him). Then I planted the phone just under where we're sitting now, shoved all the way back between the wall and one of the sofa's rear legs. By yesterday morning, it was gone. It was well-hidden enough that once Ian found it, he could believe he'd missed it on a first pass. But I bet the nagging suspicion that I might've seen it has never fully left him.

He leans away, so he has a clearer view of my face. Worry pinches his forehead.

"Okay . . . what is it?"

"Well, it's been over a week now since we paused the house hunt, and I'm sure you remember that *the* house hits the market the day after tomorrow."

He sighs, but his posture relaxes. He's relieved that this is all I want to discuss.

"I know *I'm* in a much better place since we stopped obsessing about it," I say, "and I think *we're* in a better place, too, don't you agree?"

He nods, no doubt internally rejoicing at my cluelessness.

"You said you wanted your wife back, and you have her. I promise, I'm right here, and I'm never going anywhere again."

He lowers his eyes to his hand, still on my thigh. Have I made him feel guilty?

"So," I continue, "I hope you can trust that I'm coming from a much healthier, much more rational place when I say I still think we should make an offer on it."

His face snaps back up. "Margo ..."

"I know, I know. I get that it's a very, very long shot. But I just want to give it a go the right way. Write a normal, honest offer—no games, no lying—and let the cards fall where they may."

"Margo, you know they'll never sell it to us."

"You're probably right." I take his hand in both of mine. "I mean, you're almost definitely right. But I have to see this through. I have to at least try, or I'll always wonder. I just felt such a connection to that place."

I unscrew the lid the teeniest bit, letting out just enough of the heartbreak to make my eyes water.

"I could really see us there, putting our baby to sleep in Penny's adorable bedroom. And a few years down the road, you teaching her—or him—how to throw a baseball in the backyard."

"But this is exactly what worries me," Ian says, brushing a tear off my cheekbone with his thumb, his touch roiling my stomach. "I hate hearing you get your hopes up like this, when we both know what the outcome will be."

"My hopes are not up, I promise. Just let me try, Ian. We have nothing to lose. It's not like they can humiliate us any more than they already have."

"I don't think so, Margo."

The patience is retreating from his voice.

"We can write a letter with the offer, apologizing for what we did—for what *I* did."

"My answer is no."

He pulls his hand from mine.

I slouch away from him and screw the lid back on tight. I open up a different, much larger jar. Anger pours out of this one, coursing through me like blood. I take a deep breath to steady myself.

I didn't want the conversation to go like this, but I knew it probably would. I knew that saving the phone and the affair for this moment could be useful.

I stare at him, keeping my face blank. "So, where is it then?" I ask flatly.

He narrows his eyes in confusion. "Where's what?"

"Your fucking burner phone, Stringer Bell."

He jerks away from me, flushing a deep scarlet. "What are you talking about?"

Is he seriously going to insist on turning this into a struggle?

"I don't think I'm asking for very much, Ian." I glare at him. "Just for the tiniest shred of honesty—the bare minimum, really, given that you and Alex have been shitting all over our marriage for ... how long has it been? Almost two months? Jesus, what would your parents think?"

Ian's eyes stretch into unblinking orbs. He seems to have stopped breathing, then his frozen, horrified expression crumples. He buries his face in his hands, shaking his head like he can't believe this is happening. His shoulders begin to heave up and down. He looks so small, like a weak little boy.

He lifts his gaze to meet mine, his face a mess of tears and snot. He is pathetic.

"Margo, I am so sorry," he chokes out. "I am such a fucking idiot. You know I love you more than anything in the whole world. She is nothing to me. You have to believe me."

"So you love me and you just love fucking her? Am I understanding right?"

He's shaking his head again. Another sob racks his body. "You never should've had to look at that phone. I can't even imagine ..."

I cut him off. "I need you to give it to me. Right now."

He goes silent and still.

"Fine," he says. "That's fine." He rises from the sofa and heads over to his backpack, on the floor in the entry. He roots around in it before removing a wrinkled, brown paper bag from Pret. A costume for the Nokia. Sneaky motherfucker.

He returns, placing the bag on the coffee table, too ashamed to take out its contents.

"Do whatever you want with it." He sinks back into the couch. "It's over, I swear to you. I ended it today. I couldn't live with myself anymore."

I think back to what I saw outside the apartment building. I want to believe him.

"Was she the first time?"

"Yes!" He says it urgently, grabbing my hands. "Oh my God, Margo, yes. Please, *please* believe me, I've never done anything like this before. I fucking hate myself for it."

"Did you use protection?"

The possibility of that teenager getting pregnant before me erupts in my brain like an aneurysm.

"Of course! God, of course." Ian's eyes are damp again. "Hearing you ask me that makes me sick to my stomach."

I tear my hands free of his and get up. I can't stand to sit next to him any longer.

"How'd you meet her?" I ask, pacing in front of the television.

He groans. "You really want to know that?"

I pause to face him. "Oh, I'm sorry, is this too uncomfortable for *you?*"

He stares at the floor.

"Yes," I say, "I want to fucking know."

"On the sidewalk, near the office."

"You met her on the sidewalk?"

"She was holding a clipboard, canvassing for the Environmental Defense Fund."

It takes a second for this little twist to sink in. Then I start to laugh. I can't help it.

"She's a clipboard girl?"

"She's an intern."

"Ian, that is not better."

"I know," he says quietly.

"So then what? She asked if you wanted to fuck her to save the rainforest?"

He grimaces, like I'm torturing him.

"I told her I worked at the EPA. She wanted to know more about my job, whether I thought she'd be qualified for *our* internship program..."

He pauses, hoping I've heard enough. I refuse to let him off the hook.

"I don't know what else to tell you, we just kind of hit it off." He's back to staring at the floor. "I wasn't thinking. I wasn't myself. Things have just been so stressful lately, with all the house stuff, and all the baby stuff..."

He has got to be fucking kidding. The incinerator hits full blast, I feel like I could breathe fucking fire.

"Things have been stressful for *you*?" My voice trembles. I am losing control. "I'm sorry, I didn't realize your life has been so hard." I begin to pace again, like a caged animal. "I must've forgotten—are you the one who had a needle jabbed into your vagina and your eggs suctioned out? And is it *you* who drops whatever you're doing the second a halfway decent listing hits the market?" I let my eyes sear into the top of his head. "Have I just been hallucinating this whole time that it's been me doing these things, killing myself to build a real life for us while you fuck around?" I'm not sure when I began shouting. "Can you at least fucking look at me, Ian?"

He does as he's told.

"I'm sorry," he whispers. "I...that came out wrong...I...I know this has all been harder on you. But it's been hard for me, too." He clears his throat, working up some courage. "And sometimes, I feel like you don't see that."

"So you decided to fuck an EPA groupie?" I scream it at him, not giving a shit if the neighbors hear. But Ian refuses to match my rage. He just looks defeated.

"Tell me what to do, babe." His voice quivers. "How do I fix this?"

The gravity of the question knocks some of the wind out of me. We will never be the same again. I know that. We'll be a broken vase that's been glued back together. Forever damaged—but still intact. Still mostly passable as a very nice vase (especially from behind the right Instagram filter).

Certainly still better than no vase at all.

*Perfect house. Perfect baby. Perfect dog. Shitty husband.*

Still an almost-perfect life.

"I don't think you can ever fix it. Not entirely," I say, my voice back to a normal volume. A fresh batch of tears emerges along Ian's lower lashes. "But you can start by helping me get us the fuck out of this apartment. It's killing us."

He nods.

"We need a fresh start. A reset."

More nodding.

"I'm calling the lender tomorrow to make sure our financing is in order. And on Thursday, you're going to sign your name on that offer, and we're going to cross our fingers and hope for a goddamn miracle."

"Okay," he agrees. "Let's do it."

# 26

The countdown is over. My future starts today.

The listing appears at exactly nine o'clock. I've been at my desk in front of the floor-to-ceiling window for the last half hour, refreshing and refreshing Redfin, and now here it is:

5423 Stonebrook Ave., Bethesda, MD 20816
4 beds. 2.5 baths. 3,100 sq. ft.
$1,250,000

*Welcome to the most charming home in desirable Grovemont! This classic 1940s Colonial was meticulously renovated and expanded in 2019 to include a chef's kitchen with custom cabinets, Carrara marble countertops, and Thermador appliances, and a primary suite to rival any five-star hotel. A spacious rear deck with a built-in gas grill is your summer entertaining dream. Complete with a cozy, wood-burning fireplace, white-oak floors throughout the main and upper levels, and a professionally landscaped backyard. The unfinished basement, with full-height ceilings and a separate entrance, awaits your personal touch. The ideal au pair suite?*

*Extra play space for the kids? A luxe home office? The possibilities are endless. This is the one—just 20 minutes from downtown DC!*

When I see the lead photo, a current of adrenaline crackles through me. It's the day of the dinner-party disaster, preserved in time—the house in its most flawless state, ready for its closeup. The crisp white paint. The glossy black shutters and front door. The window boxes, lush and overflowing. The shockingly green grass. A perfect, sunny scene that feels like it happened in another life.

I click through the rest of the slideshow, forty-eight shots in all. There are several of the kitchen, its creamy marble countertops seeming to stretch on forever thanks to the camera's wide-angle lens. The fireplace glows in the living room, lit just for the photos. Penny's room—staged with a few highly curated toys, and the tulle-skirted dress she wore at dinner hanging on the closet door—looks like a coral jewel box. They've captured every part of the magical owner's suite: The huge, sun-filled bedroom. The double bathroom vanities. The soaking tub. The obscenely beautiful closet. They've saved the backyard for last. The camera was focused on the flagstone patio, the flawless lawn just beyond it. But my eye still travels to the tire swing, barely visible in the upper righthand corner of the shot.

Flipping through these, I can practically hear the frantic phone calls going out to agents all over town, and the slamming of front doors as couples just like me and Ian drop whatever they're doing to make a mad run for Grovemont. It'll take an hour tops for the place to be absolutely mobbed. But all of those people will be wasting their time. Because only the best offer wins—and finally, that offer will be mine.

I email the listing to Derrick, then follow up with a text: *The house is online. Just sent it to you. Ian and I are standing by to sign the* *offer. As discussed, $1.3 million. No contingencies. We can close on the sellers' timeline.*

He writes back: *Super. Paperwork coming your way now.*

"Ian!" I yell over my shoulder. "The listing's live. Derrick's sending the contract."

"Cool," he calls from the bedroom. "I'll hang out here till it shows up."

As if he has a choice. Ian's been dancing around like a toothless circus bear the last couple days—waking up early to brew the French press, taking the Prius to the car wash, doing our grocery shopping for the first time probably in over a year, bringing home flowers *and* cupcakes.

My phone vibrates on the desk. It's Derrick.

"Hello?"

"Hey, Margo, just a small hiccup." He's trying to hide that he's nervous. "I called their agent to let her know we're planning to submit. But she says they're not taking offers until Monday at the earliest. The sellers want to wait till after the weekend, so they can review all the contracts that come in at the same time."

"Did you tell her who your clients are?" I ask, voice low so Ian doesn't overhear.

"No, I just said you love the house and you're planning to come in at your best and final number."

I glance over my shoulder again to make sure Ian is still in the bedroom. "This after-the-weekend business doesn't apply to us. Like I told you, we know the sellers, and I've worked out an arrangement with them."

"Yeah, I know you said that. But she seemed pretty adamant."

Annoyance shoots through me. "I don't care how she seemed, Derrick. We're making an offer *today*."

"All right," he says. "You're the boss. Back to you soon."

The paperwork hits my inbox seconds later. Ian and I pass my laptop back and forth on the couch, taking turns digitally initialing and signing it in all the required places, like we've done eleven times before. By now, the act of promising to fork over our life savings feels almost mundane.

Once we finish, Ian turns to me. "We did it!" he says, in the affected everything-is-fine voice he's been using. "Fingers crossed, right?" Then he leans in for a kiss.

I recoil. "Maybe when they accept."

He blinks a couple times, then awkwardly stands. "Okay, well, I have to get going."

"Yep," I say, "me, too."

...

I'm leaning against one of the massive columns in The Bexley's cavernous lobby. The most important moment of my life is unfolding and here I am, acting like it's just another workday, just another meeting with clients.

Hotel guests rush around me, roller bags rumbling behind them across the black marble floors. I refresh my email and text messages for the millionth time while I wait for Jordana and Taylor—they're Ubering together from the office, I came straight from the apartment. Still no updates from Derrick.

The magnitude of the morning didn't fully hit until I locked the apartment door behind me. *Holy shit*, I thought, *the next time I walk through here, this will all be over*. My whole body felt instantly lighter. Even now, I feel like I could float all the way up to the giant chandelier suspended from the vaulted ceiling. It may have taken almost nineteen months. My marriage may have barely survived. But my escape is officially under way. I am about to start my dream life at last.

Just before eleven, Jordana and Taylor breeze through the doors, sunlight streaming in behind them. I check my messages one more time—still nothing, but it always takes a while to hear back about these things—then hurry over to meet them.

We find our clients at a round, pink-marble-topped table in the Rivière dining room. It's too early for the lunch rush, so we mostly have the place to ourselves. Oliver, CEO of Mythos Group, is still in town from Amsterdam, his chin-length, white-blond hair slicked behind his ears. He's flanked by Charles, The Bexley's graying general manager, and Chef Xander, who somehow, despite his Michelin star, is one of the thinnest people I've ever seen. Serina is here, too. She gives me a wave.

Once Jordana, Taylor, and I take our seats, a server appears with champagne. Oliver thanks her—the deepness of his voice always startles me.

"We've had a brilliant launch, thanks to the Bexley team and our friends here from Buzz," he says to the group. "So, cheers to all of you." He lifts his flute; the rest of us follow his lead. "But there's always excitement around an opening, right? That's the easy part. The real work is in keeping the momentum going."

My phone vibrates in my front pocket. I specifically chose these wide-leg trousers so I could keep it there, in case Derrick texted. I wriggle my fingers in to retrieve it.

"I know Margo already has a media dinner in the works for Rivière. But the next play, I think, is to start cycling in some influencers for overnight stays," Oliver continues. "I want them in the nicest suites, with the most outrageous views, eating Xander's whole menu, posting that shit to their stories all day long."

We all nod.

"Absolutely," Jordana says. "My team has already started drafting a list of our first-choice picks. We can go over it here, if you want, and start the outreach as soon as we have your sign-off."

I peek at my phone, now resting by my thigh on the orange velvet of the dining chair. The text isn't from Derrick. It's from a number I don't recognize.

"Yes, brilliant," says Oliver. "Charles, you'll need to coordinate with Jordana to carve out the right blocks of time, in the right rooms, for these people." Charles nods. "And we won't want them here until after La Vue opens, of course. That's the other critical agenda item for today—we need to finalize the details for the event next month."

La Vue is going to be the hotel's rooftop bar. It has a 1970s Parisian vibe, so we're planning a Studio 54 night for its grand opening.

"We just confirmed the same DJ who did the hotel opening," Taylor chimes in. "She's very excited about the theme. And I wanted to talk to you about possibly bringing in some performers as well—I found these professional disco dancers. Let me pull up a video, they're just awesome . . ."

While everyone focuses on Taylor, I tap in my passcode, moving the phone from the seat to my lap, so I can read the message more easily.

It nearly stops my heart.

*It's Curt. Got your number from Jack's phone. I can't tell him without proof. Send a photo or there's no deal.*

He means a photo of the plagiarized paper, but he's not dumb enough to put that in writing. Cold sweat rises on my skin. I'm a fucking moron for leaving West Virginia without it. Why didn't I press Dottie harder?

I cannot afford to melt down here, but the room is spinning. The ringing in my head is back, and growing louder. I drink in a long inhale, then silently count down the exhale—four, three, two, one—willing my breathing to slow, willing the room to still.

"Margo?"

I lift my gaze from the phone screen. Six pairs of eyes stare back at me.

"Margo?" Jordana says again, her face contorted into some combination of exasperation and concern. "Did you hear what Serina just asked?"

I clear my throat, fighting through the pain in my skull.

"I didn't, I'm sorry." I force an embarrassed smile. "I seem to be a bit light-headed."

"Are you okay?" Serina asks, sounding truly worried. "You do look pale."

I catch Taylor rolling her eyes.

"I'll be fine," I say, waving Serina off. "Probably just the champagne on an empty stomach. Please go ahead—I'm so sorry—what was your question?" I notice Xander signal one of the servers.

"Oh, it's just a silly idea I had. I wondered if you thought we should do more of those private cocktail tastings, with whichever reporters you think might appreciate it, leading up to the La Vue opening. I thought maybe it could help build some anticipation."

It's a great idea. The kind of idea I should've offered, not the client.

"That's terrific, Serina, I would love to work with you on that," I say.

She smiles. The server drops off a croissant in front of me. I pick off an end, shooting a grateful look at Xander. But I have no appetite. I'm nauseated with anxiety.

Jordana pulls out her laptop so we can review her spreadsheet of influencers. While it starts up, I excuse myself to the ladies' room. It's a relief to be alone. I brace myself against the marble vanity—the same black stone as the lobby floors—and shut my eyes. What am I supposed to write back to Curt?

When I open them again, my complexion looks even pastier. The greenish cast coming off the emerald tile walls doesn't help.

I reread his text: *Send a photo or there's no deal.*

All I can do is bluff.

I tap out: *Go ahead and test me. See what happens.*

I survive the rest of the meeting in a kind of numb fog, doing my best to surface with a word of polite agreement or a thoughtful "hmm" at the right moments, Jordana periodically tossing nervous glances my way.

Curt never writes back.

. . .

"You guys want the good news first, or the bad news?"

Ian and I are both back at the apartment—the jail cell that simply refuses to loosen its fucking grasp—hovering over my phone resting on the kitchen counter. Derrick is on speaker. It's nearly six o'clock, and he's only just gotten a response from Jack and Curt's agent. The house has been on the market for nine hours now, which means dozens of people have trooped through it, measuring for their awful furniture, imagining themselves sleeping in *my* bedroom, cooking on *my* Thermador range, watching their awful children play on *my* tire swing. It's more upsetting than thinking about that clipboard cunt fucking my husband.

"Bad news, I think," says Ian, looking to me for confirmation. I shrug. What difference does it make?

"Okay, well, the sellers aren't taking your offer today," says Derrick. "Their agent says there's just way too much interest. At least six other buyers have already said they're planning to bid, and there's still an open house to get through on Saturday."

Ian squeezes my hand. "Got it," he says. "And how is there possibly any good news?"

"Well, they're not *rejecting* your offer either," says Derrick. "They've agreed to keep it in the mix to see how it stacks up after the weekend. Sounds like they're making Monday at five o'clock the offer deadline."

I feel the rage start to churn. This is my fucking fault. We're about to lose this house, and I will never forgive myself.

I sink to the kitchen floor, my face in my hands. Ian crouches next to me, rubbing my back. I will probably never know how Curt convinced Jack to let our offer even get this far. But I do know the only reason they're still stringing us along—Curt is doing exactly what I dared him to in my text. He's testing me. If I really had the paper, of course I would send him a photo of it now and put us both out of our misery. All Curt's doing is confirming that I don't have the evidence to back up my threat.

"Be honest, what are our chances?" Ian asks Derrick.

A long sigh curls out of the phone.

"Miracles sometimes happen," he says, "but given the intense interest, I don't think one point three million is going to get the job done."

## 27

Ian didn't dare protest when I told him I was calling in sick today. He just nodded and placed a glass of water on the nightstand. That must've been three hours ago, at least. I made him close the linen blackout curtains that I hung to cover the apartment's cheap mini blinds, so it's hard to say how late it is now. My phone slid off the mattress and underneath the bed at some point. Getting up to search for it seemed asinine. All that thing does is deliver bad news. Or, in this case, *no* news, a far more sadistic form of torture.

It'll take three more of these agonizing days to hear anything—a slow, pointless march toward inevitable devastation. Tomorrow, hordes of happy, hopeful people will prance through the open house. Then on Sunday, they'll return, home inspectors in tow for a look under the hood. That way, they'll be able to waive the inspection contingency in their offers, *on top* of paying cash and bidding the price up to some grotesque number. Their contracts will roll in throughout Monday, dwarfing ours, until 1.3 million American fucking dollars somehow looks like an insult. How many bids will pile up this time? A dozen? Twenty-five? Nine fucking hundred?

And where will I be at the end of it? Probably still here, tangled in these sheets, my phone pinging from a dust-bunnied corner under the bed with a text from Derrick that I can't bring myself to read because I know it'll be the fatal blow: *Sorry, guys, it wasn't meant to be.*

I let out a groan so loud and anguished that if the neighbors are home, they must think I'm either dying or having very weird sex, then I roll onto my stomach and let my face smush into the pillow. I ponder how long it'll take to run out of oxygen, but of course I chicken out at the first twinge of discomfort. Now I'm shifting around, trying to relax, but a sharp pain feels like it's literally piercing through one of my boobs. *What the hell?* I jolt back upright and recline onto my back, cautiously groping around my chest in the dark. When I press, even gently, both my breasts feel tender. Maybe I'm starting my period?

I squint in the harsh bathroom light. My reflection, once it comes into view, is alarming—sweaty black hair matted against pale skin, a bluish tint beneath my eyes, saliva crusted onto the corner of my mouth. Worst of all, I don't even care.

I slump onto the toilet and inspect my underwear. No sign of blood. But I do have to pee, badly.

Before I go back to bed, I hunt around under the sink for the Listerine. I may not care that I look like death, but I definitely care that my mouth tastes like it. I push aside a spray can of Lysol and a bag of cotton balls before I see it, tucked behind the drainpipe: a pregnancy test.

My boobs are sore.

And I don't have my period.

Crouched down, staring at the hot pink First Response box, I count back on my fingers, struggling to figure out whether I'm late. I've been so preoccupied I haven't been paying attention. Maybe it should've come last week?

The last time I took one of these was a couple of months after I froze my eggs. It was a Sunday and we'd gone to Le Dip for brunch. I ordered my usual, but the garlicky Boursin cheese in the center of the omelet didn't taste right. It was mostly bland, with a hint of bitterness. Before sending it back, I made Ian try it, and he had no idea what I was complaining about.

We were almost too afraid to say it aloud—we didn't want to jinx it—but we both admitted we thought I might be pregnant. We thought maybe the egg retrieval had taken enough of the pressure off that it had finally just happened. On the walk home, we stopped at CVS and bought a box of three pregnancy tests. We tried to play it cool, promised each other we'd keep our expectations low. But after the first two came back negative, we were both close to tears. It seemed cruel to put ourselves through the third one, so here it still is, long forgotten under the bathroom sink. (Salt in the wound: I realized the next day that nothing tasted good because I had Covid.)

Now I chug the water that Ian left by the bed, then bring the glass to the kitchen for a refill. A half-full French press still sits on the counter, so I down that, too. The microwave clock, plus the particular shade of sunlight from the living room window, inform me that it's nearly two in the afternoon.

Within fifteen minutes, I have to pee again. I've been through this routine too many other times—unwrapping the stick, holding it in place, feeling all the excitement and all the anxiety. But this time is different.

I am terrified.

When I'm done, I sink to the bathroom floor, the gray porcelain tile chilling my bare legs. I tuck my knees into my ratty, oversize Nats T-shirt—an old one of Ian's—like I used to do as a kid. The blank stick is in my hand, but I already know the result. I feel it in every cell.

After three minutes, the two pink lines make it official.

*No house. Shitty husband. A baby who'll have to sleep in the closet.*

The tears come fast and unrelenting. We are prisoners here. And now our baby will be, too. After all these months, she is right on time for her mother to completely fail her.

...

I wake up shivering, curled into a ball, still on the bathroom tile. The positive test lies next to me. As I drag myself up from the floor and into the kitchen, my stiffened joints pop and crack.

It's after five now. I snag a cold piece of leftover pizza from the refrigerator and take it into the living room, not bothering with a plate or even a paper towel, because nothing fucking matters anymore. In front of the floor-to-ceiling window, still only in a raggedy T-shirt and underwear, I stuff the slice of pepperoni and black olives into my puffy face—an image sure to haunt the dreams of anyone unlucky enough to look up from the sidewalk below.

As the procession of after-work commuters begins to swell, I wonder if any of them are planning to bid on the house. That guy with his earbuds in, talking with his hands, could be going over the details of an offer with his agent. The couple waiting at the crosswalk, hunched over one of their phones, looking way too fucking happy, might be scrolling through the listing photos. They look like the types who could win it easily. Brooks Brothers. Weekends in St. Michaels. Parents who taught them to ski. Maybe they'll get hit by a car.

A speck of red coming down U Street catches my attention—Ian's bike helmet. I've always worried about him getting hurt, riding home during rush-hour traffic like this, but now I couldn't care less. In fact, an old-fashioned tumble over the handlebars, or maybe a meet-up with a carelessly opened car door, sounds like decent entertainment.

Alas, he reaches the corner unscathed, gliding up onto the sidewalk, swerving around pedestrians. As he gets closer to our building's entrance, the rear, curbside door of a black sedan parked out front flies open. It has a Lyft sticker on the windshield.

A girl in a cutoff denim miniskirt, with messy, dark-brown hair, steps out. Ian sees her at the same moment that I do.

Alex.

He brakes hard, then climbs off his bike. He walks it briskly toward our building, extending a palm in her direction, shaking his head angrily, clearly telling her to stay away. But she ignores him.

She runs up and pulls on his sleeve, mascara streaking her face, throwing a tantrum like a child in the candy aisle. People walking past turn and stare. She's a wreck.

Ian puts down his kickstand and grabs hold of Alex's shoulders, keeping her at arm's length while she sobs. He's saying something—but not yelling, otherwise I would probably be able to hear at least some of it—his eyes darting around nervously.

When she takes a small step backward, he tries again to leave, but she's too quick. She lurches forward, clinging to his shirt, her expression frantic. Ian closes his eyes and waits for her to finish talking. He only opens them again once her mouth finally stills.

Whatever he's saying to her now appears to be calming her down.

She smiles.

She is fucking smiling.

When he's done, she nods, then walks back to the Lyft. Ian glances around one more time, then pulls up his kickstand and disappears into our lobby.

Pain builds behind my eyes. What the fuck did I just witness? My pulse whooshes in my ears; then the ringing sound overtakes it, louder than ever, like an entire surround-sound speaker system melting down. I race to the bathroom before Ian can walk in.

I turn on the shower and lock the door. I snatch the positive pregnancy test up from the floor and shove it back into the First Response box, back behind the drainpipe under the sink.

"Margo?"

He's calling me from the kitchen.

I freeze on the other side of the locked door. I need to think, but the throbbing behind my eyes is all-consuming. I strip off the old T-shirt and get into the shower, cranking up the temperature. The hot water on my skin melds into the rage, pure and scalding, coursing just beneath it. My vision is turning fuzzy, my balance is off. An imaginary wave swells beneath me, sending me stumbling backward. Groping along the tile to keep myself steady, I lower myself to the shower floor, squeezing my eyelids shut, then stretching them back open, in a lame attempt to reboot my vision.

I see only static, followed by light. White and blinding. Flooding everything. Impossible to tell if it's inside of me or outside. As it burns brighter and brighter, it ratchets up the pain in my skull and the screeching in my ears. The noise grows so deafening that it drowns out the running water.

How long am I like this, crouched like a closed fist, the water pooling around me? Maybe only seconds. Maybe several minutes. And then—the light is just gone.

The patter of the shower returns gradually, as if someone's turning up the volume. I blink open my eyes and see water beading on subway tile. The throbbing in my brain dissolves, like soapsuds swirling down a drain.

I feel warm all over—but not burning, not scalding—it's pleasant. I place a hand over my belly, and a sensation that's at first hard to recognize overcomes me. *Peace.*

As usual, I'll have to be the one who figures it all out for us. But why would I have expected anything different? Whatever it takes to solve this, I'll do it. Certainly not for Ian. But for my baby. And for me. For the life the two of us are owed.

Ian knocks on the bathroom door. "Margo? Everything okay in there?"

"Yep, fine," I say, standing to shut off the water. "I'll be out in just a sec."

# 28

Jack and Curt couldn't have designed a more perfect Saturday for their open house: fluffy clouds, brilliant sun, a debatable need for a light jacket. The home itself looks incredible. The window boxes have been replenished. Not a blade of grass is out of place. Theresa the listing agent—I recognize the Colgate smile and straw-hued helmet of hair from her website—stands on the front porch, ushering in anxious people from a line that stretches to the curb and up the sidewalk.

Several groups of three—couples with their agents—are scattered around the yard, locked in intense conversation, sneaking paranoid glances at the competition. All of them are surely debating the same thing: how aggressive they'll have to come in now that they've sized up the mob.

I've been taking in this chaos from the passenger side of Natalie's red Volkswagen Golf. We've driven up and down this stretch of Stonebrook Avenue five or six times, searching for a parking space. It's like Black fucking Friday out here, but finally, a Tesla is vacating a spot a half block down from the house. Natalie flips on her blinker to claim it, signaling to the driver of an oncoming Subaru that he'd better hit the bricks.

"This is insane," she says, as she straightens out in the space.

"Now you can see why Ian refused to come to another one of these things," I lie.

She scoffs. "I just can't imagine why anyone would put themselves through this. I mean, this house isn't even anything that special."

My skin goes hot before I remind myself that it's not worth feeling insulted. Natalie wouldn't know good taste if it smacked those obnoxious Versace sunglasses off her bronzer-caked face. Ignoring her, I put on my own aviators and pull down the brim of my Nike baseball cap before we get out and take our place in line.

The plan came to me in bits and pieces at first, and then in one big burst, as I lay wide awake listening to Ian's snoring compete with the late-night commotion of U Street unfolding below us. By the time a sliver of sunlight peeked between the curtains, I knew exactly what I needed to do—and it started with getting to the open house today.

"Thanks again for tagging along," I say to Natalie, as a couple with a baby strapped to the dad's chest joins the line behind us. "I bet this'll move pretty fast."

"Oh, this is fun for me," Natalie says, grinning. "It's like a glimpse into the domestic hell that I narrowly escaped."

Sure, Nat, judge me all you want.

In about fifteen minutes, we've inched our way down the sidewalk to within a few yards of the flagstone path that leads to the front door. That's when I hesitate, bringing a hand to my stomach: "Ugh."

"Are you okay?" Natalie asks.

"I'm not sure. I feel nauseated all of a sudden."

There are still a dozen or so groups ahead of us. But even in my sunglasses and hat, I can't get too much closer. I'm betting Jack and Curt gave Theresa a description of me and Ian—and our sad Prius—and asked her to keep a lookout. I have to make my exit now.

"I'm so sorry, Nat, I think I have to go back to your car."

"Really?" She twists up her face. "Do you think it's something you ate?"

"Actually," I lean in and lower my voice, "please don't say anything, I haven't even told Ian, but I just found out I'm pregnant. I think it might be morning sickness."

Her eyes expand, glittering the same bright blue as the sky. "Oh my God!" she shrieks, loudly enough that I dip my head. "I'm going to be Auntie Nat! Or Auntie Natty? I think that one might be cuter."

Because this is definitely about her. She pulls me in for a hug and I groan. "Sorry, I really don't feel well. But you should still go in."

"No way, let's just go home." Natalie starts to lead the way out of line.

"Hang on." I guide us back into our spot. The couple with the baby grudgingly allows it. "We've come all this way, at least one of us should go in. And, anyway, I really need someone to scope out the competition, just so I know what we're up against if I can talk Ian into going for this place. Would you mind?"

"Really? You know you sound nuts, right?"

"Come on, just give me your keys," I say, rolling my eyes. "Please?"

She shrugs, handing them over, and I head back to the red Volkswagen.

I wait in the car for a few minutes, until I'm sure Natalie's inside. Then, keeping my head down—and steering wide of Theresa's battle station on the front porch—I make my way toward the side gate to check on the one thing I need to confirm before we leave.

# 29

"Hey, babe, did you get anything?"

Ian's on the sofa, working on his laptop, when I walk in the door. He thinks Natalie and I went shopping in Georgetown. Look at him, sitting there in that disgusting sweatshirt, growing duller and more middle-aged by the minute.

"Not unless you count an oat milk cappuccino," I say, bending to unlace my sneakers. "We only made a couple stops, mostly so Natalie could return some things."

"I'm still glad you got out for a little while. I was really worried about you yesterday."

I'd like to put my fist through the earnestness smeared across his face. This is what they mean when they say marriage is hard work.

"I think I'm allowed one day to wallow, don't you?" I say. "Especially after everything you've put me through this week?"

His expression turns wounded. "Of course you are. But I'm relieved you've bounced back so well this time. I thought you'd be in bed all weekend."

"I'm not crazy." I head into the kitchen for a glass of water. "I told you I knew it was a long shot. All I wanted was to give it our best try, and now we have."

"I'm just impressed, that's all." He refocuses on the computer screen. "I was feeling a little guilty about having to go to Pittsburgh again for the river case on Monday."

"Oh, *that's* what you feel guilty about?"

He sighs, his eyes finding me again. "Sorry, I . . ." He stops himself, shakes his head. "You know what I mean."

Has he always been such a fucking idiot?

. . .

Fritter is waiting by the door when I let myself into Natalie's apartment. She will have only left for the bar twenty minutes ago, so he hasn't had much of a chance to settle down yet.

"Hi, good boy!" I say, kissing the top of his head, since I don't think his usual ear scratch will feel very good with latex-gloved fingers. "I know, I'm early, right? I just need to take a little look around, and then we'll get going, okay?"

He stays dutifully by my side as I head into the bedroom, a scruffy black-and-white barnacle.

Blossom was the exact same way.

She slept with me every night, burrowing under the covers and pushing into my hip, even though it was summer and we didn't have air conditioning. She was smart like Fritter, too. At first, she would bark every time someone came home, but she could tell it made me anxious. I would tense up each time she did it, shushing her with a finger to my mouth. My worst fear was that a neighbor would rat us out to the landlord. But it only took a couple days for Blossom to catch on. After that, whenever someone came to the door, she'd look at me, her brown eyes silently promising that she wouldn't ruin the good thing we had going.

My mom couldn't bring herself to ruin it, either. Once two weeks had gone by, we told my dad that my friend's family vacation had been extended indefinitely. They'd gone to visit Grandma in Palm Springs, we explained, and found out she was sick, so they had to stay and take care of her. After all those years with my dad, my mom was an expert at coming up with these kinds of stories to appease him—half-truths, she called them, even though they often weren't true at all.

Even he seemed to be growing attached to Blossom. She was impossible not to love, cuddling up with whoever was on the couch. I'd taught her to "shake"—she was so eager to learn tricks—and she'd taken to offering a paw for a treat whenever she saw an opening. You would've had to have been a monster to resist. I didn't yet know that my dad was one.

Blossom was so well behaved that I'd stopped worrying about school starting. We would miss each other terribly, but my mom and I thought she could handle spending the day in my bedroom. We'd asked the salespeople at Petco for any tips that might help. They'd suggested chew toys to entertain her, and pee pads so she could do her business in an emergency without making a mess.

The night before the first day of fourth grade, I held Blossom extra close in my bed, whispering to her that we both had to be brave in the morning, but that I'd be home before she knew it. We'd go for a walk in the afternoon, I promised, then I would give her the new peanut butter treats that we'd bought for the occasion.

My mom helped me set up my room for her in the morning with everything she'd need. I gave her a big hug and a kiss. She tilted her fuzzy charcoal-gray head, puzzling out what was happening, as I backed away and closed the door.

The school day crawled by, I could hardly think of anything other than her. That afternoon, I sat in the very front row of the bus, so when it pulled up to my stop, I could be the first one off. I bolted down the steps, past Alyssa's mom with the Capri-Sun, and ran the whole way to our townhouse complex. But when I got to my bedroom, I found the door wide open. Blossom was gone.

As usual, I was the only one home. My parents were both still at work, and Mitch had gone to a friend's. I searched the townhouse, throwing open every door, every kitchen cupboard, every closet. It seemed impossible that she would've escaped on her own, but I didn't know what else to do, so I combed the whole complex, calling her name, shaking around the bag of peanut butter treats. Once I was home from school, I wasn't supposed to leave the parking lot without permission, but when I still couldn't find her, I went out into the neighborhood and wandered the streets for hours. Alyssa Sato was on her tire swing, sucking on a Popsicle, when I passed, tears dripping from my chin. She asked if I wanted her to go inside and get her mom. I really did, but I was too ashamed to say so.

When I finally got back to the townhouse, the sun was setting and my dad had returned from his shift at the hardware store.

"Where the hell have you been?" he asked.

"Looking for Blossom," I said, my face swollen from crying.

"Didn't you see that her leash was gone?"

I'd felt embarrassed then. As if a panicked nine-year-old should've had the good sense to check the stick-on hook by the door.

"She's not coming back," he said, pretending to sort through a stack of mail on the kitchen counter, so he wouldn't have to look at me.

I probably knew by then, deep down, that my dad wasn't a good man. But this was the moment when that fact became undeniable.

He'd sold Blossom, he explained, to a customer who had a dog just like her. The woman came into the store almost every week, with a Cairn terrier in her shopping cart, the same type of dog that played Toto in *The Wizard of Oz*. My dad, ever the opportunist, had recognized it as Blossom's breed—something far more valuable than a street mutt found by the dumpsters. So on that day, my first day of school, he'd talked the woman into following him to the townhouse on his lunch break to check out his bargain-priced purebred. She'd bought Blossom right there in the parking lot for three hundred dollars.

The burning filled me until I was hurling my fists against my dad's stomach—the highest I could reach. To get me to stop, he clasped both of my hands in his, tightly enough that my bones ached.

I have never forgiven myself for leaving Blossom alone.

# 30

Natalie knocks around ten o'clock Sunday morning to pick up Fritter, leftover eyeliner still smudged across her lids.

"Wanna do a movie night tonight?" I ask, handing over Fritter's leash. "I'll bring the snacks."

"That sounds amazing," she says, "but I'm supposed to see this guy."

Fuck.

"Oh, okay, no big deal," I say in a tone that conveys the opposite, casting my eyes downward.

"Hey, is everything okay?" she asks, taking a half step into my apartment.

I meet her gaze just as a row of warm tears begins to well.

"Oh my God, what's going on?" She comes all the way inside, shutting the door behind her.

"It's really embarrassing"—I sniffle—"but I think Ian might be having an affair. I could really just use a friend right now."

Something like hunger flashes in her eyes before her mouth, still faintly pink from last night's lipstick, falls open as she assumes the appropriate level of dismay. "Oh no, sweetie! What makes you think that?"

"He'll be back from the gym soon, so I can't talk about it now," I say, certain she won't be able to hold out much longer for the juicy details.

"God, you poor thing, come here." She brings me in for a squeeze. "You're obviously coming over tonight. I'll reschedule with the guy."

"Really?" A couple of well-timed tears break free as I pull away, smiling at her gratefully. "You're the best, Nat. I'll come up after dinner, probably around eight or so."

"Ugh. I don't know how you can sit through a meal with him." She lets herself out. "I'll see you later."

I lock the deadbolt behind her, then grab what I need. I stand frozen just inside the door, waiting silently for my cheating, piece-of-shit husband. Within a few minutes, he's jiggling the handle, wondering why he can't get in.

"Margo? Are you there?" he calls from the other side.

I brace myself, not moving a muscle.

"Babe?" he tries again. "It's me. Let me in."

I take a deep breath. Then I do as he says.

. . .

When I show up at her apartment just after eight, Natalie frowns and pulls me into another pitying hug. "I've been thinking about you all day."

Fritter trots over and sniffs at my knee, waiting for Natalie to release me so I can give him his usual scratch. Once she lets go, I bend to greet him, then move into the kitchen, peeling off my cross-body purse and setting down a grocery bag of snacks. I extract a mostly full bottle of Cabernet Sauvignon, holding it up for her.

"Will you drink this? It probably only has another day or so till it starts to turn, and obviously"—I pat my belly—"I can't finish it."

"Oh, that's right," she groans, already retrieving a wineglass from a cabinet by the stove. "You can't even drink right now! How are you even surviving?"

I shrug. "Honestly, I don't really know."

"Well, go make yourself comfortable and tell me everything." She gestures toward her pink velvet sofa, taking a sip of the wine, then swirling it around in the glass. "Can I get you something? Sparkling water maybe?"

"I'm fine for now, thanks," I say, choosing the end next to Fritter.

Natalie settles in on the opposite side, folding her legs onto the cushion and turning toward me. "So," she fixes me in a ravenous gaze, "I'm dying to know, what tipped you off?"

I'm not about to give her the satisfaction of knowing the real story, so I've crafted a much lamer one.

"His DMs. What else?" I laugh dryly. "His laptop was open to his Instagram messages when I got back from the open house yesterday. Which seemed weird, since as far as I know, he's hardly ever on Insta." I pretend to compose myself. "He was in the shower, so I had a minute to scroll through. Turns out he's been messaging a ton with some woman from his law school class. I didn't have time to read all of it, but it's flirty—a lot of joking about how they used to hook up at UVA . . ." I take another pause. "Sorry, it's hard to talk about."

Natalie narrows her eyes, struggling to hide her disappointment.

"Okay," she says, "what else did you find?"

"That's it. That's all I had time for."

"So, not even a dick pic? Or any evidence they've met up in person?"

"Well, no . . . Ugh, I can't even imagine Ian sending a dick pic."

Predictably, her face lights up at a chance to twist the knife.

"Oh, trust me, girl, they all send them, *especially* the bored husbands. Literally no one is more obsessed with documenting their dicks—snoop a little more in those DMs, I bet you find a *National Geographic*'s worth of erections."

"Jesus, Nat."

"I'm sorry, but I'm only trying to help," she continues, downing another gulp of wine. "Take it from me, the sooner you realize marriage is a sham, the sooner you can have a real life."

Ah yes, the very fulfilling existence that only fuckboys from Tinder can provide.

"It's a little more complicated than that, given—*you know*." I nod down at my belly.

"Oh shit, yeah, I totally keep forgetting you're pregnant," she says, and I feel the inferno spreading through my veins. "Well, that's even more of a reason to figure this out now. Ian's only gonna get worse once the baby's here and you're even less interested in fucking him."

I imagine lunging across this tacky couch and clawing my nails across her face. Instead, I run them through Fritter's wiry fur and remind myself that I only have to play nice for a little while longer.

"Do you mind if we just pick a movie?" I ask, eyes pleading. "I could really use a break from all this drama."

"Oh my God, of course, sweetie." Natalie unfurls herself from the sofa and heads back into the kitchen with her empty glass. "Whenever you're ready to talk more, just know I'm here." She holds my gaze, turning down the corners of her mouth in fake sympathy.

Mercifully, we're less than an hour into *Bad Moms* when her eyelids begin to droop. You'd think a bartender would be smarter about pacing herself, but she's already finished the wine. Once she dozes off, I creep back into the kitchen and pull the latex gloves from my crossbody bag.

The heavy silver wrench is still in the toolbox beneath the sink, right where I found it yesterday.

# 31

A fog has rolled in, making the night seem blacker than normal. I cut my headlights as soon as I turn onto Stonebrook Avenue. At nearly eleven thirty on a Sunday, I'm not surprised to find the street quiet and still, the houses dark.

I pull up in front of the dream home, about where Jack's Audi was parked that first day here, when he nearly saw me sneaking out of his backyard. Where would I be now if he'd caught me that morning? If my timing had been off by only a split second? It's funny how fate works. And that's what this is—what it *has* been, all of it, all along. Fate.

The brass porch lanterns are on, and though the curtains are drawn, I know that nobody's inside. The afternoon of the open house, when I slipped through the side gate and down to the basement to make sure the latch on the Dutch door hadn't been fixed, I overheard one of the agents on the patio talking to his clients. He said the sellers were out of town until Monday, on the Eastern Shore somewhere, so they wouldn't interfere with everyone touring the place and doing their home inspections over the weekend. And just like that, the biggest risk of this whole operation disintegrated. See what I mean about fate? It's like the house *wants* me to do this, like it's in on the plan.

*Perfect house. Perfect baby. Perfect dog.*

I check all the mirrors before getting out of the car, reconfirming that the street is deserted behind me. I close the driver's-side door as softly as I can—hood up, latex gloves on, KN-95 mask over my face—and move quickly to the rear, unlocking the hatch. After wriggling the suitcase all the way to the edge, I pull it free with one final yank, its wheels hitting the pavement with a smack that echoes down the block. I freeze, waiting for a dog to bark or someone's lights to come on. A jolt of adrenaline brings every rustling leaf, every beat of my own heart, into sharp, surreal focus.

The houses stay silent and dark.

I tug the suitcase over the curb and onto the sidewalk. I'll have to wheel it up the flagstone path that leads to the front door, then hang a right just before the porch, onto an offshoot path that'll take me through the side gate to the backyard. It's not a long way, but I'm already pretty sore from earlier.

Clutching the handle with both hands, my back to the house, my masked face watching the street, I pull the suitcase from the front. Its wheels rumble slowly over the smooth stone, just loudly enough to keep my eyes shifting manically from side to side. When I reach the turnoff, I switch my grip and face forward, towing it from behind.

I'm almost there, only a couple feet from the gate, when I see headlights slicing through the mist.

I drop between the suitcase and the front of the house. Tucked down like this, I can't see the car itself, but I can see the lights washing over the street, hear its tires mucking louder over the wet asphalt. It seems to be slowing down. Does the driver see me back here? I hold my breath, waiting for the sound of a car door opening.

But it doesn't come. The tires fade, the lights disappear.

I rise cautiously, taking a quick scan of the block before resuming my slog to the gate. As soon as I'm through it, safely in the backyard and out of range of the porch lanterns, I slump down for a break. I stretch out my hands, cramped from squeezing the suitcase handle, and shake out my arms. The air is humid after the earlier rain. Sweat clings to my back.

The flagstone path continues from the patio around the deck, to the top of the basement stairs. This will be the longest leg of the journey, but also the safest, shrouded almost entirely in darkness. The tightness in my chest eases, I bring a palm to my belly. *We're going to make it. Mommy's got this.*

At the top of the basement stairs, I pause to consider my options. It's a short flight, only eight steps, but narrow and steep. If I go first, pulling the suitcase behind me, the increased weight of it on the incline could knock me off balance. The best plan, I think, is to send it down first.

I scoot it to the edge of the landing and give it a shove. It topples over, sliding about halfway down. I maneuver around it to get to the Dutch door, pushing open the top half just like Penny showed me, then reaching down to unlock the bottom half from the inside. Now I jog back up, positioning myself behind the suitcase for one more thrust. This time, it makes it all the way to the bottom.

I drag it through the open door into the gloom of the basement; the silhouettes of stacked moving boxes, packed and ready for the voyage to London, loom like ghosts. The ceiling height really is impressive down here. Wonder what it would cost to add a bathroom?

My destination in sight—a spot at the foot of the stairs to the main level—I begin my trek across the concrete floor. But a noise—a *thud*—turns my muscles to stone, my blood to ice.

*What the fuck was that?*

I strain to listen through the darkness, my whole body a tense knot, the roaring of my pulse threatening to give me away.

There it is again. The same sound.

Sweat soaks through the back of my T-shirt now, my cross-body bag heaves up and down in sync with my rapid, shallow breathing.

*Thud.*

It's getting closer.

I place a hand on my belly. *We are not alone.*

As quietly as I can, I stand the suitcase upright and let go of the handle. If someone's upstairs, I still have a chance to book it out of here the same way I came in. Slowly, I start to turn back toward the Dutch door.

But as my exit comes into view, there are hands on my shoulders, shoving me, urgently, to the ground. A scream catches in my throat.

While I'm face down, my wrists stinging from the impact, adrenaline takes over. I scramble onto my back, preparing to face my attacker . . . just in time to see a fluffy, four-legged shadow scamper out the back door.

Not human hands. Not human anything. *Lunchbox.* The goddamn neighbor cat.

Once I stop shaking, I clamber back to my feet and finish wheeling the suitcase into position. My eyes strain through the dark for something to use as a doorstop, coming to rest on a set of free weights forgotten in a corner. I grab a ten-pound dumbbell, then run up the stairs and use it to prop the door at the top wide open. I don't see how they'll be able to miss that.

Before I leave, I pull a silver luggage lock from my bag and secure it around the suitcase's zippers. If Penny finds this first, I don't want her to see what's inside.

# 32

I had no idea what the day after would feel like. As vividly and specifically as the rest of the plan came into focus, I hadn't really been able to imagine today. Would I wake up with my alarm? Brew my usual coffee? Log in to work like nothing had happened?

As it turns out, all yeses.

The rain today is harder, more violent than yesterday's drizzle. Wind whips it against the floor-to-ceiling window, the pelting competing with the TV. I've had it tuned to channel 4 all day in case there's any breaking news worth interrupting the soap operas and daytime talk shows for. With the apartment all to myself, I can keep the volume up as high as I want. It's funny how it actually feels a little bigger in here. My only company is Fritter—snuggled up on my couch, right where he belongs.

Now it's nearly five o'clock, only minutes to go before the offer deadline. Surely, Jack and Curt and Penny must be home by now. But have any of them noticed the dumbbell and ventured into the basement?

As if it's answering my question, my phone vibrates on the desk. A text from Derrick, to both me and Ian.

*Just checking in. No word yet. Let's stay positive, but realistic. I'll call as soon as I hear anything.*

Disappointing. If they've found it, I guess they haven't started alerting the bidders yet. I refresh the police department Twitter feeds again. No updates there, either.

I write back to Derrick: *Thanks. Ian's still in depositions with his phone off, but I'll be standing by.*

The rain is full-on torrential now. A homeless woman scurries with a shopping cart beneath the awning of our building's entrance. Wonder how long till the front-desk guy forces her to move. As I watch a few other unlucky pedestrians leap around the dirty puddles forming on the sidewalk, an alarming thought enters my mind. What if somehow they *never* notice the suitcase? What if the movers come and pack it up along with everything else down in that basement, and blindly stick it on some ship headed across the ocean?

What if all of this is for nothing?

...

I could drive myself bananas imagining the various worst-case scenarios while I wait to hear from Derrick. So, as a fun little distraction, I'll let you in on some local history: the true, tragic tale of the DC Murder Mansion. It had been ages since I'd thought about it, but after Erika brought it up at lunch the other day, the details started trickling back.

The whole thing began on a bone-chilling February night seven years ago, with a teenage girl returning to her family's sprawling, French-style chateau in Wesley Heights, the ultra-wealthy DC enclave where Erika and Heath live now. The girl had been at a high-school basketball game, and because it was so cold outside, her dad had reminded her to park her Jeep in the garage when she got home, not in the driveway like usual. Presumably, he thought he was being considerate. But if the girl had parked outside, she would've tried to go in through the front door. And if she'd done that, she would've seen that it was wide open. She would've seen the blood smeared all over the foyer. She would've called 911 from the porch, or maybe from a neighbor's house. The police would've shown up in a nanosecond, given the neighborhood, and made the grisly discovery for her.

Instead, she pulled into the garage just like she'd been told and entered through a mudroom. She took off her shoes, hung up her coat, then went into the kitchen—the one designed by Zoe Estelle—and made herself a snack.

This is the problem, it turns out, with a five-thousand-square-foot house. You can wander around for a full twenty minutes before discovering that both your parents have bled out on an antique Persian rug in the formal living room.

They'd been shot to death in what police said was a random home invasion—likely a botched robbery attempt. The killer had gunned them down at the front door, but they'd somehow both managed to crawl several yards away to die.

People couldn't get enough of the story. The breathtaking violence of it. What those final few moments must've been like. The profiles of the victims, both prominent attorneys. The fact that it had happened in a "safe" (rich, white) neighborhood.

At some point, everyone started calling the house the Murder Mansion.

The market back then, in 2015, was nearly as hot as it is now. No half-decent place in a neighborhood as nice as Wesley Heights would've normally lasted more than a week without finding a buyer. Especially not one with a newly remodeled kitchen. But when the investigation wrapped and the dead couple's estate listed the house for sale, it wouldn't budge. Not a single person wanted to live there.

Eventually, a developer swooped in and practically stole it. He tore it down and packed three new houses onto the lot, all of which sold faster than Beyoncé tickets. The police never caught the killer, but my money is on that developer. Maybe the robbery wasn't *botched* after all.

The narrative that I'm crafting around the dream home isn't quite the same. For one thing, over my own dead body is anyone tearing it down. And for another, no one will have been murdered *on* the property. I contemplated briefly how I might pull that off, but even if I could've figured it out, the complexity of securing and investigating the actual scene of the killing probably would've required Jack and Curt to take the house off the market.

I couldn't have that, so a body dumped inside will have to be enough. You know, to scare away the competition.

. . .

Six twenty-five and Derrick is calling at last.

"Hey, Margo, hope you're hanging in there."

"I'm fine," I say, hurrying him along. "What's up?"

"Honestly . . . I'm not totally sure," he begins slowly. "Do you wanna try patching in Ian?"

"No, no, his phone will still be off. Go ahead, I can fill him in later."

"Okay, well, I just talked to Theresa, their agent, and she sounded pretty rattled."

Something flutters inside me. I take a deep breath.

"It sounds like there's been some sort of accident maybe. Or an emergency of some kind, at the house," Derrick continues. "She really wasn't clear. But for now, until they can tell us what's going on, they're holding off on picking an offer."

Goosebumps erupt up and down my arms. This is it then. It's really happening.

"Huh." I hope Derrick can't detect that my voice is quivering. "What, exactly, did she say?"

"Very little. Only that something had happened, and she wasn't at liberty to share anything else."

I keep pushing. "Think there was a break-in?" I need to seem curious.

"Potentially," says Derrick cautiously, "but I really have no idea. Don't you know the sellers? Maybe you could try them."

"Maybe . . . though we haven't really spoken since they reneged on their promise to look at our offer early."

Derrick chuckles. "Business and friends aren't a great mix."

"So true."

"All righty, well, you hang tight," he says. "I'll let you know the minute I hear back."

My whole body is vibrating. I'm too excited to sit down. Too anxious to possibly think about dinner. All I can do is pace from the window to the kitchen, from the kitchen to the window, over and over, chewing the thumbnail of one hand and obsessively refreshing Twitter with the other.

But the television gets to it first.

Just as the six o'clock local broadcast is about to wrap up, the anchors turn serious.

"We're going to delay your regular seven p.m. programming to bring you some breaking news out of Bethesda," says the woman at the channel 4 desk. A red banner begins to tick across the bottom of the screen: *Body recovered from Grovemont home.*

I dive toward the TV and kneel in front of it like a kid glued to Saturday morning cartoons. My heart rages so loudly I worry I won't be able to hear the report. I crank up the volume.

"We'll toss it to Chad Benson, who arrived on the scene earlier this evening," says the anchor. "Chad, what can you tell us?"

The camera cuts from the studio to a live shot. The dream house fills the screen, still immaculate even in the downpour. Even with yellow police tape strung between wooden stakes in the shining front lawn. Even with grim-looking cops milling around, and a medical examiner's van parked out front.

Chad's report starts as a voiceover, allowing the house to linger on center stage: "Thanks, Doreen. That's right, I'm here in Grovemont, a mostly residential neighborhood in Bethesda, where we just saw the medical examiner wheel a body bag out of the home you see on your screen. He was followed closely by another gentleman carrying a very large black suitcase. A spokeswoman for Montgomery County police tells me there's so far no information to share about the identity of the deceased, but she does confirm this is being investigated as a homicide."

The shot zooms out—I can tell now that the camera is stationed across the street from the house. Chad enters the frame, wearing a black rain slicker, his generically handsome face fixed into made-for-TV concern.

"I can tell you this is normally a very quiet, family-centric part of town. Neighbors here are quite shaken."

A smile tugs at the corners of my lips.

"One of them, a man who did not wish to appear on camera, says police first arrived here just after four o'clock. I should also note for our viewers that this home is currently for sale. The Redfin listing"—Chad holds his phone screen up for the camera—"says there was an open house here on Saturday. We don't yet know whether that's in any way related to what's happened here, but it does seem significant that dozens, if not hundreds of strangers have had access to the house in recent days. Neighbors tell me the property was swarmed all weekend long. The details of this horrific story are clearly still developing, but we'll be sure to bring you more information as soon as we have it. For now, in Bethesda, I'm Chad Benson, News 4."

The studio comes back into view, Doreen and her male co-anchor both shake their heads in disbelief.

"My goodness, Jim, a real tragedy seems to be unfolding there," says Doreen.

"It sure does," says Jim. "Beautiful neighborhood, too."

## 33

By morning, the murder victim in the house-for-sale isn't just the top local story. All of cable news is collectively orgasming over it. At some point, our friend Chad Benson from channel 4 started using the hashtag #BethesdaBasementBody and now that's everywhere, too—viral doesn't cover it. The story made the A block of both *Good Morning America* and the *Today Show*, and all this before they've even identified the remains. The only thing police have confirmed is that the homeowners and their young daughter are unharmed.

Who could've been inside that suitcase is pretty much all anyone's been able to talk about on my office Slack. Which is great for me, since I'm far too wired to get any work done. I never made it to bed last night; I've been wide awake, here on the sofa, flipping between CNN and all the networks for hours. Now it's almost noon, which means the local news is about to come on again.

My phone rings from the coffee table. It's Derrick.

"How are you holding up?" he asks.

"I think I'm just kind of numb," I say, twirling my fingers in the white patch on Fritter's back while he naps next to me. "It's all just so tragic, I can't really wrap my head around it."

I suppress a grin so Derrick won't hear the elation in my voice.

"I know what you mean," he says, letting out a sigh. "Twenty years in real estate and I've never dealt with anything even close to this."

"Yeah, it's horrific."

I'm doing my best to sound sympathetic, but good Christ, when is he getting to the point?

"Have you, um, heard anything from the sellers?" I prod gently. "I can't even imagine what they must be going through."

"Well, that's why I'm calling," he says. "Crass as it may be, business marches on, you know?"

I laugh weakly.

"Theresa called a minute ago," he continues. "She says the police should be done processing the house in a day or two. But it's hard to tell if she really knows that for sure, or if she's only trying to paint a rosier picture than what's all over the TV."

"Mmm." The twelve o'clock broadcast starts in one minute. Doesn't he realize that?

"Anyway, they had eight offers come in, including yours. Not as many as I would've guessed, probably interest rates starting to spook people."

Now we're getting somewhere.

"Five have pulled out."

*Five?*

"That's it?" My voice spikes several octaves. Fritter stirs awake as I rise from the couch. "Sorry," I say, getting a hold of myself. "Too much caffeine mixed with the shock, I think."

"I wouldn't be surprised if the others drop off soon, too," Derrick says. "But does that mean you and Ian want to stay in? Theresa was trying to politely find out—she said there's no pressure to decide right now, of cour—"

"We're staying in." I take a breath to steady myself. "Sorry, I must be really on edge. What I mean is, I'm not ready—*we're* not ready—to pull out quite yet. Let's just see what else we find out today."

The News 4 theme music starts up, the camera closes in on the anchor desk.

"I have to go, Derrick, but I'll—we'll stay in touch."

The midday anchors waste hardly any time on small talk before the woman half of the duo tosses it to Chad. He's stationed back in front of the dream house, no doubt relishing his luck in claiming such a career-making story.

"Thanks, Janice," he begins, face grim, tone appropriately solemn. "We've been getting new information all morning long about what, exactly, went on here on Stonebrook Avenue, and, of course, trying to learn more about the victim. But I want to start with one especially significant development that we can report for you, *exclusively*, here on News 4.

"I've just spoken with sources inside the Montgomery County police department who tell me we can expect to see some kind of surveillance footage at a press conference that'll take place later today. I'm told it pertains to the identification of a vehicle that may have been involved. As soon as we know the precise time of that press conference, we'll be sure to share it with you, and we'll of course carry it live."

So there's already video. I knew there would be eventually, but that was faster than I would've guessed. I'm back to pacing the length of the apartment—window to kitchen, kitchen to window, Fritter tracking me from the couch like the pendulum on a grandfather clock. I'm reviewing the particulars of that night in my mind, and I couldn't have been more careful.

I'm sure of it.

## 34

Finally, the press conference is about to come on, nearly three hours behind schedule. It's almost seven o'clock now, twenty-four hours since news of the #BethesdaBasementBody first broke. I haven't been able to decide whether the delayed start is a good or a bad sign. Maybe the surveillance footage Chad Benson teased didn't pan out? My palms are sticky, but not from fear. I'm excited—thrilled, even—to hear what they've found.

Montgomery County's chief of police—a woman, black pixie cut, almost comically petite—stands at a wood podium in a beige room, the American and Maryland state flags hanging limply behind her. The audience isn't in the shot, but the thick, low roar of voices and the snapping of cameras lets you know it must be jammed wall-to-wall with media in there. This is far and away the most successful PR campaign of my career. It's almost a shame I can't claim the credit.

I lean forward from the sofa, elbows on my knees, fingers laced under my chin, pulse thumping.

"My apologies for keeping you all waiting," the chief begins, her face stony. "We had a late development in this case that required my attention, which you'll hear about in just a moment. But first, I want to focus on a vehicle of interest that we're asking the community to help us locate."

The camera feed zooms out to reveal a large TV mounted to the wall, just to the right of the podium. So they do have the footage then.

"The video you're about to watch was taken by a Ring camera on Stonebrook Avenue, in the Grovemont neighborhood of Bethesda, three houses down from the home where, as you know, a body was recovered Monday afternoon."

The blank blue screen switches to a still shot of a dark front porch, a strip of front lawn and empty sidewalk beyond it.

"This was recorded shortly before eleven thirty Sunday night," the chief explains. Someone out of view hits Play.

Jack and Curt only have that old-school brass knocker, but I knew others on the block would have doorbells with cameras. The shot is dim, and Sunday night's fog doesn't help. But as it glides into the reaches of a streetlamp, a cherry-hued Volkswagen hatchback, headlights off, is unmistakable.

Ian clears his throat in the kitchen.

"Looks kind of like Natalie's car," he says, squinting toward the television as he leans over the counter.

He only got home from Pittsburgh a few minutes ago. He's been over there making himself a turkey sandwich ever since, because I am no longer interested in preparing his dinner.

I shush him so we don't miss anything. The video rewinds, then plays again in slow motion.

"The vehicle you see here appears to be either a Volkswagen Golf or Volkswagen GTI, red in color, with a partially visible license plate," says the chief. "Our investigators have reviewed hours of footage from this same camera, from the overnight period Sunday into early Monday, and only three cars in total appear."

Wow. Imagine living on a street that isn't the goddamn Fyre festival all night long.

"The neighbor who supplied this footage has helped us confirm that the two other cars belong to residents of Stonebrook Avenue," the chief continues. "This vehicle is the *only* one whose owner we have not yet identified, and indeed, it is the only one with a DC tag, not a Maryland one. We believe that whoever was driving it was transporting our homicide victim."

"Jesus Christ," says Ian. "Can you believe this is happening?"

I wave him off, eager to hear whatever the chief is about to divulge next.

"This car became even more interesting to law enforcement earlier this afternoon," she says, "when we were made aware of a second scene—one that we believe is also connected to this crime."

A murmuring rises from the audience, then quickly hushes. My heart bangs against my ribs.

"It is premature for me to say anything more about this second location, other than to share that we have footage of an unidentified red Volkswagen hatchback there as well. What you're about to see was captured by a CCTV camera operated by DC's Metropolitan Police Department. We are confident this is the same vehicle that appears in the Stonebrook Avenue footage."

The shot zooms out again, then refocuses on the flatscreen hung behind the chief. Someone cues up the new video. This footage is grainier and taken from farther away. But it's clear enough that I hear glass shattering against faux-wood floorboards in the kitchen, startling Fritter awake next to me.

Ian has dropped his bottle of IPA.

"This was taken at ten fourteen Sunday evening, in the 800 block of B Street Southeast, in the Capitol Hill section of the District of Columbia," the chief narrates. "Watch closely, in the bottom right-hand corner of the screen. Here comes the red hatchback now ... and just here, you'll see it pull into a parking spot."

Once Natalie's car comes to a stop, the video pauses and jumps ahead a few frames. Now the driver's-side door is opening and someone is getting out. The footage halts again, then cuts to a still frame that's been magnified several times.

A close-up of a woman exiting the car fills the screen. Her face is obscured by the graininess of the recording, plus a KN-95 mask. She wears black leggings—thanks to the shitty quality of the footage, they almost pass as real leather—and a black hoodie pulled over her head, a chunk of light hair protruding from one side.

The effect is exhilarating.

"Please take a close look at the person of interest on the screen," the chief instructs. "This appears to be a female of average height—five-four, five-five, somewhere in that range—with blond hair and a slender build."

*Slender!*

Now the recording jumps to another magnified image.

"In this frame, you can see the same individual removing a large black suitcase from the rear of the vehicle. It appears to be similar or identical to the one we recovered from the basement of 5423 Stonebrook Avenue yesterday afternoon," the chief says. "Both we and our partners within the Metropolitan Police Department are asking for the public's help in identifying this person." The flatscreen cuts from the shot of me, to an 800 number. "If you think you have any information at all about this vehicle or its driver, we are asking you to call this tip line immediately," says the chief. "I can take a few questions now."

I peek up at Ian. He grips the edge of the sink to keep himself upright, all the color drained from his complexion.

"Margo," he whispers, "what the fuck is going on?"

## 35

Before I go any further, you should know one thing: If I'd had a choice, I would've killed Ian. As a feminist, it's important to me that you understand that. I blame him. I hate him. But it would've been impossible to cover those tracks. And I can't qualify for the mortgage on a $1.3 million house without him.

Plus, there's no way he would've fit inside Natalie's suitcase.

Alex lived in the nicest part of Capitol Hill, with historic brick sidewalks and handsome nineteenth-century architecture. Comparatively, her apartment building was a dump (and crucially, not the kind of place that has a doorman or a front desk). Still, the rent for a studio in that neighborhood should've been well out of reach for a clipboard girl at an environmental nonprofit. Her family must have money, though I can't say for sure. It's not like I could've Googled her and risked leaving more of a digital trail. It was easier, anyway, knowing almost nothing about her, aside from the fact that she was fucking my husband.

As I rounded the corner onto her block Sunday night, the asphalt, slick from the early-evening rain, reflected the orange glow of the street lamps. I slipped into the open parking space a few row houses away from her building, then double-checked that my mask and gloves were secure, that enough of the blond wig—the same one I wore at celebrity karaoke night all those years ago—was visible. I collected the suitcase from the back and looked quickly in both directions to confirm I was alone. Of course I was nervous. To keep myself focused and tamp down the fear, I repeated the steps of the plan over and over in my head. Not so different, really, from preparing for an important client pitch.

I wheeled the suitcase down the sidewalk, then up the ramp to the building's front entrance. At the intercom, I fished the digital recorder from my reporter days—ancient, but still in fine working order—out of my crossbody bag and punched in the digits for unit 201. I shook with adrenaline as the speaker crackled to life.

"Hello?"

Her voice sounded younger than I expected. There was an uncomfortable pinch in my stomach. Like I said, I really do blame Ian for this whole mess, but my hands were tied.

"Hello?" Alex said again, after I'd hesitated. "Is someone there?"

I held my recorder up to the intercom and pressed play: "Babe? It's me. Let me in."

Ian's voice. From earlier that day, when I'd locked him out of the apartment.

"Oh!" She sounded delighted. "Okay, just a minute!"

There was a buzzing noise, then the click of the double glass doors unlocking.

I rolled the suitcase to a small elevator off the shabby lobby and took the quick, rickety ride to the second floor. Before reaching Alex's unit, I extracted the large silver wrench from the suitcase's front pocket. The one I'd found in the red toolbox beneath Natalie's kitchen sink.

What happened next unfolded like a dream that I watched from outside myself, my consciousness a numb, impassive witness while my body did the work.

Alex, at the door, silky blue shorts and a white tank top.

A single, solid thud to the head before a scream could erupt from her delicate face.

The twitching of an arm, the fluttering of an eyelid, on the parquet floor of a tiny, studio apartment.

A pillow from the bed—kinder, not so messy—to finish the job.

The underwear that I'd found on Natalie's closet floor (extremely irresponsible when you have a dog) shoved into Alex's sheets. Another pair left in the hamper. A clump of hair from Natalie's brush stuffed into the shower drain, her toothbrush tucked into the top drawer of the bathroom vanity.

A Nokia burner phone—the twin to Ian's—sitting on a nightstand, stashed in a crossbody bag.

Surfaces wiped.

Suitcase . . . packed.

A blonde in a face mask and a black hoodie tugging it, two-handed, back to the elevator.

Leveraging it with all her might against the back bumper of a red hatchback to get it inside.

Then, finally, driving north out of the city, to a perfect house, in a perfect place.

# 36

I have never seen Ian look so afraid. I almost wish I could take a photo and show him.

"You remember the Murder Mansion, right?" I say, still seated on the sofa.

His expression contorts. He croaks out a single word: "What?"

"Come on, you remember. The one nobody would buy after they found those poor people slaughtered inside?"

Sweat slicks his forehead, his skin unnervingly gray. He hunches over the sink now, as if he might get sick.

"Erika reminded me about it the other day," I explain, "and then I saw your girlfriend in front of our building. So I thought, sure, why not take care of that problem *and* kill the competition for the house all at once?" I shrug. "You know I've always been a multi-tasker."

"I . . . I'm calling the police," he chokes out. "You're out of your mind."

I figured he'd react like this. But he'll come to his senses.

"I think you should stop and seriously consider how that'll work out for you. I mean, do you really want to raise your hand and volunteer that you were fucking the dead girl? You know it's the boyfriend like 99.99 percent of the time, right?"

He stares at me, unblinking, and takes a hard swallow.

"Oh, and that reminds me, we'll need to get rid of your new burner"—I let my eyes wander over him—"wherever you're keeping it."

Whatever guilt I might've felt when I first heard Alex's voice crackle through that intercom dissolved as soon as I scrolled through her phone. They'd been texting that whole night, while I was upstairs at Natalie's. Ian's old Nokia is out of battery and stashed inside the drawer of my nightstand, so it was obvious he'd gone out and bought another one. Asshole.

"But Alex . . ." He closes his eyes and takes a deep breath, beating back a wave of nausea. "Alex had one, too," he manages to get out.

"You think I don't already have it?"

His face relaxes for a split second, before tensing up again: "My DNA will be everywhere."

"Just what every wife wants to hear." I get up and join him in the kitchen. He staggers away from me, as I reach past him to fill a glass of water at the faucet. "You need to trust me, Ian. As long as those burners are the only thing connecting you two, the police won't even know to look in your direction."

"But what about Jack and Curt?" he says. "Think about it—after everything we did to them? Don't you think they'll point to us?"

I laugh. "Absolutely not."

"How are you so sure?" His head tilts the way Fritter's does when he's trying to work out what I'm saying.

"Because," I help him along, "they need *someone* to buy their house. Once everyone else drops out, we'll be their only option. If they turned us in, they'd be sending their only buyers to prison. They'd be stuck there forever."

Ian's jaw goes slack, the fight in his eyes deadens.

"This could end my career," he whispers, mostly to himself, I think. "It would be better . . ." He stares at the floor, nodding rapidly. "Yeah, I think it would be better if we cooperated . . ."

Jesus fucking Christ, I really do have to do all the critical thinking around here. I punch him in the biceps to snap him out of it. He looks up at me, stunned, eyes watering.

"Don't be an idiot."

"Margo . . . I'm . . . I'm not like you. I can't live with this."

I let out a long, exhausted sigh, then spin away from him, heading for the bathroom. Fritter hops off the sofa and trots after me. There, I dig behind the cleaning products and cotton balls and extra toilet-paper rolls, back behind the drainpipe underneath the sink, until I reach the First Response box. I pull out the test, still declaring my happy news in the form of two bright-pink lines.

Holding it out in my flattened palm, I return to the kitchen and present it to Ian.

In an instant, a *Below Deck* episode's worth of drama plays out across his face. His brow scrunches in confusion as he studies the stick, then stretches back out in horror. But when he lifts his gaze to meet mine, I see it—just a flicker, but undeniable. *Joy.*

"Is that . . ." he stammers. "Are you really . . ."

"Do you want to be in jail for the birth of your child?" I ask, my eyes locked into his. "Or, worse, you want me to give birth in a prison cell? You want our baby ripped away from us, her life destroyed before it can even start?"

Tears pour out of him now. Sloppy, silent blobs rolling in fast succession down his cheeks. Good boy.

Before either of us can speak again, his phone—the legit one—dings from the kitchen counter. Mine chimes from the coffee table at the same time.

He peers down. "It's my mom," he says weakly.

"What does she want?"

His voice shakes as he reads her text aloud: "Hi, kids, I've been hearing about the Bethesda Basement Body. Isn't that where you're house hunting? I thought it was supposed to be safer there."

"Keep it short," I instruct him. "'Yes, it's awful,' whatever. Nothing too emotional."

He nods, his face ashen. Then he lurches toward the sink and pukes up his turkey sandwich.

# 37

Ian spent the night on the couch. Notice I didn't say he slept. I could hear him crying off and on through the bedroom door until dawn. It was reassuring to know he was still there, and not out doing something stupid. I was up anyway, reading through the theories and hot takes swirling around online. I'm finding all of it pretty delicious.

The internet sleuths have really outdone themselves, picking over every shred they can find about the owners of 5423 Stonebrook Avenue. They've taken an especially frenzied interest in Curt—an altogether delightful little wrinkle that I admit I didn't see coming. Right away, they found Dottie's review of his book. Amazon has since deleted it, but the screenshot of *DO NOT TRUST CURTIS BRADSHAW* has been retweeted more than half a million times. I hope Dottie's enjoying that as much as I am. It's a cornerstone of one of the most popular theories on Reddit: that a defrauded investor from Curt's hedge-fund days dumped the body in his house as a warning.

Of course, now that they've identified the victim, a new theory—the one that I designed—should come together fairly easily.

Police from both Montgomery County and DC made it official

at a joint press conference this morning: The remains in the suitcase belonged to Alexandra Stapleton. She was twenty-three years old. Alex to family and friends. A recent DC transplant. A passionate environmental studies major at the University of Vermont. Beloved daughter and sister. Blah, blah, fucking blah. The only part that really matters is she looks like Lyla Garrity from *Friday Night Lights* in the photos now looping on every channel. And there's nothing the media loves more than a beautiful young white woman who's met a violent end.

Chad Benson, News 4, is probably concealing a raging boner behind those pleat-front khakis when the anchor tosses to him from the studio. He's no longer cemented in front of the dream home. He's on Capitol Hill now, in front of Alex's building. I turn up the volume and lean in from the sofa.

He's recapping more of what we learned from the joint press conference—that one of Alex's neighbors called 911 after noticing her door ajar, that police connected the apartment to the body based on photos found inside. But I'm distracted by the pile of flowers and stuffed animals visible just over Chad's shoulder, a memorial to Alex that's already on the verge of overtaking the front steps. The way this is playing out, the Bethesda Basement Body is on track to become a far bigger story than the Murder Mansion ever was.

Chad's going over the details of a candlelight vigil planned for tonight, when my phone rings beside me. It's Derrick.

I've been dying to call him, but I didn't want to raise suspicion by seeming too thirsty. Better to wait for him to come to us.

"Hi, Margo," he says somberly. "Horrifying news about this poor girl, isn't it? So much potential. What a waste."

I roll my eyes. "Really unthinkable."

"So . . . I'm just checking in," he says, trying to sound casual. "I haven't wanted to push, but I kind of thought I would've heard from you by now."

"Oh?"

"Well, yeah. I assume you guys want to pull the offer, but I can't legally do that until you confirm—"

"What about the other buyers?" I interrupt him. "Have the rest of them dropped out?"

Ian sticks his head out of the bedroom, registering who I'm talking to. I put Derrick on speaker.

"Well, yeah. Of course they have," says Derrick, sounding perplexed by the question. "At this rate, they'll probably have to burn that place to the ground."

Ian strides quickly over to the sofa now. "Derrick?" he interjects. "Thanks so much for calling. You're right, we're withdrawing our offer, too."

"Sure, that's what anyone would do in your—"

"No, no, Derrick." I glare up at Ian, daring him to speak again. "Give us just a second, okay?"

I mute the phone, my eyes lingering on the screen to make extra sure I've properly silenced our end of the call. Now they burn back into Ian. "What the fuck?"

"I can't do this, Margo. It's too much, what you're doing to Natalie. What you did to—" He chokes up before he can say her name. "I just . . . I can't live in that house."

How many times am I going to have to explain this to him?

"We've gone over this, Ian. If we don't buy it, Jack and Curt will have zero reason not to tell the police about us. *Zero*. And, anyway"—I rest a hand on my belly—"this isn't about you anymore."

The lying, cheating father of my child stares at me for a few seconds before his face collapses in on itself. His eyes drop to the floor, as he begins to weep softly. Maybe it did work out for the best that I couldn't kill him. Living might be a worse punishment.

I unmute the phone. "Derrick, are you still there?"

"I'm here. What's the verdict?"

A smile breaks loose across my face.

# EPILOGUE

We're keeping this room coral.

Somehow, I always sensed I was having a girl, but when the ultrasound confirmed it this morning, I was still ecstatic. It still felt like a surprise. And now we won't have to do a thing in here. The floral wallpaper on the ceiling can stay, too.

Whenever Ian gets around to putting it together, I'm planning to float the crib right here in the middle of the space. I ordered it as soon as I made it past the first trimester—I couldn't wait a second longer. The changing table will go over there, under the window. Three months in, and I still can't get over the view. I'm sure a lot of people would say it's nothing special. Just some nice big trees, some pretty houses with tidy lawns. But when you've been staring from the other direction for so long—from the outside, looking in—there is no greater pleasure than standing within the walls of your very own forever home, looking out onto the street where your daughter will one day learn to ride her bike.

We got to move in sooner than we'd anticipated. Jack and Curt accepted our offer, no negotiating required, then pulled Penny out of school and hightailed it to London. The couple next door—Lunchbox's owners, a nice pair of empty nesters—told me the moving company sent a crew to finish packing up once the police were gone. Jack, Curt, and Penny never set foot inside this house ever again.

All the neighbors, not only Lunchbox's parents, are super friendly. Whenever I take Fritter for a walk, someone stops us to chat. At first, they'd always steer the conversation toward the house, hinting around for some macabre detail. "Terrible what happened there," they'd say, "are you settling in okay?" Or, "How wonderful to have some new energy in that place after... *you know*." Yeah, not subtle. But they seem to be calming down now. Certainly, they can all agree we got one hell of a deal.

In fact, since we didn't have to compete, we had enough money left over to finish the basement, as long as we do most of the labor ourselves. Ian has thrown himself into it. He spends almost all his nights and weekends down there, really any time he's home, framing out the new bathroom, adding drywall and proper flooring. "I just need it to look different," he keeps saying. And that's A-okay with me. Whatever it takes to keep him occupied till the baby arrives.

Fritter loves it here, too. On nice days, he'll nap for hours in the sun on the deck. Sometimes, just watching him out there makes me cry. The hormones probably have something to do with that. But it also just feels so good to give him the life he deserves.

He doesn't seem to miss Natalie at all.

It was later that Wednesday, the very same day we told Derrick that we still wanted to buy the house, when the train of cop cars came flying down U Street. As soon as the first one braked in front of our building, I knew they were there for her. The footage with her partial plate had been circulating for less than twenty-four hours, but how many red Volkswagens with two number 7s on the tag can possibly exist in DC?

The scene couldn't have been pleasant when the police kicked in her door. Natalie had been in the tub for two days by then.

I'd gone upstairs that Monday morning, right after Ian left for Pittsburgh. I knew Natalie would still be on the couch, out cold from the five crushed-up Xanax that I'd mixed into the wine. Someone needed to let Fritter out.

After we got back from our walk, I dropped him off at my apartment, then returned to hers. When I shook Natalie by the shoulders, her eyelids barely opened. "Thirsty" was the first thing she said. So I fixed her a tall glass of watered-down vodka—and stirred in a spoonful of the powdered ketamine that I'd found in her medicine cabinet.

Once I was done running the bath, her eyes were closed again. She didn't resist at all, draping a heavy arm around me, as I dragged her to the bathroom and peeled off her clothes. If she ever came to while I was holding her under, I didn't notice.

A week or so after they found her body, the US attorney held a press conference laying out the prosecution's theory of the crime.

Natalie, he said, was obsessed with Alexandra Stapleton. They'd had a fling, the evidence showed, and it appeared Natalie couldn't let it go. Investigators found her DNA inside Alex's apartment, including from hair in the shower drain and on a pair of underwear tangled at the foot of the bedsheets. A large wrench left just inside the front door came from a toolset belonging to Natalie. It matched the blunt force trauma to Alex's skull.

Investigators pulled Natalie's cell phone data, which confirmed she'd been at both locations the night of the murder. The fob to our building's parking garage registered that she hadn't returned home till after midnight.

As for her connection to the Bethesda basement, her phone also revealed that she'd been to the home for the open house and taken numerous photos of its interiors. Perhaps, the US attorney theorized, in the throes of a psychotic episode, Natalie had latched onto the idea of "living happily ever after there" with Alex.

"It appears she could not live with herself after taking Miss

Stapleton's life," he concluded, "and so we are left with not one, but two grieving families. While my office is pleased to bring this case to such a speedy resolution, this is not the outcome any of us would have hoped for. I'd like to extend my deepest condolences to both families, and my heartfelt gratitude to our officers here in the District, as well as our law enforcement partners in Montgomery County, for their tireless work to get justice for Alexandra Stapleton."

The public devoured every morsel of this, just as I knew they would. Two hot white women? A hookup so intense it ended in a murder-suicide? A B-plot about real estate? I mean, come the fuck on, I dare you to craft a more compelling narrative. The real tragedy here is that I won't get a cut of the inevitable movie deal.

Naturally, it raised some eyebrows when Ian and I went under contract on the house—quite a coincidence that the buyers would've lived in the same apartment building as the killer. But I had an easy explanation when the police came over to question us about it. Through tears, I told them how guilty I felt about the whole thing. After all, *I'd* been the one to show Natalie the listing, I explained—been the one to put the idea in her head that it could be "the dream house," the perfect place for a "happily ever after." (Yep, the US attorney stole that line from me.) If only I'd never told her that Ian and I were planning to make an offer on it, maybe none of this would've happened.

"And then I just took her at her word when she said she was going out of town and needed me to take care of her dog," I'd said, face snotty, Fritter at my feet. "I don't remember if I even asked her how she was doing when she dropped him off."

The detectives—there were two—both insisted I stop beating myself up. Natalie, they said, was very sick, and there was no one to blame but her.

When the toxicology report finally came back—revealing she'd overdosed on an impressively wide range of substances before drowning—it only got harder for anyone to defend her. While announcing the results, police shared that they'd found a supply of party drugs, including the ketamine, in her apartment, salacious new info that sent the internet sleuths back to work. They dug up Natalie's divorce filings, a messy affair in which she accused her ex of repeatedly cheating, and he laid out how the woman he loved had spiraled out of control and broken his heart. His private investigator had observed Natalie getting high at clubs, and his lawyers had gotten an affidavit from her old boss confirming the Molly incident—which, of course, all made it easier for the online mob to believe she was unstable enough to be the Bethesda Basement killer.

It was strange, the commenters conceded, that the police never explained how Natalie and Alex met. Never detailed a dating app connection, or a text message history. Still, several pointed out, Alex was clearly a closet case, so maybe she'd been paranoid about leaving a digital trail.

Speaking of which, I got rid of those burners before we moved. I smashed them up and scattered them around—a few pieces into the Potomac River, some bits into public trash cans at opposite ends of town. It felt cathartic, like spreading the ashes of my old life. No one will ever find them, and let's be honest, no one will ever look. Aside from a handful of internet obsessives, everyone is content with how quickly this wrapped up. The police aren't about to reconsider a case with a mountain of evidence. They have enough to deal with, the way crime is skyrocketing in the city—every day there's another shooting, and the homelessness problem is out of control. Whenever I watch the news, I feel more grateful to live here in the safety of the suburbs—away from all the craziness, away from all the danger.

And now with that drama behind us, I can finally focus on what really matters. I briefly considered switching the walls in here to a pale mint—something not so gender-specific—but after this morning's big reveal, the coral just feels meant to be. I think I like it even better when the sun gets lower, the way it turns a little more orange in this light.

"Fritter, come on, time to go out."

My happy little muppet gets up from the floor of the empty nursery and follows me downstairs. Even though I'm hardly past the first trimester, the summer humidity already feels so much more oppressive than it used to. These sunset walks are about the only ones I can bear.

One perk of being pregnant, at least, is that everyone is nicer to me. Take Jordana. I wasn't yet ready to tell people at work about the baby, but when she called me into her office a couple months ago, I sensed I might not have a choice. She'd barely gotten the words out—"Margo, we need to discuss your performance"—when I cut her off.

"There's something I need to discuss, too," I'd said cheerily. "I'm pregnant! Finally!"

Her face fell, as she presumably did the math: not great strategy for a woman CEO to fire an expectant mother, especially not one who'd have to explain to so many loyal clients that she'd gotten the ax mere seconds after sharing the happy news.

To her credit, Jordana recovered well. "That's just wonderful," she said, eyes wide. "Let's talk about what the rest of the team can do to support you."

Work is going a lot better these days anyway. I'm much more focused now that we're properly settled in here. I find Fritter's leash hanging from its hook in the coat closet (I have a *coat* closet now!). He waits patiently while I snap on his harness, then slip on my Birkenstocks. We're nearly through the front door when a faint buzzing stops me. I stand perfectly still, straining to detect its origins.

As I take deliberate steps back toward the closet, it grows louder. I'm getting warmer.

When I open the door, my gaze instantly falls on the source. Ian's brown leather backpack, in a heap on the floor. I lift the front flap and reach inside. The tight lump of rage unfurls itself, pulsing to life, when I see what I've pulled out.

A crumpled-up Pret bag, something vibrating inside.

Down within the depths of the basement, a power saw screeches on. Fritter whines at the high-pitched sound. A familiar throbbing starts up again behind my eyes.

# ACKNOWLEDGMENTS

When I think of you, the reader, holding this book in your hands (or listening to it in your car, or flipping through it on your Kindle), I am overwhelmed with gratitude. Thank you so much for coming—I sure hope you had a good time.

Getting this novel into the world would've been much harder and much less fun without Nate Carlile. Thank you for cheering me on, covering too many dog walks, keeping me fed, and never once complaining while I locked myself away on weekends to write eighty thousand words that could've amounted to nothing. Thank you for being my number-one hype man and brainstorming partner. Thank you for the title! I love you; marrying you was the smartest decision I've ever made.

Maybe the second smartest? Querying Meredith Miller at UTA. I'm so glad you emailed me back! Thank you for being the fiercest advocate anyone could ever want in their corner. Ethan Schlatter, thank you for completing our little dream team—and for your amazing ideas and sense of humor. Thank you both for believing in me and this book, and hustling tirelessly to convert so many others into believers, too. And shout out to Samori Cullum for keeping everything running smoothly!

Ryan Doherty, you and Celadon changed my life. Thank-you seems inadequate—but thank you from the bottom of my heart for betting on me. All my gratitude to you and Faith Tomlin for your careful stewardship of this novel.

Thank you also to Deb Futter, Rachel Chou, Christine Mykityshyn, Jennifer Jackson, Jolanta Benal, Molly Bloom, Chloé Dorgan, and the many other brilliant people at Celadon and Macmillan who've worked so hard, in so many capacities, to elevate this novel.

Of course, none of this would be possible without my mom, Debbie Kashino, my first and biggest fan. Thank you for always encouraging my love of writing and creating, and instilling in me the confidence to go after big things. Thank you for the forty years you devoted to teaching, making the world an immeasurably better place for the rest of us.

I hope that my grandparents, Louise and Shiro Kashino, would be proud to see their last name on the cover of this book. Any time something seems too hard, all I have to do is remember that they're a part of me, and I know I'll find a way through. I will always be grateful to you, Grandma and Grandpa, and I will never take your sacrifice for granted.

I think Kris Hiraoka has read every word of mine that's ever been published. Thank you, Auntie Kris, for always asking the best questions, giving the kindest feedback, and having multiple types of M&Ms and gummy candy at the ready.

My deepest gratitude to the rest of my family and the friends who feel like family across Seattle, Portland, DC, New Haven, and Ohio. Sharing this with you makes it so much better.

To my intrepid TV rights team at UTA—Mirabel Michelson, Olivia Fanaro, Matt Waldstein, and Dylan Cano—I will never forget the surreal three-week marathon we ran together. Thank you for carrying me over the finish line.

My thanks to Melissa Chinchillo at UTA; Kate Burton and the team at C&W for your deft handling of the translation rights; and

Ullstein, HarperCollins Holland, and Prószyński Media for bringing *Best Offer Wins* to your countries.

Bobby Mostyn-Owen and the team at Doubleday UK, your vision and enthusiasm for this book blow me away. Thank you for being my dream partner on the other side of the pond, and all my thanks to Kerry Nordling at Macmillan for making it happen.

During my journalism career, I was fortunate to work alongside many brilliant colleagues who made me a better writer, but none more so than Kristen Hinman. As my editor for eight years, you turbocharged the storytelling instincts that powered this novel. Thank you for always pushing for more.

Mimi Montgomery, I am incredibly lucky to count you as a friend. When I first started writing this book, I knew next to nothing about publishing a novel. You changed that in one lunch—telling me what to read and what to listen to. And then, a few months later, you gave the most insightful feedback on my first draft. I will be grateful to you forever, and I can't wait for everyone to meet your Margot.

Ken Germer and Jeff Gay, it has been a particular treat to have you along for this ride. Your friendship and support mean more than I can say.

Tammy Greenwood and my classmates at the Writer's Center, thank you for reading the beginnings of this novel and giving me the tools to keep going.

Tony Lupo and Courtenay Ebel at ArentFox Schiff, thank you for your generous and smart counsel.

Chris Hobbs and Marshall Stowell, many thanks for the crucial bit of fact-checking.

And finally, a very special shout-out to Bexley, Clancy, Kyrie, Olive, and Penny for inspiring the four-legged characters in this book, and, in a few cases, lending your names to people and places in these pages. Mostly, thank you for making my life so much happier.

## ABOUT THE AUTHOR

Marisa Kashino was a journalist for seventeen years, most recently at *The Washington Post*. She spent the bulk of her career at *Washingtonian* magazine, writing long-form features and overseeing the real estate and home design coverage. She grew up near Seattle, graduating from the University of Washington with a degree in journalism and political science. She lives in the DC area with her husband, two dogs, and two cats. *Best Offer Wins* is her first novel.

**CELADON BOOKS**

Founded in 2017, Celadon Books, a division of Macmillan Publishers, publishes a highly curated list of twenty to twenty-five new titles a year. The list of both fiction and nonfiction is eclectic and focuses on publishing commercial and literary books and discovering and nurturing talent.